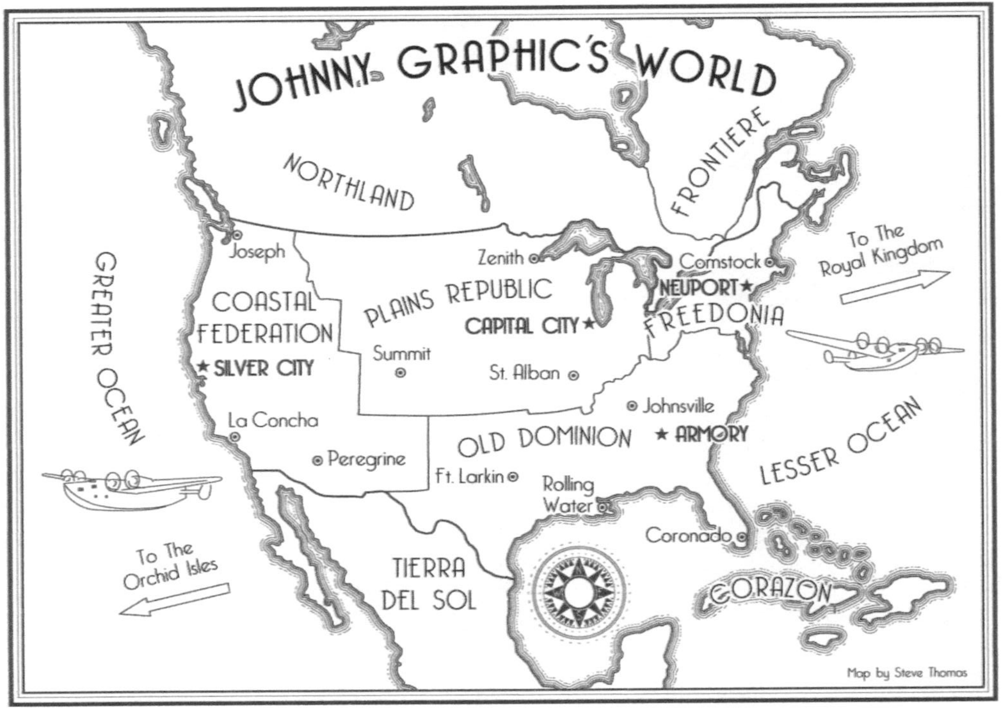

JOHNNY GRAPHIC'S WORLD
NORTHLAND
FRONTIERE
GREATER OCEAN
Joseph
Zenith
Comstock
To The Royal Kingdom
NEUPORT ★
COASTAL FEDERATION
PLAINS REPUBLIC
CAPITAL CITY ★
FREEDONIA
★ SILVER CITY
Summit
St. Alban
La Concha
Johnsville
OLD DOMINION
★ ARMORY
LESSER OCEAN
Peregrine
Ft. Larkin
Rolling Water
To The Orchid Isles
Coronado
TIERRA DEL SOL
CORAZON
Map by Steve Thomas

JOHNNY GRAPHIC

AND THE ETHERIC BOMB

D. R. MARTIN

JOHNNY GRAPHIC ADVENTURES BOOK 1

CONGER ROAD PRESS
MINNEAPOLIS

ISBN: 978-1-7355067-1-5

Cover Art and Design & Map © 2012 & 2020 Steve Thomas

Visit johnnygraphicadventures.com, drmartinbooks.com, and facebook.com/johnnygraphicadventures
Contact the author at drmartin120@gmail.com

PROLOG

TUESDAY, OCTOBER 1, 1935
SILVER CITY, COASTAL FEDERATION

TWENTY MOUNTED GHOST WARRIORS charged through the stormy night sky. Through torrents of rain and deafening thunder. Through lightning bolts and blasts of hail.

Burilgi, their leader, rode out in front on a brown gelding. With seeping, empty eye sockets he surveyed the wrathful heavens. Many centuries dead, the wraith did not feel the chill and damp that would have pained an ordinary mortal.

After long hours pounding southward, the ghost troop soared out of the storm and into ragged clouds that reflected a salmon-colored dawn. Burilgi bent his bloody, eyeless gaze downward.

Spiderwebs of dirt roads spread out beneath him. Then came thousands of little houses on grids of streets. Automobiles belched smoke and puttered along. Farther to the south, a huge city glittered on the shore of a vast ocean.

The troop of Steppe Warriors flew in over the metropolis and scattered. Burilgi made his way to an abandoned herbalist's shop in a part of the city where immigrants from the Jade Kingdom had settled. There he waited.

Some hours later, he heard a key snick into the lock of the shop's front door. It swung open as he watched from his hiding place in the wall.

In stepped a tall, heavy white man—a living man—who wore a long black coat. His head was perfectly, glisteningly bald. The only hair he seemed to have was a trim white mustache. He didn't even have eyebrows.

Fishing a flashlight out of his pocket, the man shot a beam of light around the room. Nothing was revealed but dusty display cases and cascades of cobwebs.

"Burilgi, are you here?" the man asked quietly.

The eyeless ghost emerged out of the far wall.

The very instant the bald man saw the wraith, he gasped and took a step backward. His narrow slits of eyes opened wide. He stood there stock still, except for the constant twitching of his left hand. Finally composing himself, he asked, "Are you all here?"

"All twenty." Burilgi's voice sounded like sandpaper rubbing on stone.

"You know your mission."

"To exterminate the enemies of our khan. Now tell me where to find them."

THE EXQUISITE PEARL TEMPLE sat on a narrow side street in Silver City's teeming Jadetown. Burilgi entered the temple's meditation chamber from the rear, through brick and mortar and iron, a spear in his hand. Butter lamps flickered here and there among the sculptures and tapestries.

At this late hour in the evening, only one person remained in the chamber—a thin, elderly man kneeling on a prayer rug before a large golden statue of the sacred one. He wore a shabby, wrinkled jacket of light blue, trousers of threadbare khaki, and a white shirt. A few strands of gray hair trailed across the top of his head.

"Mongke Eng," hissed the specter.

The old man lifted his head, gingerly rose to his feet, wobbled, and turned around. He had a face very much like Burilgi's—but without the cruelty and hatred. Mongke Eng focused his rheumy eyes on the ghost and nodded.

"Where are your guards?" snorted the specter. "I was told you would have guards."

"None are needed," replied Mongke Eng.

"Why not?"

"Because I am dying anyway."

Burilgi tilted his head. "Of what?"

"Cancer. In my blood. Better to die quickly, I think."

Burilgi couldn't help but admire the old man. "To bravely face death at the hands of your enemy is honorable."

"But why am I your enemy?"

"Orders from the khan."

Mongke Eng looked astonished. "You have a new khan? A new leader? Remarkable. There has not been a khan in over three centuries."

Burilgi saw the face of the old man transform itself—from dismal acceptance of his doom to bright-eyed fascination. As if he was delighted to learn something new and wonderful, even in the very last moments of his life.

"You are from the era of Semei Khan, unless I am mistaken," said Mongke Eng. "Circa 1220 to 1250. Am I right?"

"Yes."

"From the army of the One-Armed General? Your uniform is most distinctive. The rampant wolf that you wear on your tunic was unique among the Steppe armies. The bronze-pointed leather helmet, as well."

The Steppe Warrior said nothing.

"Can you see without eyes?" Mongke Eng asked with sincere curiosity.

"Would I be here if I could not?"

Mongke Eng smiled at the terse reply. "What is your name?"

"Burilgi."

The old man chuckled. "Destroyer? Your parents called you Destroyer?"

"A good name," the ghost said. "You know why I am here."

Mongke Eng nodded tiredly, like a man ready for a long, long sleep. "You've killed at least three others—and now me. Who is next?"

"Someone called Melanie Graphic."

The old scholar shut his eyes and shook his head. "But she's so very young."

"She must die, too, old man. The khan has given me my orders."

Mongke Eng was about to say something else when the spear caught him in the chest, tumbling him backward into the statue of the sacred one.

CHAPTER 1

WEARING A BROWN CLOTH CAP and shabby overcoat, Johnny Graphic trudged along the north side of Superior Avenue, head down. *I can't believe I'm doing this*, he thought.

No one noticed him. The people bustling around were far too busy chattering among themselves. If shoppers wondered about the square object in the canvas bag slung over his shoulder, they didn't say so. If they were curious about the peculiar grin that kept breaking out on his round, freckled face, they didn't mention it. And as far as he was concerned, that was just fine. They had no idea they might be seeing his photo in tomorrow's newspaper.

Johnny still couldn't imagine never having to go to school again—unless he wanted to. He'd spent a year studying hard and had passed the high school exams on his very first try. And here he was, at twelve and a half, taking photos for the *Zenith Clarion. He was an honest-to-goodness newspaper photographer.* The youngest ever in the history of Zenith, the second biggest city in the Plains Republic.

His seventeen-year-old sister, Melanie, had warned him—in that gloomy way of hers—that he'd be missing some of the best years of his life by getting out of school early. The way he looked at it, staying in school meant missing five years of taking pictures. Now that would *really* be sad.

From the time he was a little kid, Johnny thought that shooting photos was something almost magical. Frame the shot. Focus. Press the shutter at just the right moment. Then, when the prints came back from the drugstore, the things and people you saw through the viewfinder would be on paper, captured forever. Every time he opened up that envelope and saw his newest pictures, it was like getting presents on his birthday.

At first, the idea that formed in his head seemed too impossible, too incredible. But as he studied every newspaper photo he could get his hands on, he began to think, *why couldn't I do this?*

And now he was. Getting paid for his pictures in the newspaper. Getting a byline under his shots—"Photo by Johnny Graphic."

The photo editor at the *Zenith Clarion* had hired Johnny at first to do a simple freelance assignment. Then another and another. A press conference at the Zenith Geographical Society. The launching of a new lake boat down at the shipyards. Triplets born at Hilltop Hospital.

But today was the first time he had been given an important assignment, a *dangerous* story. Miss Maude Beale, managing editor of the *Clarion*, had personally told Johnny what it was all about and what he had to do and why he was the best "man" for the job.

And there he was, wearing his first disguise. The shabby, filthy coat. The tattered newsboy cap tugged down over his head. The dirt he'd purposely smudged on his face. He looked just like a poor, homeless kid. Too bad Miss Beale had nixed his idea of a mustache.

Maybe, he daydreamed, he'd even get on the front page.

He was just plodding past a newsstand when a headline on the *Clarion* late edition stopped him in his tracks.

Ghostly Murder Mystery: Who Killed the Etherist?

Johnny grabbed a copy. He scanned the article and let out a gasp. The subhead read: "Silver City etherist run through with a spear."

The article went on to say that Mongke Eng had been slain the evening before. Police didn't know who was responsible for the death, but suspected renegade ghosts—possibly ancient warriors that had been seen in the vicinity.

Johnny put the paper back down, shaking his head. Mongke Eng was a family friend. Johnny had met him several times and thought he was a nice old guy. Like Johnny's sister Melanie, Mongke Eng was an etherist, or "wraith handler." Johnny explained to people that etherists were professionals who hired ghosts or fired ghosts.

In fact, right now Mel was out in the suburbs somewhere, trying to evict a particularly noxious specter from someone's house. She probably hadn't heard about what happened to Mongke Eng. As soon as he was done with the assignment, Johnny had to get home and give her the bad news.

Out of nowhere a very large, strong hand grabbed him by the collar and twisted him around.

"What the heck!" Johnny yelled, struggling to break free. Then he looked up into the long, acne-scarred face of the biggest, tallest policeman he'd ever seen.

"Shouldn't you be in school, young man?" the officer said in a voice that rumbled like a foghorn.

"I tested out," Johnny answered. "Earned my high school diploma a couple months ago."

The officer scowled. "I'll need some proof."

Johnny glanced down the busy sidewalk behind the policeman. A throng of pedestrians flowed along on both sides of them, like a stream around a boulder. Just then he saw a ghost rider on a ghost horse trotting toward him. The bearded rider, looking very grim, had his saber drawn as if ready to attack.

Johnny was one of the few people on Superior Avenue that afternoon who could see the wraith. Only two or three in a hundred humans had the gift of etheric sight.

When he noticed the ghost approaching them, Johnny shook his head violently and threw up his open left hand, as if to say, *STOP*. And the spectral rider did just that.

The officer squinted down at him in puzzlement. "Are you okay, kid?"

"Here, just a minute," Johnny sputtered, putting down his backpack and reaching into his coat pocket. He fished out a new leather wallet and flipped it open. Beneath a clear celluloid window was an official-looking card bearing the signature of the Superintendent of Zenith Public Schools. It had a tiny photo of Johnny glued in the upper right corner and it stated: *John Joshua Graphic, having earned the Zenith Public Schools high school graduation equivalency certificate, is hereby relieved of any further requirement for regular attendance in school session. Granted this 23rd day of July, 1935.*

The policeman took the wallet and examined Johnny's get-out-of-school card. "Not right that a kid your age ain't in school," the copper grumbled. "Guess you're legal, though." He let go of Johnny's collar and handed back the wallet. "Just don't get into any mischief," he said, and sauntered away.

Johnny stuck his wallet back in his pocket and picked up the canvas bag. He glared up at the waiting ghost rider and frowned. "What were you going to do, Colonel? Cut his head off?"

Dead now over seventy years, the ghost still maintained his ramrod military posture. A barely visible smile broke out among his whiskers. "Are we just going to stand here, then, Master Johnny? Don't we have work to do?"

JOHNNY FOUND the four sewer workers sitting around an upended wooden cable spool, down a shadowy alleyway. Just as Miss Beale had said he would find them. They were playing poker, cracking wise, and drinking beer straight out of the bottles—right in the middle of what ought to have been their afternoon shift. The game so occupied them that it took half a minute before one of the men noticed Johnny standing there. "Get outta here, kid," he snarled.

Johnny just slouched there and waited for the men—all in dirty brown overalls, tin hats, and tall, black rubber boots—to stop noticing him. When they finally did, he reached into the canvas bag and pulled out his Zoom 4x5 press camera. The film and flashbulb were ready to go.

He lifted the camera up to his eye, framed the picture at just the perfect instant, and pressed the shutter release. A bright explosion of light filled the alley.

With roars of outrage, the sewer men rushed at him.

Johnny was already halfway down the alley, his legs pumping, his feet pounding the pavement. But the men were catching up. No way could he outrun them.

Suddenly he threw a hand high into the air. The colonel hauled him up into the saddle and they galloped off down the street.

Johnny saw the startled looks on faces all around, as he bounced along five feet above the street with no apparent means of support. Glancing back, he caught sight of one of the sewer men angrily throwing his tin hat on the sidewalk.

"Spooks!" the worker hollered in disgust, as if it were the filthiest word imaginable. "That kid's in cahoots with spooks!"

Johnny was tempted to shout back a retort. Instead, he held tightly to the ghost horse's luxuriant mane and laughed in giddy relief.

Holy maroley, he thought, *I really did it.*

CHAPTER 2

JOHNNY *DID NOT* ENJOY flying with Colonel Mac-Farlane and his ghost horse, Buck. Not one little bit.

To tumble off Buck from the height of several hundred feet, Johnny figured, would be every bit as fatal as falling off a cliff or a tall building. Gravity doesn't care how a fellow got up there.

But after reading the headline on the front page of the *Clarion*—about Mongke Eng getting murdered by ghosts—Johnny knew he had to tell Mel the bad news as soon as he could. Mel really respected the old man, and hearing about his death from Johnny might soften the blow. The streetcar and bus would take too long. So after turning in his film at the newspaper office, he asked the colonel to fly him home.

Home was a ten-mile flight from downtown Zenith. The Graphics' house, Birchwood, was a couple hundred yards up from the rocky shore of Great Lake, the largest freshwater lake in the world. From Lake Highway down by the shore, the brick house could barely be seen through the evergreens, birches, and poplars that filled its big front yard.

The instant they touched down on the driveway, Johnny hopped off the ghost horse and rushed up the porch steps. He threw open the front door and shouted, "Mel! Are you home yet?"

No one answered.

Johnny trotted into the living room, tossing his camera bag onto the sofa. "Mel?"

Again, not a peep from anyone.

He went back into the hallway and ran up the stairway two steps at a time. Maybe Mel was back, working in her bedroom. When she was really busy with a project, it took a stick of dynamite to get her attention. But when he peered into her open bedroom door, no one was there. Just her stuff. A cluttered desk and bookshelves. Her upright piano. Her bed, neatly made up, with the crossed army sabers up above it, hanging on the wall. The landscape painting by the Contessa di Altamonta, the famous ghost artist and friend of their mom.

"Master Johnny?"

Johnny nearly jumped out of his skin. He twirled around and saw Mrs. Lundgren standing in the hallway by the bathroom door. Pale and translucent, the ghost housekeeper held a real bucket in one hand and a real mop in the other. Her apple-doll face showed a look of worry.

"What's wrong, child?" she asked in that peculiar whispery tone. "Is anything the matter?"

"I'm looking for Mel, Mrs. Lundgren. Something important's come up and she needs to know about it."

"I believe Miss Melanie said she would be back by suppertime."

"Thanks, Mrs. Lundgren," Johnny said, and headed back downstairs. He went out on the front porch and sat on the long oak bench, waiting for Mel's return. It wasn't very long before someone arrived home—but not his sister.

Puffing up the driveway on her balloon-tired bicycle came Nina Bain, attired in a khaki safari jacket and stout skirt of olive drab. Her short, black corkscrew curls bobbed with every pump of the pedals. The dark-skinned girl and Johnny had been best friends ever since she and Uncle Louie had come to live in the big brick house—right after Will and Lydia Graphic had vanished.

Johnny thought it was swell, how Uncle Louie had been granted custody of Nina after her father died. That kind of made her Johnny's honorary cousin. The two were about the same age and natural allies in the fight against sober adult points of view. Johnny sometimes called her "Sparks," because she was a dedicated ham radio operator. She had her radio gear up in the attic and a tall antenna on the roof.

Almost out of breath, Nina rested her bike against the side of the porch and joined Johnny on the bench. "So how'd it go?" she asked, taking off her backpack and laying it on the floor.

"It went okay, Sparks, but it was a little bit scary. First time I've taken shots of people who don't want their photos taken."

"Is your picture going to be on the front page?"

"Yup, they said it would be."

"That's great. So what happened exactly?"

And Johnny told Nina about the whole adventure. At several points during his narrative, she shook her head in amazement. But when he finished she had a kind of funny expression on her face. "What?" he said. "What's wrong?"

She narrowed her eyes. "The Johnny Graphic I know would be grinning and jumping up and down. You seem awfully subdued, considering you're getting your first front-page photo credit. Smells a little fishy to me. You have a bellyache or something?"

"I wish that's all it was," Johnny said. Then he told her about Mongke Eng.

MELANIE GRAPHIC didn't make it home for supper that evening. By the time she finally came through the front door at half past ten, almost everyone else had gone to bed. But Johnny was waiting for her in the entranceway.

She looked utterly exhausted. Her limp, black hair was limper and stringier than usual, and the circles under her eyes more pronounced. She wearily took off her green plaid jacket and hung it on the coat rack, then headed toward the kitchen, giving her brother a half-hearted wave.

He hopped out of his chair and followed her. "Bad haunting?" he asked.

"I'll say." Mel yawned, making straight for the refrigerator. She pulled the door open, extracted a bottle of milk, and found the cheese-and-sausage sandwich Mrs. Lundgren had made for her.

Johnny sat down opposite his sister at the table. "So what happened?"

"People sometimes don't know how lucky they are, not seeing and hearing ghosts," she said after her first mouthful of sandwich. "New family bought an old house in Hector Town. The daughter can see ghosts. Of course, she can hear them, too. Moved into a place with a screamer, and the mom and dad didn't know it beforehand."

Johnny winced. Screamers were ghosts that howled and screeched pretty much non-stop. Not because they couldn't stop, but because they were angry with everyone and everything.

"It wasn't easy," said Mel, "but I got him to move to an abandoned mansion about a mile away. I convinced him he'd sound even louder in a big, empty house like that. Took a while, though." She chomped another bite of sandwich and regarded Johnny with a quizzical look. "You seem suspiciously grim. Do you want to tell me something?"

Johnny looked at his seventeen-year-old sister. She had the same spray of freckles across the cheeks and nose as he did. But her eyes were hazel, not blue; her hair black, not dark blond. Sometimes they almost didn't look like siblings. She resembled their mom. He was a lot like their pop.

"What is it, Johnny?" Mel asked, suddenly concerned.

He took a deep breath. "They killed Mongke Eng. A ghost assassin in Silver City. The article in the *Clarion* said it was some kind of a warrior."

He expected her to be shocked, but to his surprise she wasn't. She merely slumped down in her chair.

"Steppe Warriors," Mel said, almost in a whisper. "They're called Steppe Warriors. Now that you know about it, I might as well tell you everything."

Johnny's mouth dropped open. "'Everything'? What do you mean, 'everything'?"

"It's not just Mongke. Five other members of the Hausenhofer Gesellschaft have been murdered by ghost assassins. The first two or three, we hoped it was just some grisly coincidence. But now..." She trailed off.

What Mel had just said hit Johnny like a ton of bricks.

It wasn't just a single etherist who had gotten himself killed. It was specifically members of the group to which Mel belonged—the Gesellschaft. There were only about twenty-five of them in the outfit. And now six were dead. This was a lot worse than he had thought.

If someone was targeting members of the Gesellschaft, then Mel's life was in danger, too!

CHAPTER 3

"WHY DIDN'T YOU say something?" Johnny asked with a flash of anger.

Mel pulled herself upright and stared back at her fuming brother. "You went through so much when Mom and Dad disappeared. We didn't want to put you through the wringer again."

"I handled what happened to Mom and Pop pretty good for a kid. Did you think I'd fall apart if I found out I might lose you, too?"

"You're not going to lose me," Mel said, trying to reassure Johnny that he wasn't about to become an only child, as well as an orphan. "Besides, why would anyone want to kill someone like me? It's utterly insane."

Her words didn't calm him.

"I mean, six people murdered," he said. "And you're in the same small group as them. It doesn't take a genius to figure out that these ghost assassins might come gunning for Melanie Graphic."

"We all just hoped that this thing would blow over. Hoped that you'd never even have to know about it."

"And what do you mean by 'we'?" he asked, still bristling. "Who else knows?"

"Uncle Louie knows. Colonel MacFarlane knows. He gave orders to the troopers to set up pickets around the house twenty-four hours a day."

That made Johnny feel a little better. The colonel and his Border War ghost soldiers would definitely keep a sharp eye on Mel. But it didn't feel good knowing that everyone had left the kid brother in the dark.

"Dame Honoria knows, of course," added Mel. "That's why she cut short her visit here and went down to Capital City. To talk with the authorities."

Johnny thought about the situation for a moment. "Someone has to be controlling these warrior ghosts, or whatever you call them."

"Steppe Warriors," Mel said. "Well, that's how it works, isn't it? Specters can't operate in the real world unless a living person asks them to."

"But why would anybody want to eliminate a bunch of musty old etherists?"

"Hey, watch it!" Mel gave her brother a crooked, little grin. "You think I'm musty and old?"

"Naw, not you, Sis. But you gotta admit, just about everyone else in the Gesellschaft is. At least everybody I've met."

"Well, apart from insulting my friends, you make a good point. Why murder us? We're harmless. All we do is study how ghosts can come out of the ether into the real world and function as if they were alive. How can Mrs. Lundgren make me a cheese-and-sausage sandwich? A woman who died thirty years ago? How can the colonel and his men play poker all night in the basement, with real cards and chips?"

Johnny smiled. The colonel and the boys sure did love their poker games.

"Something one of you did or said maybe threatened someone,"

Johnny speculated.

"But what?" Mel asked. "What could it possibly be? I've got to admit, I don't have a clue."

Johnny let his sister finish her sandwich and drink her milk in silence. Then he took a deep breath, puffed himself up—because he didn't like what he was about to say.

"Doesn't seem there's much else to do but cancel the trip out to La Concha. Wouldn't be safe."

Mel looked at her brother in astonishment. "*Ab-so-lute-ly not,*" she said. "In case you've forgotten, Iron River Mining Company has gone bankrupt. Mom and Dad's contract with Iron River has been our meal ticket ever since they vanished. Now it's out of business. No more checks in the mail.

"Sorry, Johnny, but what I'm earning plus what you're earning plus Uncle Louie's salary from down at the aeroboat port just isn't enough. We have to pay for this big, beautiful house. If we don't start making about twice what we're making now, the bank will repossess Birchwood."

Johnny, of course, knew all this, though he usually tried to put it out of his mind.

"If my hypothesis about the physics of etheric light transmission is proved correct," said Mel, "we could make a bundle."

Mel had spent long hours trying to develop a formula for a movie film that would actually photograph ghosts—something that had been utterly impossible up to now.

"Couldn't you just do the research here in Zenith and send it to Megatherian?" Johnny suggested. "Instead of going out to La Concha?"

Mel shook her head. "The studio wants to put me together with its film chemists to see if we can actually make an etheric film. And I've got to be there in their laboratory."

Johnny's face suddenly brightened. "Is it true that Donnie Anderson wants to make a movie with Megatherian?"

Donnie Anderson had been Johnny's favorite cowboy star. That is, until the unfortunate actor had taken a fatal tumble off his horse two years before. Johnny wanted nothing more than to see the singing cowboy back in the saddle and up on the silver screen again, strumming away on his guitar.

"That's just a rumor," she said. "But I know there are five or six ghost stars who are ready to get back in front of the cameras."

"I really want to go to La Concha," Johnny admitted. "Taking pictures of movie stars would be incredible. And Miss Beale at the *Clarion* said she'd buy every shot I take. But you know, I'd rather have a big sister than a big pile of money. We don't have to go. It's too dangerous. We can find some other way to keep the house."

Mel shook her head. "It's really sweet that you're worried about me, Johnny. But a fat contract with Megatherian would solve all our money problems. My mind is made up. I'm going to La Concha."

CHAPTER 4

AS THE MORTON MONARCH touring car pulled away from the big brick house, Johnny spied Mrs. Lundgren floating out through the front wall. The ghost housekeeper waved and shouted, "A safe journey, children."

A few moments later, the big convertible was zooming south on Lake Highway. Johnny sat in front, feeling both excited and uneasy. Looking at things from his normal point of view, this trip could be really amazing. Meeting movie stars. Taking their pictures. How could a news photog not love that?

But that annoying, grown-up voice inside his head—ever more insistent since he had tested out of school—kept saying, "Boy, oh boy, not a good idea."

Driving the car was a tall, muscular man in blue dungarees, tan work shirt, and a Zenith Blue Sox cap—the "S" resembling a lightning bolt. Louie Hofstedter had dark, slicked-back hair and a square face with lots of wrinkles from smiling all the time. But that afternoon Johnny noticed that his uncle wore a glum expression.

The gals, as Uncle Louie called them, were all in the backseat. Nina had arrived home from school barely in time to ride with them and was still wearing her navy blue sailor dress. Beside her sat Mel, intently reading the latest letter from Megatherian Studios and making notations in pencil in the margins.

Squeezed in next to the two girls was Dame Honoria Gorton Rathbone, looking as if she had just eaten a sour pickle. But she usually did look that way. Quite famous in the Royal Kingdom, the heiress of the Gorton's Little Pills fortune had helped win females the right to vote back in the late teens. More recently, she had been collaborating with the dead author Sir Chauncey Holyfield, shepherding his bestselling scientific romances into print.

Johnny thought she wasn't that bad an old stick, for someone almost sixty. Practically a member of the family—and Johnny's own godmother—Dame Honoria had spent two full weeks with the Graphics during her tour of the New Continent. Uncle Louie and Mel had even thrown a big dinner party in her honor, where the great lady held forth for hours and enjoyed showing off her necklace with the giant black diamond, known as the Star of Gilbeyshire.

After a slow slog through rush-hour traffic, the Morton Monarch finally pulled onto Superior Avenue, just as its gaudy neon signs and theater marquees started blinking on. Johnny adored Superior Avenue. It was always lively, always hopping. The sidewalks were crammed with people going to the stores and restaurants, to the movie palaces and nightclubs. Streetcars rattled along the length of Zenith's main shopping street, and cable cars trundled noisily up and down the city's steep central hill.

Johnny glanced over his shoulder. Half a block back, passing through autos and streetcars and pedestrians, trotted Colonel MacFarlane, up on Buck, his chestnut bay ghost horse. Behind him rode the entire First Zenith Brigade—every trooper present and accounted for. That was the only concession that Johnny and Uncle Louie could wring out of Mel—she'd allow the colonel to come along on the journey west, just in case.

Uncle Louie swung the convertible left onto Lake Street and cruised into the Bowery—a very different, darker place than Superior Avenue.

The Bowery always gave Johnny an uneasy sort of feeling. It showed what could happen to folks if things went bad—often through no fault of their own. It made him grateful for everything he had, even without his parents around.

But he had to admit, he felt conspicuous here, in his nice blue wool suit, red silk tie, and gray fedora.

Ragged, defeated men and dreary, frumpy women gathered in clumps in front of saloons and fleabag hotels. Lots of ghosts floated around, too—the specters of drowned sailors, starved children, desolated people of all kinds. The living and the dead gazed at Johnny, and in his mind he could almost hear them asking: *Why do you have so much, boy, and we have so little?*

A few minutes after crossing the Aerial Bridge onto Zenith Point, the big touring car pulled up to the main concourse of the George Babbitt Memorial Flying Boat Port. On its landward side, the terminal building was a broad edifice of cream-colored limestone decorated with giant relief sculptures of water birds. On the bay side, a number of aeroboat docks extended out onto the water, all but a few of them occupied by seaplanes great and small.

Uncle Louie steered the auto into a spot under the long canopy. In a wink he and Johnny had every piece of luggage on two porter carts—one for Dame Honoria, who was flying east to Neuport, and another for Johnny and Mel's flight west to La Concha. After shaking Dame Honoria and Johnny's hands, Uncle Louie gave Mel a big bear hug.

"Take care now and keep your eyes peeled," he told his niece and nephew, climbing into the Monarch. "If needs be, let the colonel do his job."

As the touring car pulled away, Nina hollered, "Johnny, don't do anything I wouldn't."

"Will if I want to, Sparks," he shot back.

THE ZEPHYR LINES Night Goose to La Concha didn't depart until late in the evening. So Mel and Johnny had time to escort Dame Honoria through the bustling air terminal and right to her flying boat.

Johnny's godmother was short and heavyset, her perpetually overcast face resembling that of a gloomy horse. She wore a gray lady's suit with a skirt that reached mid-calf.

The noblewoman stopped just shy of the ramp up to her aeroboat, pulling Mel and Johnny off to the side. A stream of travelers trudged by them and into the four-engined Como Eagle.

"I beg you, Melanie, one last time," Dame Honoria said, her voice grave and quiet. "Please postpone your trip. Jules and B. J., Elmer and Anna, Deng and Mongke. All murdered." She peered intensely at Mel. "You are every bit as vulnerable as they were, as I am."

"I know you're trying to protect me," said Mel. "But we need to make more money. Megatherian Studios looks like the best chance that we have."

"At the risk of repeating myself," Dame Honoria said, "I would be only too happy to pay your mortgage for as long as needed."

Mel gave her a vigorous hug and kissed her on her fuzzy cheek. "You are a wonderful, wonderful old dear," she said with a sad smile. "And I love you absolutely to bits. You've been so good to us since Mom and Dad disappeared. But we cannot accept any charity. The Graphic family does not accept charity."

As Mel released her, the older woman nodded slowly, accepting defeat.

Johnny couldn't help piping up. "Dame Honoria, aren't you worried for yourself? You're in danger, too."

"But I'm not seventeen," she said. "I don't have a whole half century ahead of me. And with my sweet Percival gone these last five years, much of life's joy has faded."

Johnny knew just how awful it felt to lose two parents. But Dame Honoria reminded him that it couldn't be much easier to have your only child taken away. On that very same terrible night, in that very same terrible place that took Will and Lydia Graphic. They and Percy Rathbone vanished from their tents in the midst of a raging blizzard on Okkatek Island.

"Will you be staying in Gilbeyshire, then?" asked Johnny.

"First to Neuport, then Gilbeyshire. Finally, on to my dear old Gorton Island. I've work to do with Sir Chauncey. By then, perhaps, this terrible business will have blown over."

Dame Honoria sniffled. She reached into her handbag and pulled out a lavender linen handkerchief, then dabbed at the corners of her eyes. "Well, the air stewardess is looking at me rather severely. So I suppose I'd best get on board."

She embraced and kissed Mel, then shook Johnny's hand. He could tell she wanted to hug him, but was grateful that she didn't. Getting hugged by old ladies was not one of his favorite things.

"Godspeed, my dear ones," she said, and then tottered up into the blue and silver flying boat.

CHAPTER 5

JOHNNY'S WINDOW SEAT gave him a clear view of the bottom of the Night Goose's vast starboard wing, along with its four engines. Mel plopped down next to him and quickly nodded off to sleep.

As usual, she was wearing her "protective coloration," as Uncle Louie described it. This time it was a beige silk blouse, gray gabardine trousers, scuffed brown moccasins, and white ankle socks. Over her shoulders she'd tied an old gray cardigan sweater. With all those neutral colors, thought Johnny, his sister almost disappeared. Of course, that was just how she liked it.

"Solitary" didn't begin to describe Mel. She only left the house to do a job—like that haunting up in Hector Town—or to hit the research library at the Zenith Institute of Etheristics. Her two best friends from school had steady boyfriends now, so she rarely saw them anymore. Johnny wished that Mel didn't have so much to worry about. She deserved to have some fun, too.

Before long, a tugboat chugged up, and slowly towed and nudged the giant aeroboat out into the taxiing channel. Johnny watched the process with fascination. When the tugboat retreated, the Goose's eight engines roared to life, one after another, making a tremendous noise. The airliner proceeded south, then made a broad U-turn into the main north-south runway. As soon as the aeroboat's nose was put into the wind, the takeoff run began.

Johnny yanked off his fedora and stuck his face right up to the porthole. His heart pounded. He loved to fly—so long as it wasn't on a ghost horse. The dark water foamed white under the Goose and trailed off behind it. Buoy lights flashed by. The wing gradually lifted, pulling the pontoon off the water. On the far side of the bay, lights atop grain elevators and iron ore docks winked red in the night. Long, low lake boats sat in broad pools of yellow light, taking on wheat and soybeans and corn. Headlights zoomed up and down West Bay Road.

With a mild lurch, the giant seaplane lifted up from Zenith Bay, gained some altitude, and turned gently toward the west, right over the vast Acme Iron Works, glowing red in the night. As the Goose began its slow climb to ten thousand feet, Johnny could see Zenith's nighttime glow disappear back to the east.

He pulled out his backpack from under the seat in front of him and extracted a plastic bag from one of the outside pockets. A wicked grin danced across his face.

A few days earlier he'd visited Zoltan's Costumes and Makeup, hoping to spot some nifty disguises for work. He made Zoltan show him the new line of human-hair mustaches from the Kingdom of Ithia.

"You're too yunk for deese, Chonny," Zoltan had told him. "You look zilly."

Johnny glared at the elderly shop owner. "I still want it. Everyone likes to know what they look like in a mustache."

One glance in his bedroom mirror told him that Zoltan knew his stuff. Johnny looked plenty "zilly." But he had an alternative use in mind for the hirsute decoration.

As Mel and most of the other passengers slumbered, Johnny

pulled the object from its bag. He daubed it with spirit gum. Then he leaned over and delicately placed it on his sister's upper lip, pressing lightly.

Heart pounding, he withdrew his fingertips. Would it hold?

Mel snored a little and rolled her head to the side.

"Gotcha!" Johnny whispered, digging out the new issue of *Astounding Stories with Duke Donegan*. He reached up, flipped on the light, and started to read. Before long, he was snoring, too.

IT WAS THE SAME NIGHTMARE he'd been having for years. Ever since Mom and Pop vanished on Okkatek Island.

He was lost in the wilderness. Scrambling for his life through deep snow. And, of course, he was stark naked.

He staggered along the bank of a frozen stream and heard the howling of the ice wolves that pursued him. He could almost feel their hot breath on his shoulders. He could almost sense their long, yellow fangs going for his throat. He spun around and saw the first wolf break through a screen of pine trees, surging toward him.

Then out of nowhere came a great BOOM.

Someone was shooting cannonballs at him.

Another thunderous BOO-OOM resounded through the wintry woods.

Time, Johnny's dreaming self decided, *to wake up*. He winked open his eyes and felt instant relief.

It was okay. He was in his seat on the Night Goose, heading for La Concha. Everything was—

BANG.

BOOOOM.

The explosion came from outside the cabin. Johnny's heart, pounding like a bass drum, leapt up into his throat. He peered out the porthole and the most amazing thing happened.

One.

Two.

Three bronze arrowheads punctured the bulkhead next to his seat.

Whunk.

Whunk.

Whunk.

Inches from his right ear.

Then they dissolved into wispy nothingness.

CHAPTER 6

HORRIFIED, JOHNNY SAW that one of the propellers had stopped turning, the engine trailing smoke. Down below, ghost riders in pointed helmets circled and swooped.

He had to wake up his sister. *Fast.* He swiveled and punched her in the arm.

"Aaaa-oow!" She jumped up out of her seat and banged her head on the overhead compartment. She whimpered in pain. "You little worm, I'm going to wallop you!"

"Trouble!" Johnny snapped. "Big trouble! Window! *Now!*"

Growling and rubbing the rapidly forming knot on her head, Mel leaned over and looked out. It didn't take her long to comprehend their dire situation.

"We're under attack," she gasped. "*By Steppe Warriors!*"

Johnny took another look, just in time to see the ghost attackers plummet earthward and out of sight.

Almost all of the one hundred and twenty seats in the big passenger compartment were occupied. Several people had woken up and were peeking through the portholes on both sides. Air stewardesses and stewards brought up the lights and circulated, reassuring people that everything was under control.

Johnny knew all too well that things weren't under control.

"I'm going up to the flight deck," Mel said.

Johnny stared up at her, his mouth beginning to form the sound "Oops."

He'd forgotten about the mustache.

"What?" Mel snapped.

"I'm coming with," he announced, grabbing his camera bag and sticking his *Zenith Clarion* press card in the band around his fedora. A fellow never could tell when there might be a news-worthy shot that needed taking.

The stewards and stewardesses were so occupied with the other passengers that they didn't notice Mel and Johnny sneaking up the steep, tight ladderway and onto the flight deck.

"The Goose is one of the safest flying machines in the sky," bellowed a frizzy-haired woman in the pilot's seat. "The Goose has never crashed. Now, tonight, we have two engines blow out within seconds of each other. Two more and we go down."

She had on headphones and a microphone, and probably didn't need to shout. But Johnny couldn't blame her. He'd be shouting, too.

"Dash it, Danny, we have to get down on the water," the pilot continued. "Summit's five hours west. That's too far. And we're too big to splash down anywhere else—we might never get air-borne again."

The co-pilot, sitting in the right-hand seat, carefully worked some levers at the bottom of the main control panel. Their radio-man sat behind them. He was broadcasting an emergency call.

"Then it's gotta be back to Zenith, Hilda," the co-pilot shouted.

Johnny jammed his elbow in Mel's ribs and gestured at the pilot. "Tell her what's happened!"

Mel took a very deep breath and yelled, "Excuse me!"

With headphones on, neither of the pilots nor the radioman could hear her. No one had even noticed the two kids.

So Johnny decided to take charge. Mel was just not pushy enough. He tramped over to the radio operator and tapped him on the shoulder. A wiry, middle-aged man with a prominent Adam's apple, the fellow jumped, looking startled. Ripping his headphones and mic off, he gaped at the two siblings. "You can't be up here," he said. "Get back to your seats right now, or you're in big, big trouble."

"Everybody on this aeroboat is in big, big trouble," Johnny barked back. "We think we know what happened, why your engines conked out."

"You know *what?*"

"My brother here saw what happened," said Mel in a loud voice.

"You're not pulling my leg, are you?" asked the radioman.

"We're deadly serious," she replied.

The radioman lurched to his feet and quickly got the pilot's attention. She glared at the two young interlopers and said that this had better not be a joke. "A hundred thirty lives are in danger here," she warned them.

Mel sucked in another deep breath. "Ghosts are shooting arrows at your flying boat, ma'am."

"Captain Merrick!"

Mel cringed. "Sorry, Captain Merrick. My name's Melanie Graphic and I'm an etherist, a ghost wrangler. From what I can see, we're under attack by ghosts shooting etheric arrows. They've pierced an engine—"

"Two engines," the co-pilot said, looking up at Mel. He was a trim young man with olive skin and almond-shaped eyes. "But how can their arrows hurt us? If they're ghosts?"

"Because some living person has given them the job of shooting us down," answered Mel.

Johnny saw the co-pilot's eyes suddenly focus intently on Mel's upper lip. *Uh-oh,* the young photographer thought, *he's noticed the mustache. Hope he doesn't say anything. Because this sure wouldn't be a good time.*

"And I think they've put some arrows through the cabin walls," Mel continued. "I'm very much afraid they're after yours truly. I belong to a group called the Hausenhofer Gesellschaft. Steppe Warriors have murdered six of our members. The only theories we have are that—"

Captain Merrick cut her off. "Am I right to assume that your theories won't provide any practical help right now?"

"Um, well, no," said Mel.

"Then forget 'em, Miss Graphic. Is there anything you *can* do?"

"I think my ghosts are already on the job, Captain."

"*Your* ghosts?"

Johnny piped up. "Horse soldiers, Captain. First Zenith Cavalry Brigade. Dead since the First Border War."

The captain shook her head in disbelief. "At least," she groaned, "it'll be an interesting way to die."

CHAPTER 7

GALLOPING ALONG outside the flying machine, Colonel Horace MacFarlane went from one of his horse soldiers to another, barking out their orders.

"Form a perimeter," he shouted in the blasting wind. "All 'round. They'll be back. Don't chase 'em. That's what they want. At all costs, keep 'em away from Commander Graphic and her brother. Let's show these people what the First Zenith Brigade is made of!"

The Steppe Warriors had darted up from below and down from above—perfectly coordinated, highly effective tactics. They came standing in their saddles, arrows nocked, bowstrings pulled and released in blinks. It took just a matter of seconds. *Caught us properly by surprise*, the colonel thought.

The boys did get off a few shots with their revolvers. But the attackers were too swift. As quickly as they'd come, they slipped away.

Having never been in a real fight with ghosts before, the colonel recalled what he knew of the laws of the ether. Specters use the same weapons that they used when they were alive. And a bullet or arrow wound still smarts something fierce, even if you're a ghost. But it can't kill a specter, who is already dead. One death—that's all a fellow gets. However, an etheric head or leg sliced off will cripple a ghost for eternity. Chop him to tiny pieces, and he will find himself in the most horrible torment imaginable.

Not for the first time, the colonel marveled at how well things had turned out for him. He certainly never could have imagined being dead these seventy years and tonight finding himself in a battle among the clouds. It felt excellent, fighting the good fight yet again.

Of course, no sensible person would ever want to get stuck in the ether. You couldn't eat. Couldn't drink. Couldn't smell. Couldn't taste. Couldn't sleep. Couldn't dream. Most of all, the colonel missed breathing. He ached to feel the sweet friction of air going down his throat, into his lungs and out again.

You couldn't touch or hold anything. Couldn't play the piano. Couldn't cradle a baby to your chest. Unless a living person asked you to.

For the first sixty years of his death the colonel felt cut off from anything vaguely meaningful. He'd wished many a time he could kill himself—and have another chance at dying properly. Which, alas, he could not do. If you don't vanish into the great unknown when you first die, you're trapped in the ether forever.

Then he had met someone up the shore of Great Lake, north of Zenith. About ten years ago. Someone alive. Someone who changed everything for Horace MacFarlane.

He remembered that moment as if it were yesterday. He had been sitting on a jagged gray boulder when he heard a small voice say, "Hello, mister. What's your name?"

Looking up, he saw a skinny young girl standing before him, perhaps six or seven years old, in a summer frock of pastel green. She had sad hazel eyes, with little flecks of amber. There was a spray of freckles across pale cheeks, and she wore long black hair plaited down her back. The colonel's heart had stopped pumping six decades before, but he could have sworn that it started up again when the girl talked to him.

"Colonel Horace MacFarlane," he had said, standing up to his full six feet. He doffed his campaign cap and bowed. His blue officer's jacket had holes and blood stains from the shrapnel that had killed him. He observed with interest that the child didn't seem scared.

"And to whom do I have the pleasure of speaking, young lady?" he asked.

"Melanie Graphic."

"Very pleased to meet you," the ghost said.

The little girl kicked at the pebbles underneath her feet. "We're having a picnic down the beach, Colonel. Want to meet my mom and dad and little brother? They can see ghosts, too."

"I would be honored," the old soldier replied.

It had been absolutely the best day of Horace MacFarlane's afterlife.

And as he finalized the Brigade's defenses, the colonel was determined that tonight should be the best night.

The lives of Commander Graphic and Master Johnny depended on it.

CHAPTER 8

"WHY DOES THAT KID have a camera?" Captain Merrick asked, finally noticing Johnny's Zoom 4x5. "I don't allow pictures to be taken on my flight deck."

"My brother's a news photographer for the *Zenith Clarion*," Mel replied.

Upon hearing that, the captain gave Johnny one of those disapproving looks that he knew so well. He'd seen it many times since he'd started in the newspaper game. He could almost read her mind: *Why aren't you in school? You're missing the best years of your life, young man.* Johnny was so tired of that attitude.

"I'd *really* like to take a few shots," he explained. "This is big news, Captain. Just a couple of pictures of you and your co-pilot. If we make it through, you'll be glad you agreed."

The co-pilot prodded Captain Merrick in the shoulder. "Let him take his pictures, Hilda. Can't do any harm showing the heroic pilots at work, can it? The boss might even like it."

Johnny took the co-pilot's point and hammered it home. "It'd be a swell thing to have for the history books. I mean, this attack is a big deal and everyone's going to want to see a photo of you and your co-pilot, Mr. ummm—"

"Officer Danny Kailolu," the young co-pilot said.

"All right, all right," the captain agreed with a frown. "Just a couple shots. That's all."

Johnny understood only too well that this was no comic book adventure. If the Steppe Warriors took out two more engines, the big flying boat would go down—with Mel and himself and everyone else on board. But that didn't mean that he should stop doing his job. If everyone survived, he knew these shots could end up on front pages all around the world. And the two pilots would be big heroes.

He squeezed by Mel in the dim, cramped cabin, sneaking another peek at her fuzzy upper lip. He groaned under his breath, regretting his stupid prank. How was it she hadn't noticed yet?

Johnny held the Zoom 4x5 up over his head, aimed down at the captain and co-pilot, and pressed the shutter release. The bulb made an audible *pooosh* sound as it went off, blasting the cabin with light.

After another shot, the captain told him to go back to his seat. But Johnny argued that having another pair of ghost-seeing eyes up on the flight deck could only help. Again, Danny Kailolu took his side and the captain yielded.

"Now get ahold of Jonesville," she ordered the radioman. "Have them telegraph Babbitt Tower. We should be getting back on toward dawn. Tell 'em we have two engines out. Nothing about ghosts and cavalrymen and bows and arrows. No details!"

Captain Merrick gently turned the steering yoke toward starboard and began the Goose's long, slow about-face. The deck tilted, the stars shifted lazily in the sky, and the moon disappeared for a time, reappearing on the other side when the aeroboat arrived at its new course and altitude.

Mel and Johnny leaned over the pilots' shoulders, scanning the night sky. The troopers of the First Zenith Brigade held position all around the giant flying boat, shimmering eerily in the moon-light as they galloped along. Johnny wished the captain and Danny could see them. It was an amazing sight.

With absolutely no warning, a rain of silvery arrows plum-meted out of the heavens—making a dreadful drumbeat on the aluminum skin of the aircraft.

"Here they come again!" Johnny screamed.

He saw the attacking Steppe Warriors do everything they could do to bring down the giant flying boat. And the First Zenith Bri-gade did everything possible to keep them away.

The two opposing troops of ghost soldiers circled, shifted, soared, and dived through the moonlit sky.

Bows snapping. Arrows flying. Revolvers banging. Sabers slashing.

Somehow, the dead combatants managed to keep up with the flying boat, which was cruising along at about two hundred miles per hour. They were easy for Johnny and Mel to see because—like all ghosts—they glowed green in the dark. Of course, the captain and the co-pilot couldn't see a thing.

Before long, only the colonel and one of the Steppe Warriors were pounding along in front of the aeroboat. The rest of the bat-tling specters seemed to have fallen behind.

The two remaining ghost soldiers slashed and cut at each other. Again and again. Thrusting, chopping, parrying. It scared Johnny, thinking what could happen to the colonel.

Finally, with a spot of luck, the colonel won the advantage, hacking his saber deeply into the Steppe Warrior's neck. In a flash, the colonel's opponent tumbled off his mount and vanished from view.

Johnny blinked, and the colonel disappeared as well. Johnny was amazed that so much could happen in just a matter of minutes. The sky had been raging with battling ghosts, but now it was calm and empty in the moonlight. It was, ironically, a beautiful night to be airborne.

He glanced at Mel—still, alas, mustachioed—and said, "I don't see them anymore, do you?"

She shook her head. "They're all gone."

"Gone?" the captain asked in her loud voice. "The ghosts are all gone?"

"Well, for now," Mel said, scanning the sky. "They went at it pretty hard at first, then fell away. I bet by now they've gotten scattered all over the place."

"You think we're safe then?" the radioman bellowed from his panel of controls.

Mel shook her head. "Not by a long shot."

"Who was winning?" the captain asked.

"Since we haven't crashed," Johnny said, "I'd wager that the colonel and his troopers put up a pretty good fight."

That's when engine number one on the starboard wing let out a resonant BOOM, like a giant firecracker under a garbage can.

"Blast it!" Captain Merrick swore. She leapt up out of her seat, glaring at the flame and smoke billowing from behind the slowing propeller.

"Starboard one," Danny Kailolu shouted, glancing out of his side window. "Shut her down!"

The captain pulled back one of the throttles with a loud snap, and rapidly flipped a series of switches on the broad control panel.

Just then a woman's blood-curdling scream came from back in the passenger cabin.

Johnny rushed to the flight deck door, threw it open, looked down, and gasped.

"*Mel-a-neeeee…*" he yelled. "You'd better come quick!"

CHAPTER 9

FROM THE FLIGHT DECK STEPS Johnny and Mel saw an astonishing and frightful scene playing out in the passenger cabin.

Facing away from them was a Steppe Warrior with braided black hair down his back. He moved purposefully among the center rows of seats. He held his horse's reins in his left hand and the animal followed along docilely. The wraith was hunting for someone among the agitated passengers—through whom he passed invisibly, with no one realizing it.

In his right hand he gripped a curved sword, tipped backward, resting on his shoulder. The blade dribbled black oil. Johnny wondered if that sword damaged the third engine.

In the aisle off to Johnny and Mel's right, a steward was trying to revive an unconscious young woman. Johnny figured that she must have been the source of that awful screech—no doubt she could see ghosts. And he didn't blame her one little bit for fainting.

He whispered in Mel's ear. "Get back up on the flight deck, Sis. I'll try to get rid of him."

Mel sharply shook her head just one time and stepped down into the passenger cabin.

Before Johnny could say anything more, she hollered, "I think you're looking for me!"

The eyes of every passenger rotated from the woman who had been screaming—now unconscious—to Mel. Johnny knew just what they all must have been thinking: *Why does she have a mustache?*

A few passengers answered her declaration, assuring her that they *weren't* looking for her. A slim, ruddy-faced steward began to approach Mel. But Danny Kailolu had just come down from the cockpit and ordered the man to leave her alone.

The Steppe Warrior slowly turned and regarded her with empty, bleeding eye sockets. Johnny had never seen a ghost so terrible to look at. And Johnny had seen many ghosts.

"Sir, we need to talk," Mel said, with a quaver in her voice. "Who sent you? Why are you killing my friends? If you have a problem, I'm certain we can come to some reasonable arrangement."

Johnny wished Mel had kept her mouth shut, but he was prepared to get between her and the ghost, if he had to. He wondered, over the course of a few heartbeats, what kind of weapon a Zoom 4x5 camera would make.

The wraith dropped the horse's reins and walked slowly forward toward Mel, through center seats and passengers, halting fifteen feet short of her. Peering out through his stomach was the face of an elderly female passenger, unaware that she and the medieval assassin simultaneously occupied the same space.

The Steppe Warrior held his gaze—such as it was—on Mel. Then he tilted his head in amusement. A ghastly smile turned up the corners of his lipless mouth. He chortled deeply, menacingly.

"Do all the women in your family grow such splendid mustaches?" he hissed.

Johnny shuddered and stole a glance at his sister. She looked quite baffled. An idea popped into his head straight out of nowhere. Mel's life might depend on what he was about to do. Hoping no one would notice him, he slowly sidled off to the left aisle.

"What?" said Mel. "Mustaches?" She put a finger to her upper lip and gave a little gasp.

The Steppe Warrior's dreadful smile vanished. He moved toward her, raising his saber for the killing stroke.

That's when Johnny brought his camera up and jammed down the shutter release. The flashbulb went off, creating a dazzling burst of light. Almost all the passengers blinked wildly, some rubbing or covering their eyes. And just as Johnny had hoped, the explosion of light distracted the Steppe Warrior for several very precious seconds.

Snarling with anger, the ghoulish specter pivoted to his right and lunged at Johnny with his blade. Johnny leapt backward, stumbling and falling into the lap of a startled passenger.

No one but the Graphics and the Steppe Warrior witnessed what happened next.

With a furious shout of "CHARGE!" Horace MacFarlane and Buck came blasting through the back of the cabin. The colonel slashed powerfully at the flank of the little Steppe horse with his saber. The terrified animal screamed piteously and dove straight through the cabin floor.

The eyeless Steppe Warrior turned, roared, and launched himself straight at the colonel. But the colonel had too much momentum and speed. As the Steppe Warrior's blade came up in a vicious backhand, the colonel's came down with full force, parried it, and sliced his opponent's upper arm.

Before the colonel could come around again, the Steppe Warrior shrieked in pain, and just as his Steppe pony had, dropped like a rock through the cabin deck.

Johnny struggled to his feet, apologizing to the poor gent who had caught him. For a moment he thought the colonel was going to pursue the Steppe Warrior. But instead, the old horse soldier halted in mid-passenger cabin, leapt off Buck, and rushed to Mel.

"Are you all right, Commander?" the ghost officer asked with a tone of extreme concern. "Are you hurt?"

Johnny arrived a second later and asked a similar question.

Then it was Danny Kailolu's turn. "Miss Graphic, what just happened?"

Wide-eyed and dazed, Mel looked from the colonel to Johnny to the co-pilot. She gestured at the empty air over the first rows of seats, where dozens of shaken passengers were chattering away. "He didn't want to talk," she said with a look of shock. "He was going to kill me. He was *actually* going to kill me."

Somehow, Johnny managed to quickly flip his camera's film holder and snap in another flashbulb. With a flare of light and another *pooosh* he took a picture of Mel's startled face.

"Who was going to kill you?" Danny asked, almost as wide-eyed as Mel. "One of the ghosts?"

"I think that I need to sit down," she said, going frighteningly pale.

The co-pilot managed to catch her just as she blacked out.

CHAPTER 10

TUESDAY, OCTOBER 8, 1935

ZENITH

THE ZEPHYR LINES NIGHT GOOSE came in over Zenith Bay just after dawn, battered and cruising slowly, having lost three engines. She splashed down in the South Bay and was met by a flotilla of tugs, police launches, and boats with news reporters and curiosity seekers. Johnny watched the whole business from one of the starboard portholes and took several pictures.

A little over an hour later, he and Mel found themselves in a windowless meeting room in the bowels of the National Office Building. The man who had taken them off the aeroboat—Managing Agent Wilton Crider of the National Police Bureau—trod through the door. Behind him came a tall, meaty man in a black suit. Except for a little white pencil mustache, he didn't have a hair on his head, not even eyebrows. The man's left hand twitched constantly.

"This is Assistant Director Santangelo of the Ministry of Etheristics," said the pugnacious, red-haired Crider. He plopped down across the table from Mel. "Miss Graphic, I need you and your brother to tell me—"

"We haven't done anything wrong!" Johnny protested.

"No one said you did," replied Crider.

Johnny didn't care for this situation one bit. It was terrifically unfair. He was a member of the press and they couldn't haul him off like this unless they were going to arrest him. They couldn't keep Mel and him from talking with their Uncle Louie and Johnny's colleagues from the *Clarion*. But they had.

"Then why're you keeping us here?" he grumbled.

"You and your sister are material witnesses in a criminal investigation," said Crider. "Let's just begin at the beginning, Miss Graphic. Tell me about the Hausenhofer Gesellschaft."

Mel nodded tiredly. "Before he died in the Great War, Oskar Hausenhofer posed a question: Just how, scientifically speaking, can wraiths touch and affect the physical world? Some kind of physics is operating here and there has to be a rational answer. Our small group looks for that explanation."

"And what have you actually discovered?" sneered Santangelo. "Scientifically speaking." His left hand continued to twitch incessantly.

Johnny, as a rule, liked most of the people he met—alive or dead. He thought of himself as a friendly sort of person. But this Santangelo character somehow gave him the creeps. And not just because he was showing Mel that snotty attitude. This guy wasn't to be trusted.

"Have we uncovered the basic secrets of the ether?" asked Mel, scowling at the bald man. "No. But thanks to the work of my parents, we've harnessed the intrinsic glow of ghosts to allow them to prospect for metals far underground. And to diagnose illness inside living human bodies. I was flying to La Concha to work on an etheric photo film that might let us photograph wraiths."

"But you still don't know the basic science," the bald man said. "You still can't tell us why an oral contract between etherist and ghost allows the ghost to operate in this dimension."

"That may be true," Mel allowed. "But I fail to see how that has any bearing on the Gesellschaft murders. And this attack on the Night Goose has to be part of that."

"There've been two more Gesellschaft killings overnight, Miss Graphic," Crider said grimly.

Mel almost came up out of her chair. "No! Who?"

Crider took a telegram out of his pocket and unfolded it. "John Addison in Neuport. Machine-gunned by a gangster ghost. And Hans Wallin in the Duchy of Steinberg. You would have been the ninth."

Tears formed in the corners of Mel's eyes. Johnny reached over and patted her arm. *She sure has had a bad night*, he thought. But there would be no "I told you so" from him.

Crider let Mel collect herself, then continued. "Is there anything that members of your group could have done or written about that could be perceived as a threat by others? I'm trying to get at the motive for these crimes."

Still sniffling a bit, Mel said, "I've read every article ever published in *The Annals of the Hausenhofer Gesellschaft*, and I can't imagine anything our members have said that could provoke others."

Johnny looked across the table at Crider and Santangelo, and felt pretty proud of Mel. She was holding her own against those two tough guys. But then, he always knew she had guts. He'd seen plenty of that in the days after Mom and Pop were lost.

"Here's an idea," Mel said, sitting up straighter in her chair. "Why would a ghost be willing to do such bloody work? What reward would motivate him? Of course, the ghost of a psychopath or some other monster might enjoy killing again. But most of these murders are being done by dead soldiers—men of discipline. What would motivate them? I'm wondering if we have to consider the Two Impossible Things."

Crider looked puzzled. "The Two Impossible Things?"

"They're practically an obsession for ghosts," Mel explained in a rush. "Approximately ninety-seven percent of living humans who die move on to heaven or the great unknown or whatever you want to call it. Their spirits, souls, essences are gone, vanished from this world and the ether. No one knows where they go or how. But the remaining three percent end up as ghosts."

"And the Impossible Things?" asked Crider.

"The First Impossible Thing is to become alive again. The Second Impossible Thing is to pass over to the great unknown. No human or animal ghost has ever returned to life, nor passed from the ether into the unknown realm. So far as we know."

Johnny regarded his sister with admiration. Did that girl have a big brain, or what? It made perfect sense. What else would a ghost really want, but to get out of the ether?

"You're suggesting that someone has figured out how to achieve one of the Impossible Things?" said Crider. "And he's using that to reward these wraiths?"

Mel thought about it for a few seconds, then nodded. "I suppose I am."

CHAPTER 11

THE VERY MOMENT Johnny sauntered into the sprawling *Zenith Clarion* newsroom, his fedora tipped at a rakish angle, people started shouting from all over.

"Hey Johnny! Glad you're okay!"

"Way to go, kiddo!"

"We got the exclusive, right?"

Reporters, editors, copyeditors, copy girls and boys, secretaries, and sub-editors mobbed Johnny as if he were a baseball hero or a movie star. His back was slapped too many times to count. *I could get used to this*, he thought.

No one paid much attention to Uncle Louie, Nina, and Mel, who trailed in after him. Uncle Louie and Nina had extracted the two siblings from a scrum of reporters and photographers on the front steps of the National Building. Then they drove directly over to the Clarion skyscraper on First Avenue.

From the far end of the newsroom came a hoarse, powerful bellow. "Back to work, people."

Johnny's head swiveled around.

Standing in front of his glassed-in office was Carlton Cargill, the *Zenith Clarion*'s editor-in-chief. An unlit cigar rolled from one side of his mouth to the other, and back again. His face looked flushed and angry. But Johnny remembered that the chief's face always looked flushed and angry. Maybe it was because he always wore suits that fit his fireplug figure a little too tightly.

"Blast it, let the kid through," Mr. Cargill ordered. "We've got business to conduct."

Out of nowhere, Maude Beale appeared and took Johnny by the arm, shooing the crowd out of their way. "I haven't seen Mr. Cargill this excited since the Vivaldi quintuplets story," the managing editor whispered in Johnny's ear.

Johnny turned back around and gestured to Mel, Uncle Louie, and Nina to follow him.

They all trooped across the newsroom—its dozens of typewriters now clacking away—and Johnny introduced the others to Mr. Cargill and Miss Beale. The chief ushered them into his office, which looked out onto the skyline of Zenith. The four visitors plopped down on the sofa.

"Hamburgers, fries, and sodas are on the way," Mr. Cargill said, sitting down facing them. "Thought you might be hungry after your little powwow with Agent Crider."

The chief turned to Miss Beale, who perched on the corner of his desk. "Have you briefed Johnny and his sister yet?" His cigar was still rolling back and forth.

"Not in any detail, Chief." She briefly readjusted her loden green felt cap, with its gorgeous pheasant feather angled jauntily to the rear.

Mr. Cargill took the cigar out of his mouth and held it like a pencil. "I admit I was dubious about you at first, Johnny," the gruff editor said. "A twelve-year-old kid shooting news? But you've produced the goods. Never seen a young shaver take to the business so quickly. And that trick of yours, riding the ghost horse. Splendid! Swell picture, too—those goofball sewermen playing their cards and drinking their beers on the city's dime."

Johnny shrugged modestly. "Just doing my job, Chief."

"Now, Melanie, Johnny," the editor continued, suddenly looking very serious. "You kids don't have to give the *Clarion* an exclusive for the Night Goose story. You could walk down the street to the *Herald-Tribune* or the *Journal* and get a couple of nice, fat checks. But what happened last night is the biggest news out of Zenith since the Vivaldi quintuplets were born here last year."

Miss Beale winked at Johnny: *See, toldja.* He grinned back.

"And I want your story in the *Clarion*," Mr. Cargill said. "We'll give you both contracts and a nice hunk of cash."

Johnny was excited, almost vibrating. This could be a huge break, a dream come true. A contract meant he was halfway to getting on the *Clarion* payroll as a staff photographer. And there was hardly anything he wanted more.

"I think we should do it, Mel," he said. "Something big's going on, and it's real important that people find out what happened. Nobody could tell this story better than you and me."

Johnny knew Mel had hoped that when the Gesellschaft's name hit the front pages, it would be to report some huge discovery that would benefit mankind. She had told him, as the Night Goose limped back to Zenith, that she didn't approve of the idea of writing about ghosts as thugs and assassins. It would only reinforce the hostility that many of the living feel toward specters. Johnny understood that prejudice against ghosts was way too common, as if it was their fault they died and got stuck in the ether.

"I think Johnny's right when he says something big is going on," the exhausted ghost wrangler agreed. "This'll give us a chance to explain why the Hausenhofer Gesellschaft matters. And why we have to get to the bottom of this terrible plot."

She looked from Johnny to Uncle Louie to Mr. Cargill and

gritted her teeth.

"Let's do it," she said. "Do you have a typewriter I can use?"

CHAPTER 12

LATE THAT EVENING Mrs. Lundgren greeted her two "babies" on the front porch with hugs and kisses and blubberings. She said she'd listened to radio news reports and had been dreadfully worried. "But you're safe now," said the ghost housekeeper, as they all trooped inside.

Within a matter of minutes she had whipped up some chicken sandwiches and plopped the plates down on the kitchen table. Uncle Louie filled everyone's glasses with root beer, then nodded to Nina. "Old Bean, you do the honors."

Nina hoisted up her glass. "A toast to the illustrious Miss Melanie Graphic, for valor and bravery in the face of extraordinary danger."

"To my big sister," Johnny added with a grin.

They clinked their glasses all around and took hearty slurps.

Johnny heard a mild "harumph" from the far corner of the kitchen. He and Mel turned their heads simultaneously. Colonel MacFarlane stood next to the pantry door, snapping to attention and saluting. "To the commander, *huzzah!*" he barked in that odd, papery voice of his. "The bravest woman I've ever known, alive or dead!"

Mel forced a weak smile. "Well, it didn't seem brave at the

time. Stupid, more like."

Everyone tut-tutted her and said that no, *brave* she had been and they would take no guff on that point.

After the sandwiches and potato chips had been thoroughly demolished, Mel yawned a prodigious yawn. "Johnny and I have been awake for forty hours. I just want to climb into bed and sleep for a year or two. But first, I have a question for my kid brother."

Johnny sat up straighter. He had a bad feeling about this.

"Why," Mel asked, narrowing her eyes, "did you put that mustache on me?"

She was scowling at him and so were Uncle Louie and Nina. Even the colonel and Mrs. Lundgren didn't look too happy with him.

Feeling his cheeks redden, Johnny knew he had no one to blame but himself. "You were out like a light. And it was *soooooo* tempting. And..." He trailed off. "You're not still mad, are you?"

"Normally, a stunt like this means you're washing dishes every night for a month," Mel said, still looking grim.

Uncle Louie nodded gravely and took a long sip of his root beer.

Johnny was genuinely appalled.

"And no radio," Mel continued.

"No radio?" A shock wave went through Johnny's body. How could a guy live without his radio? No *Duke Donegan Show*? No *Captain Justice*? No football games?

Mel crossed her arms sternly. "But right now what you're going to get is—"

Johnny cringed.

She jumped out of her chair, pulled her brother to his feet, and gave him a bear hug. Then she planted a big, embarrassing smacker on his forehead.

Johnny squirmed out of his sister's grasp. *She's gone totally bonkers*, he thought. *Rubber room material!*

Suddenly, everyone was laughing.

"Okay, Mr. Graphic," Mel teased. "Let's go over what happened when the Steppe Warrior was getting ready to slice and dice me."

Johnny thought back to those very memorable moments on the Night Goose. "You were at the front of the cabin and shouted at the ghost. The Steppe Warrior turned and walked toward you. He had his sword out. But instead of moving in for the kill, he stopped and laughed. If he hadn't stopped—"

"And why did he stop and laugh?" asked Mel.

Johnny thought about it. Then he grinned. "He was surprised by the mustache. On a girl!"

"Exactly!" trumpeted Nina. "And if he hadn't been surprised, he wouldn't have stopped. And if he hadn't stopped, the colonel would've arrived too late."

"And the commander might have been killed," added the colonel.

"And you would have ended up an only child," said Uncle Louie.

"Your stupid two-dollar mustache saved my life," Mel said. "In all the excitement I never even felt it on my lip. I was wondering why people kept staring at me. So, my turn now." She grabbed her root beer off the table and hefted it high. "To John Joshua Graphic and his exclusive one-year contract with the *Zenith Clarion*."

"To Johnny," Uncle Louie said, "and a lifetime of great photographs."

"To the eagle-eyed lensman," Nina chirped, beaming with pride at her best friend.

After the kitchen quieted down, Mel stretched her arms above her head. "Bed for me, I think. G'night."

"Remember," Johnny said. "Lunch tomorrow with Mr. Cargill."

Offering a nod and a wobbly wave, the pony-tailed etherist vanished down the hallway.

"You know, Uncle Louie, it's just not fair." Johnny stared into his root beer, now going flat, along with his mood. "I mean, what'd Mel do to deserve almost getting slaughtered by a ghost?"

"Well, John," answered Uncle Louie, "sometimes life just grabs you by the scruff of the neck and gives you a good, hard shaking. There's nothing you can do except try to hold on and make it through. Like when your mom and dad disappeared. You can't even imagine how you'll survive something so awful. But you do."

Johnny's eyelids suddenly felt incredibly heavy. He wasn't sure he'd ever been this tired. He yawned and put his head down next to the empty root beer glass. He was asleep before his forehead clunked against the varnished oak.

CHAPTER 13

WEDNESDAY, OCTOBER 9, 1935

ZENITH

WHEN JOHNNY WOKE UP, dazzling sunlight was pouring through the window, making his entire bedroom glow. He sat up, rubbed the sleep out of his eyes, and squinted at the alarm clock on the bed stand. It was already ten o'clock.

Thirteen minutes later he came trotting down the main staircase in his brown tweed herringbone suit—face scrubbed, hair combed, teeth brushed. He strode into the kitchen and found his sister at one end of the table and Uncle Louie at the other.

"We thought you'd be up earlier, lazybones," said Mel. "Figured you'd want to see this as soon as possible." She held up the front page of the *Zenith Clarion*.

Johnny's eyes practically popped out. He snatched the newspaper out of his sister's hands, sat down, and examined the front page in detail. It looked amazingly impressive.

In heavy black type the headlines shouted:

AEROBOAT TRAGEDY AVERTED! GHOSTS ON RAMPAGE!

GHOST WARRIOR BATTLE HIGH OVER THE WESTERN PLAINS!

ZENITH ETHERIST DEFEATS DEADLY SPIRITS, SAVES 130 LIVES!

Exclusive Personal Account By Melanie Graphic, M.E., N.A.C.E

Additional Commentary by Col. Horace MacFarlane, First Zenith Cavalry Brigade, Deceased

Exclusive Photographs by Johnny Graphic

Below the headlines came three stark images. One showed Captain Merrick sweating at the Johnson Goose's controls. The next depicted Mel at the end of her ordeal, a look of utter shock on her mustachioed face. And the last was a photo of one of the damaged engines.

Mel's story wasn't that long, only about seven hundred words, with a few hundred more from the colonel in a shaded box. The old ghost soldier gave a ripping account of the battle in the clouds and his confrontation with the eyeless Steppe Warrior. At the bottom of the page Miss Beale's report recounted what the National Police Bureau was doing about the Steppe Warrior attack and the apparent worldwide conspiracy to murder members of the Oskar Hausenhofer Gesellschaft.

"Miss Beale called a couple hours ago," said Uncle Louie, sipping on his coffee. "The entire sunrise edition sold out by seven. They're printing additional copies of the regular morning edition and doing an extra edition for this afternoon."

"The story's been picked up by dozens of newspapers and radio stations around the world," Mel added.

Though Johnny was terrifically excited, Mel didn't look like she was enjoying the attention of millions of newspaper readers. Which, he thought, made perfect sense. *Let's see. Your friends get murdered. You almost get slaughtered, as well. And your mug is on front pages everywhere wearing a fake mustache—not a good look for a girl. She was sure a good sport to let them print that shot.*

"Here, this just arrived," she said, handing him a small yellow envelope. "From Dame Honoria."

He pulled out the telegraph—its printed message taped on the yellow paper—and read the shocking news:

JUST SAW STORY OF YOUR CLOSE CALL. ARE YOU SAFE MY DARLINGS. ARRIVED IN NEUPORT AND ATTACKED BY GANGSTER GHOST WITH MACHINE GUN. BARELY ESCAPED. I AM ALL RIGHT. NOW BACK TO GILBEYSHIRE AND ON TO GORTON ISLAND. TELEGRAPH YOUR NEWS BOTH ADDRESSES. LOVE HONORIA.

Johnny already understood they were involved in a very serious predicament. But all of a sudden, the gravity of the situation sunk in with deadly earnestness. Somebody really meant to kill all these etherists, including Dame Honoria and his sister. And he had to do everything he possibly could to stop it.

AT TONY WELLER'S CAFÉ on Superior Avenue, Johnny, Mel, and Uncle Louie were escorted up the staircase by Tony himself, and ushered into a small private dining room. Carlton Cargill, Maude Beale, and a woman from Zephyr Lines had already arrived for the lunch date they'd scheduled the day before.

When the three of them came down the staircase an hour and a half later, Johnny was still in a daze.

"So does this mean," he said when they emerged out onto the bustling downtown sidewalk, "that we're *really* flying around the world?"

Uncle Louie reached inside his jacket and pulled out a folded document. "Once I sign our contract here, that's exactly what it means."

Mel kept a stone face as they strolled by Freeman's Book Store, windows chockablock with all the latest best-selling mysteries and romances. Johnny, though, couldn't help but feel energized.

He could hardly believe it. They were going to investigate as many of the Hausenhofer Gesellschaft murders as they could, and send back their stories and photos. Silver City, Orchid Isles, Tor Chan, Old Continent—*here we come!*

The *Clarion* was hiring Mel and Uncle Louie, as well as Johnny. Zephyr Lines would provide a long-range Como Eagle aeroboat for two months. Danny Kailolu—co-pilot of the Night Goose— would captain it. An experienced flying boat aviator himself, Uncle Louie would be the co-pilot. While Johnny took pictures, Mel would write exclusive dispatches. Colonel MacFarlane and his troopers would come, too. Best of all, Nina got the assignment of running the long-range radio. She was going to positively pop a cork when she found out she was getting out of school for two months to fly around the world. And Johnny would have someone interesting to talk to on the trip.

On the walk back to their car, the trio kept hearing *Clarion* newsies hawking the paper on the street.

"Aeroboat tragedy aaaa-voided! Attack of deaaaaadly specters!"

"*Clarion* exclusive! Midnight horror in the clouds!"

"Local girl saves the day! Exclusive photos by Johnny Graphic!"

No one seemed to recognize Mel—until she was about to climb into the big Morton Monarch touring car.

Suddenly, a towheaded tyke in short pants and fuzzy brown sweater ran up to her, eyes wide, finger pointing. The little brat twirled a nonexistent "mustache" on his own upper lip. He giggled wildly and ran off down the street.

Mel frowned at her brother and uncle. "I was afraid that might happen. Maybe instead of becoming more famous, we should just all go hide. The ghost assassins would never find us."

"Listen, Mel," said Johnny, "we could get killed no matter where we hide. They could find us anywhere we go. I say the best defense is a good offense."

Mel sighed. "Let's just go home," she said, as she climbed into the back seat. "I know we'll be safe there."

CHAPTER 14

SUNDAY, OCTOBER 13, 1935

ZENITH

THE NEXT FEW DAYS teemed with activity. Meetings were held. Itineraries were planned. Financial arrangements were made. Potential stories were discussed. The world travellers went shopping for the supplies and equipment they would need. When Sunday evening rolled around, an exhausted Johnny flopped onto his bed and fell asleep almost instantly—still wearing his tan corduroy slacks and blue cotton shirt.

Sometime well after midnight an annoying metallic clangor woke him up. At first he wondered if the noise came from a remnant of a dream. But when he realized it was emanating from the bedroom next to his, he jumped to his feet in the dark.

Bolting out into the hallway, he threw open Mel's door and froze at the sight. Mel was battling for her life! With a Steppe Warrior!

Something boiled up inside Johnny, out of control. Pure, red-hot anger! He wanted to tear this blasted ghost from limb to limb. But if he tried to enter the room to help, he might end up distracting Mel. So he did the only other thing he could think of. He turned and screamed. "Help! Colonel! Uncle Louie! Mel's fighting a Steppe Warrior!"

After Johnny shouted, the ghost launched a series of slashing strikes with a curved sword. And it was clear that Mel had all she could handle, deflecting them with her own army saber. Just *parry...parry...parry.* She backed toward the door that Johnny had flung open. He felt on the verge of panic, watching her weakening defensive moves.

What could he do? *What could he do?*

For a start, he ran toward the top of the staircase and switched on the hallway lights so his sister could see clearly. He knew that the light would help her even the odds.

The two sword fighters erupted into the hallway, raining sword strikes on each other.

With incredibly bad timing, Uncle Louie—half asleep, barefoot, and in his bathrobe—stumbled out of his room and almost into the middle of the fight, narrowly avoiding Mel's whirling infantry saber. "Jumpin' Jiminy!" he exclaimed, and nipped back through the door.

"Mel's fighting a Steppe Warrior," Johnny shouted from the top of the staircase. "I'm gonna try to help her. You yell for the colonel."

"You got it, John," Uncle Louie hollered back. "Colonel Mac-Farlane! Colonel MacFarlane!"

One of the globe lights on the ceiling shattered into hundreds of shards when the Steppe Warrior's sword hit it. The wraith was backing Mel down toward where Johnny stood. Mel could stay upstairs and get trapped by the ghost at the far end of the hallway. Or she could tread backward down the broad staircase, just as the movie star Trevor Sheridan did in his famous duels up on the silver screen. Or she could gamble it all and launch a fierce attack.

But Johnny didn't know how much longer his sister could last. She was breathing heavily and groaning with every strike and parry. Her face was equal parts terror and concentration.

Johnny had to give her a break, some kind of an edge.

He bolted into his bedroom and reappeared with his Zoom press camera. By that time, the two combatants had neared the top of the staircase. From behind the Steppe Warrior's back, Johnny could see Mel's grimly intense expression. Darting quickly, he slipped past the Steppe Warrior—barely evading a cut by the ghost's blade—and wiggled his way behind Mel. Hoping the diversion would work one more time, he lofted the bulky camera above his head, and aimed it so the bulb would go off right in the ghost's face.

"Mel!" he yelled, almost in her ear. "Flash!"

He pressed the shutter release.

The Steppe Warrior gasped at the coruscating corona of light. For a mere one and seven-eighths seconds the ghost was distracted.

Which was just enough.

With a guttural roar, Mel rushed at the would-be assassin with a powerful flurry of diagonal slashing cuts.

The curved blade flew out of the Steppe Warrior's hand and clanged down the hallway. Wearing an expression of deepest loathing, the wraith charged at Mel with bare hands.

Out of pure reflex, Mel grunted and cut downward. The noise that followed was a terrible, sodden kind of percussion—the same sound Johnny had heard in the butcher's shop.

A horrific wailing filled the enclosed space of the upstairs corridor. Only then did Johnny realize that the Steppe Warrior was a girl. She fell to her knees. Her right arm, her sword arm, rested on the carpet, twitching and pulsing. She bayed at the ceiling like a wounded animal and pawed at her right shoulder with her left hand.

Just then, Colonel MacFarlane flew up through the hallway floor, saber drawn. He regarded the scene with a mixed look of horror and regret. He caught Mel's eye and shook his head. *Sorry, ma'am*, said his expression, *late again.*

Johnny peered more closely at the girl ghost, and almost recoiled. He could tell how she had died. Her face was covered with smallpox pustules. What a horrible way to go.

After half a moment, the dismembered soldier looked up at Mel and composed herself—still holding onto her right shoulder. "I have failed," she said with resignation. "Take my head."

Panting, Mel said, "Answer. Me. This." She paused to suck in a couple more breaths. "What is your name?"

"Checheg."

"Why are you doing this?"

"It is the will of the khan."

"Who is the khan?"

"Our emperor, our king, our general."

"What does he want?"

"He has united Steppe Warriors from many generations. We have waited centuries for him. He has given us purpose again. He is leading us into battle, so that we may properly die."

The ghost paused, glaring darkly at Mel. "No more questions. Just do it," she said. She pulled off her helmet, shut her eyes, and stretched out her neck.

Mel sniffed. "Don't be ridiculous! I've already cut off your arm. Isn't that enough?"

"I would have cut off your head," the wraith said, "if I had prevailed."

"I don't doubt it," Mel snapped. "But you didn't win, did you? *I did.* You're a barbarian, and I'm not. And I don't cut people's heads off, even if they're dead. Even if they deserve it! What I want you to do is go back to your khan, whoever he is, and tell him that Melanie Graphic's coming after him. And then she's going to put him out of business! Now, *scram!*"

The ghost slowly stood up, and regarded Mel and Johnny with a look of utter hatred. Then she stooped to pick up her severed arm and flew straight up through the ceiling.

For a few seconds, no one said a word. Finally, Uncle Louie, standing in his bedroom door, whispered, "Is it gone?"

Both a little shell-shocked, Johnny and Mel nodded in unison.

At the far end of the hallway a door creaked open and out tottered Nina, in her purple bathrobe. She rubbed her eyes and frowned crankily at her guardian and two friends.

"Do you people have any conceivable idea of how late it is?" she scolded. "You woke me up!"

THE WHOLE HOUSEHOLD gave up on the notion of getting any more sleep. Johnny, Mel, Uncle Louie, and Nina trooped down to the kitchen, where Mrs. Lundgren served them hot chocolate. As they sat around the table, Mel described her near brush with doom.

"I was just lying there in the dark," she said. "Couldn't sleep. Thinking about the trip and the murders and everything else."

And pondering a couple of months with Danny Kailolu, I bet, thought Johnny. He couldn't help noticing on the Night Goose that she seemed to like the guy.

"Finally, I rolled over and was just drifting off, when my piano plinked in the darkness. I could tell there was someone else in the room. I knew it couldn't be the colonel or Mrs. Lundgren or any of the boys."

"No ghosts allowed in the commander's room without leave," said the colonel, who was standing next to the icebox. "And properly so."

"I lay there scared to death," Mel continued. "Thought my heart was going to burst. But thank heaven I remembered my army saber, hanging right over the bed. I jumped up and unsheathed it, then flipped on the light. That's when I saw Checheg. She had an arrow aimed at my chest."

"She was by herself?" asked Nina.

Mel nodded, then laughed.

Nina frowned at her. "What's so funny? Doesn't sound humorous to me."

"She asked me a question that gave me a little more time to think, to plan what to do."

"What question?" asked Johnny.

"She said, 'Where is your mustache?'"

"So the old mustache trick paid off again," Uncle Louie said, grinning. "Just like the old flashbulb trick."

"It did indeed." Mel playfully slugged her brother on the shoulder. "Thanks again, Mr. Graphic."

Johnny laughed along with everyone else, but he wasn't feeling very jolly. He wished he could think of something that would put this horror show to an end. The next time Mel found herself in peril, she might not make it.

"So what happened then?" Nina asked.

"I insulted her," answered Mel. "I impugned her courage. Said that it was just cowardly to shoot me with an arrow from such a close distance. I challenged her to a sword fight."

"Canny tactic," said the colonel, smiling and beaming with pride. "She couldn't have realized that you're a fair sword fighter."

Mel smiled up at the ghost officer. "You ought to know, Colonel. You trained me. All those summer afternoons out on the lawn. I never in a million years thought they'd turn out so useful."

CHAPTER 15

SUNDAY, OCTOBER 13, 1935

PALOA ATOLL IN THE GREATER OCEAN

BAO NEVER FORGOT the day she became a ghost.

The raiders had come to her village, and one of them chased her into the jungle. He caught her, grabbed her around her neck, and strangled her. His hands were terribly strong and hard. Everything went black.

When she woke up, Bao clambered to her feet, feeling weirdly light and nimble. There was a girl who was lying by the base of a tree. Arms and legs askew.

The girl on the ground wore a shabby blue shift. Just like Bao's.

She had on a black headdress. Just like Bao's.

She had a crescent-shaped scar across the bottom of her left foot. Just as Bao had.

And she was quite, quite dead, Bao's mysterious twin.

Finally, Bao understood. She screamed and shouted, but no one came. She tried and tried to cry, but no tears would form in her eyes.

For the little girl ghost the centuries crawled by as slowly as tortoises—every moment a torment. If there was anything like hell on earth, being in the ghost world was it. Nothing that was good was allowed.

Happiness.

Love.

Pleasure.

All impossible.

However, when the dead shaman found Bao up in the mountains, huddling by a rocky stream, he promised her something she wanted above all else.

"If you come with me," he said, "I can end your suffering. I can send you to your gods."

That is how Bao found herself flying eastward across the great ocean with hundreds of other wraiths—a great, ghastly gaggle of ghosts. For the first time in centuries she talked with someone in a friendly way. He was an odd sort of specter called Lord Hurley of Evansham, or "Evvie." He had died at the age of sixteen. She liked him because he made her laugh, a rare treat for a ghost.

Toward noontime on the last day of their journey, Bao and the others spied something that made no sense, off toward the edge of the world's curvature.

"Has an island sprouted a volcano?" shouted a woman ghost.

"The germ of a typhoon," suggested Evvie.

"Perhaps the jungle is on fire," someone yelled from the rear.

The phenomenon came from an atoll—a ring of small islands in the middle of the vast ocean. From the surface of one of the islands arose a ribbon of silver, gray, and white. It undulated and pulsated, floated from side to side, grew thin and tall, and then compressed itself down toward the ocean. It broke apart and came back together. Bao had never seen anything like it.

As they flew closer, everything became clear.

Thousands of ghosts had ascended into the clouds. They were trying to hold steady over the sandy outcropping of land beneath them. Wraiths had crowded the surface of the little island. There was barely any more room anywhere, but up.

Somehow, though, Bao and her new friend found a bare spot of sand near a clutch of barrel-roofed buildings made of some kind of metal that Evvie called "tin." Scurrying between them were living humans in short white robes and broad-brimmed straw hats, carrying parchments and strange devices. In the center of the compound, a wooden tower a hundred feet high was crowned by a small, square hut with a thatched roof. Bao could make out a woman climbing up a long ladder attached to one of the tower's supports. At the top, the woman crawled into the tiny hut.

Near the entrance to one of the tin shelters a fearsome-looking wraith warrior—with a black braid down his back and a pointed helmet on his head—held the reins of a ragged little ghost pony. Bao gasped when he turned around. The man had no eyes, only seeping, horrible eye sockets. How in the world, the girl ghost thought, could he see anything? But clearly he did, glaring malevolently at anyone who dared to stare at him.

Just then the door to the shelter burst open and out lurched a person who was not a ghost, but was a strange-looking creature nonetheless. Or so Bao thought.

His long, hard face, with its jutting jaw and dark burning eyes, swiveled around, surveying the legion of ghosts. He walked in an ungainly way—his body at odds with itself, as if it couldn't quite decide how it wanted to move.

"My khan," the eyeless warrior said, prostrating himself on the sand before this bizarre individual, "I bear tidings. Some for good, some for ill. Mongke Eng is dead. But Melanie Graphic lives."

CHAPTER 16

SATURDAY, OCTOBER 19, 1935

ZENITH

MEL'S ACCOUNT of her saber duel with a wraith called Checheg made many a front page—along with Johnny's picture of her after the fight, disheveled but triumphant. Exciting as their journalistic success was, it didn't bring them any closer to getting to the root of the etherist-killing conspiracy.

That's why Johnny agreed to go downtown with Mel and Uncle Louie on a beautiful Saturday morning that deserved something better than sitting in a musty old office. He figured that Managing Agent Crider of the National Police Bureau had some important news for them. Maybe, Johnny hoped, they had found the evil mastermind behind the conspiracy. Because there had to be an evil mastermind somewhere, just as there always was on the *Captain Justice Adventures* radio show.

So, at about ten o'clock, Johnny found himself sitting in, well, a musty old office. Next to him were Uncle Louie and Mel. Crider, standing by his desk with arms crossed, had a wind-burned face that gave nothing away. Assistant Director Santangelo of the Ministry of Etheristics sprawled in Crider's own chair behind the desk, his piggy eyes narrowed, a sneer on his lips. His left hand was still twitching.

Johnny couldn't put his finger on why, but Santangelo practically smelled of trouble.

A few minutes late, Carlton Cargill swept in as if he owned the place. "Well, Crider," he managed to bark, even with the unlit cigar in his mouth, "here I am." He nodded at Johnny, Mel, and Uncle Louie, and briefly studied the agent and the stranger. "What's this all about then?"

"I'd like you to meet Ministry of Etheristics Assistant Director Santangelo," said Crider. "Santangelo, Carlton Cargill, editor-in-chief of the *Zenith Clarion*."

The two men said their how-do-you-dos, reached across the desk, and shook hands—quickly, as if neither enjoyed it.

"So," Mr. Cargill said, plopping down in the empty chair next to Uncle Louie, "what've you found out about the Night Goose attack? Got any new leads?"

"Actually, Cargill," said Santangelo, "that's not why we've asked you here."

Johnny groaned. *They wasted my morning!*

Uncle Louie frowned and shushed him. Johnny was tempted to frown back, but didn't.

Mr. Cargill raised his eyebrows, then gently set his unlit cigar on the edge of the desktop.

Santangelo cleared his throat and tented his fingers under his chin. "It's come to our attention—"

"Meaning who, exactly?" Mr. Cargill snapped.

"The Ministry of Etheristics, Mr. Cargill. It's come to our attention that your newspaper and Zephyr Lines intend to mount a little aeroboat expedition to investigate the Hausenhofer Gesellschaft murders."

Johnny and Mel looked at each other in surprise. How had Santangelo found out?

"And what of it?" the editor asked.

"We are fortunate," Santangelo began, sounding like an orator starting on his favorite topic, "that ghosts who engage in the human sphere almost always perform functions that are constructive, vital, affirmative. From nursemaid to street sweeper to—"

"No speechifying, if you please," Mr. Cargill grumbled. "Get to the point."

Johnny grinned. If there was anyone who could handle this character, it was the chief.

Santangelo untented his fingers—half of them twitching—and glowered back at the editor. "My point is that ghostly crime is exceedingly rare. No one among my colleagues can recall a ghost crime of the magnitude of the Night Goose attack. No one."

"Practically a military operation," Mr. Cargill observed.

"Yes. Practically."

"That's why it's an awfully big story," Johnny blurted, unable to contain himself.

Mr. Cargill chuckled and nodded. "The boy's right. An awfully big story."

"So I take it you *are* contemplating an expedition of some sort?" Santangelo asked.

Johnny noticed for the first time that Santangelo had perfectly sharp little canine teeth. Like a vampire—not that anything as unbelievable as vampires actually existed.

"I'm officially informing you that the investigation into the Night Goose attack is now in the hands of the Ministry of Etheristics," Santangelo said in an ominous tone. "I would hope that we could count on your cooperation."

Mel spoke up. "What do you mean by 'cooperation'?"

"Our investigations, and those of our colleagues in other countries, are currently under way. We ask that you leave this problem to the professionals. Your interference could compromise our work."

"What do you mean by 'compromise'?" asked Johnny.

"It means, John my boy," Mr. Cargill said, "that Santangelo here thinks you and Melanie will gum up the works, mess up the inquiries of crack police agents all around the world." He turned to the bald man. "Is that about right?"

"Yes, about right. Minus the sarcasm."

Mr. Cargill started to say something, but Mel interrupted. "Legally what could you do to stop us?"

Santangelo's piggy eyes had opened a bit. "We have reason to believe that Zephyr Lines is flying in a special long-range seaplane sometime in the next few days."

Mel put her hand up. "Please, Mr. Santangelo, what could you do to stop us?"

"I have a national judge downstairs who is ready at a moment's notice to allow us to seize the aeroboat in question, and to prohibit you from leaving Zenith. If needs be, we can hold you and your brother and uncle indefinitely in custody."

"In jail?" Johnny yelped, shocked even at the idea of it.

"On what grounds?" Mr. Cargill growled.

"On grounds of national security," Santangelo growled back.

Johnny turned to his boss. "Can he do that?"

"It depends if *his* lawyers are better than *my* lawyers," Mr. Cargill answered. "And whether or not the judge has an ounce of common sense."

"Well, that's rotten," Johnny groaned. This whole meeting had turned really sour really fast.

"You're all playing at a very dangerous game," Santangelo warned. "This matter is way over your heads, and none of your business."

Mel's eyes shot daggers at the bald bureaucrat. "Mr. Santangelo, you weren't nearly beheaded by a Steppe Warrior with no eyes. *I was.* You didn't spend hours flying home through the dark in a badly damaged flying boat that might have crashed. *I did.* You didn't nearly get sliced to bits in your own upstairs hallway. *I did.* You don't have to go to sleep afraid because specters are hunting you. *I do.* So, I would suggest to you that what is happening is *very much* my business."

Johnny looked at his sister with admiration. Boy, did she tell that bum what's what!

"Now, now, Miss Graphic," said Santangelo, with a dainty little smile, "I'm just doing my job."

"Melanie," Mr. Cargill said, his abrasive voice unexpectedly smooth, "I think Mr. Santangelo's suggestion that we reconsider our plans makes a certain sense. Let's go back to my office, talk things over. We don't want to get in hot water with the Ministry of Etheristics, now do we?"

Mel took a deep breath and followed Mr. Cargill's lead. "No, of course we don't."

Santangelo looked pleased. Grinning in a magnanimous way, saying how sensible they were being, the bald man walked out of the office.

Johnny was almost shaking with anger. Who did this overbearing goon think he was, telling them what they could and couldn't do? Even worse, why did Mr. Cargill, of all people, give in so easily? What was *that* all about?

"Why in heckfire did you say that, Chief?" Johnny asked, turning red in the face.

CHAPTER 17

UNCLE LOUIE PUT AN ARM around Johnny's shoulder, leaned over, and whispered in his ear. "Hey there, short stuff. You don't go spouting off to your boss like that. Not if you want to keep your job. Right?"

Johnny sniffed and muttered, "Guess so, Uncle Louie." Then he turned to Mr. Cargill. "Sorry I shot my mouth off, Chief."

"John, my lad, you remind me a lot of myself when I was your age," Mr. Cargill answered. "I can understand that you feel a little hot under the collar. But sometimes we just gotta take our lumps and do the best we can do. The guy who can handle a punch is the guy who'll make it through. Now I suppose we'd better get going. Thanks for hosting this little clambake, Crider."

Crider put up his hand. "Just a moment, please. I'd like to speak with you four privately, now that Mr. Santangelo's gone. Johnny, will you please shut the door?"

Johnny did just that and returned to his seat.

"What I'm about to tell you is for background only, a rumor of a rumor that I heard," Crider said, his voice low, his eyes furtive.

"Go on," said Mr. Cargill.

"Off the record? I can trust you all?"

"Yes, sir, off the record and confidential," the editor replied gravely. "Not a word you say will be published, let alone attributed to you. We'll only use your information for deep background. Right Louie, right kids?"

Johnny, Mel, and Uncle Louie all agreed.

Johnny understood that Crider's information—whatever it was—must not be linked back to the lawman. It was a sacred trust for a newspaperman like Johnny to keep Crider's secret. But Mr. Cargill and his newspaper could use it for their investigation.

"If you ever quote me or attribute this information to me, I'll deny I ever said it," Crider warned.

Mr. Cargill nodded. "What have you heard?"

"BUT WHY WOULD the Ministry of War be interested in the Night Goose investigation?" Johnny asked.

They were huddled together in a green-upholstered booth at the back of the Angry Trout Fishhouse—Johnny and Uncle Louie on one side, Mel and Mr. Cargill on the other. Servers in long white aprons rushed back and forth, carrying trays covered with heaping plates of different kinds of fish.

"Haven't a clue," said Mr. Cargill, shifting his unlit cigar to the opposite side of his mouth. "But if Crider heard true, some general somewhere thinks our ghost assassins are a real threat to the nation."

"But that doesn't make any sense," Johnny said. "As rotten as the Gesellschaft murders are, what do they have to do with national security?"

"I don't know," Mr. Cargill replied. "But the army and air corps don't stick their noses into anything without very good reasons. And I've gotta admit, I'm even more intrigued by this affair than I was to start with. There's a lot for our reporters to start checking out. Somehow, you two kids have touched a very raw nerve in the ministries down in Capital City."

Johnny nibbled on his fish and chips and regarded Mel, sitting quietly across from him. He knew that look, when she knitted her brows together and half closed her eyes. She was formulating an idea—or hiding something.

"Mel, what is it?" he asked.

She stared down into her bowl of catfish chowder. Then she sat up straight, pulling back her shoulders. "I have a theory why the Ministry of War might be interested in this business."

Mr. Cargill put down his cup of coffee and regarded the young woman with a questioning expression. "Go on, Melanie."

"I mean, heavens to Betsy," she began. "It's a preposterous idea. Something Mongke Eng wrote in the *Annals of the Hausenhofer Gesellschaft* back in '32. Mongke was sort of a genius, you know."

Johnny nodded in agreement. His parents had worked with Mongke on several occasions and often said how much they had admired him. Mongke even helped Johnny's pop with the research that transformed the art of medical diagnosis.

"I believe that his article is why we're all being targeted for death," Mel continued. "Eliminate us, and you could control the theoretical knowledge that the conspirators wish to own."

"Okay, then," said Johnny, feeling confused. "What does that mean, in ordinary English? What did Mongke come up with?"

"Right," said Mel, clearing her throat. "Here goes—"

When she finished explaining, simplifying the science for the three nonscientists, the table seemed very quiet, amid the bustle and noise of the packed restaurant. The other three looked staggered and dazed. Even Mr. Cargill seemed at a loss for words—not his usual style. Obviously upset, Uncle Louie slowly shook his head. And Johnny wondered with amazement and horror if such a thing were even remotely possible.

"*An etheric bomb?*" he pronounced after a long, stunned silence. "Powerful enough to wipe out a whole city?"

"I know, I know," Mel said. "But I've gone over Mongke's equations a dozen times, and I'd say there's a chance that a bomb might actually work. They'd need at least three thousand wraiths, maybe more, and a containment vessel. No idea what that would look like, what it would be composed of, its size. But compress all those ghosts down to microscopic size—and ghosts can do that, you know. And they reach a critical mass. Then they form a conduit, a connection that draws energy directly from the ether and transfers it out to our universe. All in a millisecond. As a gigantic release of energy."

Uncle Louie groaned. "A bomb to end all bombs. Makes sense that the Ministry of War would want to have a few of those."

"Afraid so," Mel agreed.

"Ghosts would like it, too," Johnny said. "What ghost wouldn't want another chance to properly die, even if it means being blown up in a bomb? I mean, what if the Second Impossible thing isn't impossible after all? What if the people behind this have figured out that the bomb is a way to send ghosts to the great beyond?"

"Ghosts who've been trapped in the ether for centuries or longer might grasp at straws," Mel said. "They'd be desperate for any chance to be released."

Their waitress stopped by the booth, a plump woman with tight blonde curls all over her head. She regarded them and frowned. "Hey, whatsa matta?" she chirped. "Somebody die?"

"Nope, nope," lied Uncle Louie. "Everything's fine."

"I betcha some pie or cake'd put some smiles on them gloomy mugs, huh?" She handed out dessert menus and trotted away.

"So do we still go on our grand adventure around the world?"

asked Mel.

"Absolutely," Mr. Cargill pronounced. "You're going to visit as many places where etherists have been murdered as is possible. You're going to find out everything you can about the killings. And you're going to send back your stories and photos through World Press Association offices. We're still just operating on speculation and theory. But my reporter's nose is tingling like crazy, and it usually isn't wrong."

Mel scowled. "But how can we do anything, go anywhere, now that Mr. Santangelo's forbidden us to?"

Mr. Cargill shook his head. "No, not quite right, Melanie. Santangelo's *warned* us, but he hasn't gotten a judge's restraining order. He hasn't even talked to a judge yet."

"He lied to us?" Johnny asked with surprise.

Mr. Cargill brayed with laughter. "He's in the government. Of course he lied."

"How do you know that, Chief?" asked Johnny.

"Let's just say I have a few friends of my own down at the National Building. But just in case Santangelo really intends to stop us, we'd better get a move on."

Johnny looked puzzled. "What do you mean?"

The newspaperman grinned and rolled his big cigar back and forth in his mouth. "How quickly can you folks pack your bags?"

CHAPTER 18

AT ABOUT ONE IN THE MORNING Johnny and Mel each gave the weepy Mrs. Lundgren a peck on the cheek—a strange, tingly sensation on the lips, kissing a ghost. Then they, Nina, and Uncle Louie slipped out the back door and into the woods behind the big brick house.

Johnny carried his pigskin suitcase and had his camera pack strapped to his back. Mel laughed when she saw him, saying he looked almost comical in his dark suit, dark blue shirt, black tie, and fedora—hardly an outfit for tramping through the woods.

Mel, on the other hand, was dressed practically—in a warm gray knit jacket, her lined wool trousers, and hiking boots. Yet she appeared almost as odd-looking as Johnny, with her army saber in a scabbard around her waist. Nina wore a dark sweater and heavy blue dungarees. An experienced woodswoman from her days up north with Uncle Louie, she carried everything she needed in a worn leather backpack.

Uncle Louie led them up the deer path toward the country road two miles northeast. He carried two pieces of luggage—Mel's suitcase and his own black carpetbag.

About an hour later they emerged on the narrow dirt road. A twinkle of moonlight illuminated a well-polished automobile pulled partway off into the brush. Trudging up toward it, the quartet saw a stout, powerful man leaning against the car's grill, arms crossed.

A bullhorn voice greeted them. "You're five minutes late."

"Sorry, Mr. Cargill," Johnny said. "We had to detour around a muddy patch."

Within half an hour they were rolling up Superior Avenue—less hectic than usual, but with late-night denizens still ambling from nightclub to nightclub. A few sad, lonely ghosts loitered here and there, staring dolefully as the station wagon rolled by—trailed by the colonel and the sixteen troopers of the First Zenith Brigade. Before long the automobile cruised by the lakeboat docks and the huge Acme Iron Works in West Zenith.

Heading out into the countryside, they passed Mount Pleasant Cemetery, with its telltale green glow. This sprawling "city of the dead" was also home to a sizeable Wraithville—a ghost ghetto. Thousands of specters "lived" here, and every night the vast graveyard glowed green from the light of their etheric bodies. This was where Lydia Graphic had found Mrs. Lundgren, where Mel and the colonel had recruited several members of the Zenith Brigade.

The car traveled northwest for another hour, through brushlands and bogs, a light drizzle making a metallic patter on the vehicle's roof. No one felt like talking. In the front seat, Uncle Louie and Mr. Cargill stared through the back-and-forth of the windshield wipers. In the back seat, Mel and Nina nodded off. But Johnny was far too excited to snooze, gripping his camera backpack in his lap. He fantasized about all the great pictures he was going to take. This would be the most incredible adventure of his life.

About half an hour later, after bouncing off a blacktop road downhill onto a dirt track that wound through gloomy woods, the station wagon lurched to a halt.

"We're here," Mr. Cargill announced.

"Here" was next to a long, low country cottage built of blue fieldstone. Down a sloping lawn Johnny could see the Treport River flowing by. A dock reached out onto the water, then made a right-angle turn downriver. Bobbing easily on the river side of the dock was a streamlined, aluminum-skinned tri-motor aircraft on large pontoons, securely moored with multiple lines.

"Boy, oh boy!" Johnny said. "That's some gorgeous flying boat."

Uncle Louie whistled in admiration. "A Gianelli Z-509. About the fastest passenger seaplane in the world. Not a flying boat, really, but a floatplane. Has her own pressurized cabin. We can fly her straight to Silver City, right over the mountains."

"They brought her up yesterday afternoon," Mr. Cargill explained, as they all climbed out of the automobile. "After our lunch at the Angry Trout, I called my friends at Zephyr Lines. Thought we might need a Plan B, since Santangelo knew about the other aeroboat Zephyr was sending. And as long as a judge hasn't forbidden us to go—"

"There you are," someone shouted.

The house's double front doors had swung open and two men stood there, silhouetted against the orange, welcoming light of the front hallway.

"Come inside," one of them hollered. "You'll get soaked!"

Mel broke out in a big smile when she saw Danny Kailolu, in his sharp blue uniform. *So she* does *like him*, Johnny thought.

"Hi there, Mel," said the pilot, holding the door open for

everyone. "Like I was telling Jock here—" He nodded toward his co-pilot. "—that girl looks a lot better without the mustache."

Mel turned a little red, but didn't look mad—which relieved Johnny. Even though the mustache had saved her life, it couldn't be too much fun to be reminded of it all the time.

"I'll take that as a compliment," she said. "But I think you'll find that most girls look better without mustaches."

After introductions were made, they all trooped into the living room. "I sure hope this flight isn't as exciting as the last one," Johnny whispered up into Danny's ear,

"How could it possibly be any crazier?" the pilot whispered back.

CHAPTER 19

THE LIVING ROOM'S golden-stained timber walls teemed with hunting trophies—heads of elk, bighorn sheep, a water buffalo, bears, even a lion. Johnny was impressed and took a shot of everyone standing in front of the water buffalo. Mr. Cargill explained that the house belonged to Mrs. Throckmorton, owner and publisher of the *Zenith Clarion*. Her late husband had been quite the big game hunter.

Everyone fit comfortably on the two maroon-brocade sofas that faced each other across a vast redwood coffee table. Kerosene lamps burned cozily here and there.

"So, my friends," said Mr. Cargill, sitting down between Danny and Jock, "what're our plans?"

Danny's co-pilot, Jock Atkinson, was a string bean of a man, with a long, thin face. He spoke in the drawl of someone who had grown up in the Old Dominion. "Simple enough. We get y'all out to Silver City. Then Danny sticks with you folks and captains your Como Eagle. Mr. Hofstedter'll be your co-pilot. I believe that

Miss Bain there'll operate the radio."

Johnny winked at Nina, who was beaming. His friend had practically been walking on air the last couple of days.

"Of course I'll have a little refresher training out in Silver City," Uncle Louie hastened to add. "And Nina will get some hours in on the Eagle's radio setup."

"How soon can you leave?" Mr. Cargill asked.

"Not until dawn," answered Danny. "We can't take off in the dark on water we don't know. We could hit a log or catch a sandbar."

Mel cleared her throat. "There might be a way to get out of here sooner."

Danny peered at her curiously and raised his eyebrows. "You can't bring the sun up early, can you, Mel?"

"That'd be a neat trick," she said, "but nope."

"Then what?" Mr. Cargill asked.

"I can tell you in a wink if it'll work." She hopped to her feet and ran outside, through the front doors. A few moments later, a little damp from the rain, she traipsed back into the living room with someone only she and Johnny could see—Colonel MacFarlane.

Mel nonetheless introduced the ghost officer to the two pilots, even though he was invisible to them. As she had told Johnny many times, it was the polite thing to do. Because ghosts had feelings, too.

"I've checked this out with the colonel and he thinks it's practicable," Mel said. "He and his men can go out on the river and find a stretch that'll allow the aeroboat to get off safely. It'll take them less than an hour to do their scouting. How long a run will you need, Danny?"

"A mile with a good headwind," he said, sounding rather wary.

"A bit more, without it. But what's the point, if I can't see where to make my run?"

"The colonel and I thought about that," Mel continued. "We'll give the troopers flashlights, if we can find enough. The lads will float above the water to mark your runway on both sides. As simple as that. A safe nighttime takeoff."

Danny shook his head emphatically. "I'm really sorry, but I've gotta say no. Taking the Gianelli out on black water, in the dark, in that drizzle? Even with the help of your ghosts, it's a bad idea. And anyway, a few hours' wait shouldn't matter, should it?"

In the next room a telephone rang. Mr. Cargill heaved himself up off the sofa and went out to answer it. When he came back he was scowling even more darkly than usual.

"It was Miss Beale, my managing editor," he said, looking at the two pilots. "The Department of Etheristics has the police out looking for us. They've been to Johnny and Mel's house already. The ghost of some old lady walloped Santangelo pretty good, with a broom. Wish I coulda seen that. Gentlemen, they know your floatplane came in and refueled at South Bay Port."

"But they can't find us, can they?" Johnny asked.

"I'm afraid they know exactly where we are."

"But how could they?" Johnny was appalled.

"Miss Beale tells me one of our pilots got too talkative."

It seemed unlikely that someone with Danny's dusky complexion could turn pink, then red, but he did. "The dock manager at South Bay Port asked where we were headed," the flier moaned. "I told him an estate up on the Treport River."

"Doesn't take much to figure out who at the *Clarion* has a big, fancy cottage on the Treport," Mr. Cargill observed.

"So if we stay till dawn," Johnny said, suddenly more worried than he'd been all night, "we might not even get to go!"

Mel drew herself up. "We have to try a night takeoff. The colonel won't let us down. You have my word."

"I'm not sure it's worth dyin' for," Jock drawled.

Danny looked at his co-pilot, then at Mel and Johnny. "Listen, I'm really sorry about blabbing my mouth back there at South Bay. *Really* sorry. But if I make the wrong decision… I'm the captain of that Gianelli out there and I'm responsible for all our lives. If you could tell me what this is all about, Mel—why do you have government agents after you? What's so darned important that you'd risk your necks for it?"

"I know this may sound nuts. But I think someone, somewhere, is trying to create what I call an etheric bomb. If it exists, it would be the most powerful weapon in history—capable of utterly destroying a city the size of Zenith or Neuport. One single bomb!"

Danny shook his head. "All due respect, Mel, but you've gotta be mistaken. How could such a thing even be possible?"

Mel filled in Danny and Jock on the Gesellschaft murders, then explained her suspicions about the etheric bomb. She said that as far as she knew, the people in this room were all that stood between this horrible weapon and the lives of innocent millions.

Mel suddenly looked as if she were carrying the whole world on her skinny shoulders. "I actually hope, Danny, that I'm wrong. But can we take that chance?"

Danny looked grimly around at the others. "I don't like it, not one bit. But I guess we've got to give it a try."

At that, Mel gave her orders to the colonel. "Survey the river. Quick as you can. We need a mile and a half of clean water."

CHAPTER 20

AIDED BY THE CARETAKER and his wife, Mr. Cargill and the adventurers combed the big bluestone cottage and guest cabins, hunting for flashlights. They found seventeen that worked—exactly as many as they needed.

In less than an hour, the colonel and his troopers had finished surveying the water. Everyone gathered on the dock, the drizzle still coming down, as the colonel reported his findings to Mel and Johnny.

"We can give your flying machine a mile and a quarter of deep, open water, going downriver," the ghost said. "There's a light headwind from the southeast. But your climb brings you out perilously close to some tall trees down where the river bends. Your driver will need to pour on the power. Just follow me. I'll be right in front of you with my electric torch. Pull you up with my bare hands, if needs be." The specter laughed his papery laugh and winked.

Mel told Danny and Jock precisely what the colonel had said.

"Then you'd better give your etheric friends their flashlights and we'll be on our way," Danny said. He and Jock stepped up into the aircraft, and a few seconds later the cabin lights came on. Uncle

Louie got busy loading the luggage that Nina and Mr. Cargill were bringing from the chief's station wagon.

Mel and Johnny walked along the shore, each with a bag of flashlights, passing them up to the dead horse soldiers, showing each man how the devices worked. Then the troopers trotted off, taking up their positions on the broad Treport River—eight on one side, eight on the other. Holding the seventeenth flashlight in his left hand, the colonel positioned himself and Buck directly in front of the Gianelli Z-509.

Jock's head popped out of the aeroboat's door. "Come on board, y'all," he shouted. "We'll be ready to go in a few minutes."

Johnny turned to his boss and stuck out a hand. Mr. Cargill took it and pumped it. "Remember, John, that you, your sister, and your uncle all have letters of credit," the chief said. "Good for cash money at any bank. Any World Press Association office will help—"

"Automobiles comin', Mr. Cargill!"

They turned around to see the caretaker pointing back toward the woods. Three pairs of headlights were snaking down from the highway through pines and poplars. The police!

"Lucky I locked the driveway gate when we arrived," Mr. Cargill chuckled. "Time for you folks to hotfoot it, I think." He clapped Johnny on the shoulder. "Good shooting, John, old man."

Johnny made a crisp salute from the brim of his fedora. He couldn't have felt more pride—or responsibility. He could sense the weight of it. Well, this was what he'd always wanted. "We won't let you down, Mr. Cargill," he said with a determined nod.

"Now I'd better go greet our visitors," the chief said. "But I think I'll walk kind of slowly." He turned on his heel and began ambling up the long driveway, his hands in his pockets.

Johnny almost managed to climb the aeroboat boarding ladder

in a single bound, scampering over the last step right on Nina's heels. As soon as Mel started up the ladder she shouted, "We have company, Danny. Time to go."

"Louie, untie the lines," Danny hollered out of his cockpit window.

The old aeroboat jockey quickly undid the ropes securing the port-side pontoon. He was inside the aeroboat and sealing the pressurized door in under forty seconds.

The nose engine roared to life. Then the port. Finally the starboard propeller started turning. The streamlined seaplane slowly eased away from the dock and out onto the water, the rain drizzling down. It made a slow 180-degree turn—heading northwest, upriver against the current.

THE FLIGHT DECK was dim and far more cramped than on the Night Goose. But it was sure exciting being up there with Danny and Jock. In fact, Johnny had never seen a takeoff from this angle.

He and Mel hunched over behind the two pilots. All they had to do was stay upright and not get knocked over. They were supposed to be seated in back with Nina and Uncle Louie, but Danny wanted them to keep their eyes on the colonel—in case he made an important signal that the pilots couldn't see.

The brother and sister stared straight out through the windshield, which the wipers swiped clean of rain every few seconds. Just beyond the blur of the nose prop, the colonel and Buck trotted along easily, as if they were on a Sunday ride in the park.

Danny steered the floatplane through another broad U-turn and aimed it downstream. Ahead, two rows of flashlights, bobbing gently, flickered down the broad center of the river. The farthest lights looked fainter through the rain. In a voice that Johnny could barely hear above the din Danny said, "Okay, people, let's go."

The three radial engines roared like a tornado. The Z-509 surged downriver, past the first pair of lights. The nose came up and the water spray almost disappeared.

The colonel charged along just ahead of the central propeller, clearly visible to Johnny. As the third and fourth troopers flashed by, Johnny caught a brief glimpse of automobile headlights pulling up to the dock.

All of a sudden, the vibration of the pontoons on the river fell off to almost nothing and the aircraft's nose came down. The seaplane was skimming along on top of the water. More pairs of lights zipped by in quick succession.

"Here we go everyone," Danny shouted, easing the yoke back. The Gianelli bulled its way off the water.

"The colonel's pointing up," Johnny yelled. "We've got to climb!"

Danny responded. The nose tilted higher. The aeroboat zoomed by the last two flashlights. Rain still pounded the windshield.

Johnny saw the colonel tip Buck up almost onto his hindquarters, as if to charge up a precipitous hill.

"Steeper yet!" Mel screamed.

"He sees something!" hollered Johnny.

Danny jammed the throttles forward, drew the yoke back as far as he could, and yelled, "Don't stall, baby!"

A murky wall of firs and pines suddenly emerged through the drizzle, branches dancing in the aeroboat's headlamps. The forest rushed at them, columns of ancient green.

A loud WHUMP-THUD erupted beneath them, as brief as a heartbeat. The sickening percussion shuddered through the whole airframe—as if some giant had rung it like a gong.

The Z-509 wobbled but kept climbing.

Without warning the steep tilt of the deck sent Mel staggering. She stumbled back and fell past Johnny onto the cabin floor. He managed to deflect her a bit, so she only knocked her head a glancing blow against the navigator's seat.

"Mel, what's the colonel doing?" Danny shouted. "Mel? Johnny?"

"Mel's down, Danny!" yelled Johnny, scrambling to get to his sister. "Knocked out!"

CHAPTER 21

"MIZ GRAPHIC! MIZ GRAPHIC! You okay?"

Jock squatted down as Johnny cradled Mel's head in his lap. The co-pilot gently slapped the young woman's cheeks. Johnny was worried sick. He'd never seen his sister look so queasy and pale.

Then he realized the aeroboat wasn't climbing so steeply. It seemed as if they were out of the woods. Literally *and* figuratively. They hadn't crashed. There were no more loud thumps, so that was good.

With any luck, the treetops had not smashed their pontoons. It was the middle of the night and they had no way to see any damage from their perches in the cockpit. They'd only know they were okay *for sure* when they set this bird down. Or if Johnny could alert the colonel and have him make a mid-air inspection.

First things first, though, he thought. *Gotta get Mel upright.*

"Come on, girlie," Jock said. "I ain't never had a passenger croak on me and I ain't about to start now. Thought you were a tough little cookie, from what Danny told me."

"Come on, Mel," said Johnny. "You're okay. Wake up now."

In the dim amber cockpit light Johnny saw Mel's eyelids flutter and open. She muttered a few words, but he couldn't make them out. The engine noise was still too loud. It took her eyes a few seconds to focus, but she clearly recognized him.

"Hi, Johnny," she mumbled as he leaned in closely. "I seem to have misstepped somehow. And I'm no 'little cookie.'"

Jock grinned. "You took a tumble, that's for sure."

"So we made it up off the river?"

"You betcha, Sis," said Johnny, quite relieved. "Otherwise, we wouldn't be yakking, now would we?"

Her eyelids fluttered a bit more. "I think I'd like to rest for a while, if you don't mind."

"Just let me look at your eyes," Johnny said. He knew from adventure books that the eyes could tell you if someone had a concussion. He examined Mel's and they looked fine—the pupils were not too large and were both the same size.

"Do you feel dizzy or confused? Have a headache?" he asked.

Mel shook her head.

"Ringin' in the ears? Nausea?" chimed in Jock.

Mel said no.

"Then let's get you back to your seat," Jock said, as he hoisted her up.

After they buckled Mel in, Johnny and Uncle Louie settled back in their seats—pillows behind their heads and blankets across their laps. But Johnny had a hard time falling asleep, unlike Uncle Louie. He tried and tried, and just couldn't. He was quite wide-awake when the ranks of snow-capped mountaintops began passing by the floatplane, a bit after dawn. The view from twenty thousand feet was absolutely spectacular.

Mel woke up about that time and seemed to be perfectly fine, except for a little headache and a cranky mood. She took charge of distributing orange juice, coffee, and sandwiches—which tasted surprisingly good, especially for food wrapped in cellophane.

The Gianelli tri-motor arrived safely at the dock at Zephyr Lines' Silver City base later that afternoon. Everyone piled out to look for any damage done by the tall pine trees of the Treport River.

Just as the colonel had reported to Johnny while they were still airborne, there were scratches and dents on the pontoons, and bits of greenery stuck in seams and joints and corners of trusses. That's when they realized how close they had come to utter disaster. A takeoff climb only a few feet lower would have ended in a cartwheeling maelstrom of crushed metal and flame.

"The colonel saved our bacon," Johnny pointed out. "If he hadn't shown us where to go, we'd all be dead."

"I promise," Danny proclaimed after his inspection of the Gianelli, "that I will *never ever* take an aeroboat up in the middle of the night on an uncharted river. *Never! Ever! Again!*"

"But you did it, you and Jock," Mel said, grabbing his forearm. "You're the best pilots in the whole world!"

JOHNNY WAS AGOG at the huge Zephyr Lines base on Silver City Bay. There were scores of flying boats in wet docks and dry docks. They had flown all over the world, these aircraft. To destinations westward, such as the Orchid Isles, Majuro, Port Marlowe, Tor Chan. Back east across the fractured continent that had once been a country called the Free States—back before the First Border War. Beyond Freedonia's great metropolis of Neuport, Zephyr Lines aeroboats flew east across the Lesser Ocean, to the Royal Kingdom, La Belle Republique, and points beyond.

Johnny wanted to visit every single one of those places. And the way he figured it, his Zoom 4x5 press camera was his ticket to go.

Uncle Louie, Nina, and the Graphics said goodbye to Danny and Jock, and took a taxicab into the city, through the gathering dusk and heavy rush hour traffic. Some kind of a blockage up ahead stopped them for a time in the middle of the three-mile-long Silver Gate Bridge. It gave Johnny a chance to view the city's magnificent skyline. Silver City was the capital of the Coastal Federation, so Johnny wasn't surprised that the downtown had even taller skyscrapers than Zenith—and lots more of them.

The weary travelers checked into the Paragon Hotel and had a quick supper in the cafe in the lobby. From their tenth-floor suite they could look out at the night vista of nearby Jadetown—where Mongke Eng had died. It was a little universe of colorful, flashing neon and ornate, exotic architecture. Somewhere out there were Mongke Eng's daughters. And Johnny and Mel had to get an interview with at least one of them.

Mel and Nina went to bed at eight-thirty. Johnny hit the sack about nine, figuring that he would conk out immediately. But here he was, in this incredibly comfortable hotel bed, with his head spinning, his mind racing. There was just too much to think about, too much to worry about.

A while later he heard Uncle Louie answer a rap on the hotel room door. There was a muffled exchange of words. Johnny had no idea what it was about, but it didn't matter for now. His brain and his body suddenly decided *enough*. Off to sleep with you.

CHAPTER 22

JOHNNY PUT ON HIS SUIT and hat, then his socks and shoes. He tiptoed through the sitting room and was about to sneak out the hotel room door, camera pack slung over his shoulder, when someone cleared her throat behind him.

He spun around. There stood Nina, dressed in her travel clothes, grinning and looking very pleased with herself. He was tempted to groan, but he knew that would be a bad idea. Nina did not like being groaned at.

Johnny started to say something, but she put an index finger up to her lips and pointed at Uncle Louie, snoring away on the sofa. She came over and nudged Johnny out the door, gently closing it behind them.

"I was just going to shoot some local color," Johnny sputtered in the hallway. "You don't have to come."

Nina put her hands on her hips. "You're always going off and having adventures by yourself. Every once in a while you ought to share them! I mean, I'm practically your cousin. Anyway, if you leave without me, I'll go back in there and wake up Mel and Louie."

"You wouldn't!"

"I would."

Johnny opened his mouth, intending to say a few choice words, but thought the better of it. "Well, okay, Sparks," he yielded. "Come on."

"Let me leave them a note," she said, slipping back into the suite.

It was still dark outside. They walked through a public park across from the hotel and came upon Silver City's grand Mac-Dougall Fountain, lights still burning, with its statue of President MacDougall. He had been a tall, thin man with a haggard face and a beard. Cast in bronze, he was standing, looking somberly down, his hands clasped in front of him, the very picture of despair. Chiseled in the granite beneath his lanky figure were the words:

WILLIAM MACDOUGALL
LAST PRESIDENT OF THE FREE STATES
HERO OF THE LOST CAUSE

Back in school, Johnny had read about the capture of President MacDougall and the Free States' capital by forces of the Old Dominion during the First Border War. This event led to a peace treaty and, ultimately, the division of the Free States into four countries. The triumphant Old Dominion. The Plains Republic, where Johnny and Nina lived. The Coastal Federation. And a remnant of the Free States that survived in the northeast, now called Freedonia—of which Neuport was the capital.

The two of them emerged out of the park onto a broad avenue that bordered Jadetown. Streetlamps threw down little puddles of light, illuminating a few ghosts who were standing around—bored, listless, depressed. Johnny said "Hi" to some of them, which prompted the specters to tag along behind the two kids.

Up the avenue stood a big, ornamental gate encrusted in sinuous, climbing dragons in red enamel and gold leaf. A green metal roof the shape of a witch's hat crowned the structure.

This was one of the four ceremonial entrances into Jadetown—looming right over General Tang Boulevard. Johnny had read about them in a tourist magazine at the hotel. The two youngsters marched beneath the gate, half a dozen ghosts trailing behind—most of them immigrants from the Jade Kingdom.

For an hour, they wandered through narrow, winding streets. Vivid aromas of spices and cooking oils wafted from the open-air restaurants. Roosters crowed here and there. It seemed almost every window had someone leaning out of it, waiting for the new dawn.

The two friends talked in spurts. About the murders. About the trip. About Mel's interest in Danny.

As Nina had observed, Johnny and she *were* practically cousins. But they hadn't gabbed this much in a while.

Johnny would never forget the day Nina came to live with them.

At first she had been shy and clung to Uncle Louie. But she'd lost both parents, too. So they had that in common. By and by the two kids began to talk, and they talked a lot about having no mom, no pop anymore. Before long they were hiking the woods together. Nina tagged along when Johnny took pictures, and he hovered over her shoulder when she monkeyed around with her radios. She impressed the heck out of him by actually flying the little float-plane that Uncle Louie owned—making her first solo flight when she was only eleven. Johnny had seen her do it.

Both kids were fascinated by gizmos, gizmos of any kind. And they sure did enjoy having adventures. But small adventures. Nothing like this, Johnny thought, nothing that could get you killed. And since he wanted to live to be a hundred, he preferred adventures that were exciting but *not* lethal.

"Hey, Johnny," Nina said, as they studied a shop window full of exquisite ivory figurines, "did you worry you were going to die on the Night Goose?"

"Uh, not really. I just did what I figured needed doing. I had to keep that Steppe Warrior away from Mel as long as I could. If the colonel hadn't arrived…" He shrugged. "I'd have done anything to stop that ghost."

"But you could have gotten killed," she said. "Both of you could have gotten killed."

"Guess so. I could get hit by a truck this afternoon. Better to die for a good reason than no reason."

Nina kept staring into the shop window. "Do you think we're going to get through this whole thing alive?"

"Listen, Sparks." Johnny tried to sound confident. "Everything'll be fine. No one's gonna try to hurt us. *Promise.*"

AFTER TAKING SOME PICTURES in a market, Johnny paid for two bowls of rice, vegetables, and fish. He never could handle chopsticks, so the smiling cook found him a wooden spoon. Of course, Nina had no trouble with chopsticks.

The two youngsters gobbled up every bit, sitting on a couple of overturned wooden boxes. That's when Johnny remembered to look at his pocket watch.

"Jeez Louise!" he exclaimed. "Almost seven. We'd better get back."

It didn't take him long to realize that he had no idea exactly where they were. But he knew how to find out. Turning around, he addressed his troop of ghostly hangers-on. "Am I going in the right direction to get back to the Paragon Hotel?"

"No, young master," said a pretty girl ghost, bowing. She could have been thirteen when she died, or eighteen. Johnny couldn't tell. She had on a blue silk gown and elaborate headdress with dangling pearls. "The Paragon Hotel is on the other side of Jadetown, almost a full mile and a half from here."

"Will you take me there?"

"Certainly, young master." The dead girl lifted her daintily painted eyebrows. "May we know your name?"

He blinked. "Oh, pardon me. I'm Johnny Graphic. I'm a news photographer. This is my friend, Nina Bain."

The wraith smiled and bowed modestly. "My name is Su Li."

Johnny bowed in return, and then poked Nina in the ribs. She bowed as well, following his lead.

So off they marched, Su Li leading the way. Soon they found themselves in a larger marketplace. Johnny and Nina wove their way through gaggles of people. More ghosts had joined them.

They walked by a woman who had a table full of handsome watercolor paintings. Landscapes, flowers, that sort of thing. Her face revealed Steppe heritage. Johnny wanted to stop and look at the pictures, but he had no time to spare. He thought the woman stared at him a little oddly.

The two youngsters were halfway across the square when the watercolor painter came running after them, shouting, "Johnny Graphic? Are you Johnny Graphic?"

He pivoted around, surprised to be recognized so far from home. "Yeah, ma'am, I am. What's the problem?"

"Big problem, Mister Graphic. Steppe Warriors on the other side of the square. No one's seen them here since they killed my father."

Johnny had to think for a few seconds, then his jaw dropped. "You're one of Mongke Eng's daughters?"

She nodded briskly. "Yes, Betty Mongke."

"Steppe Warriors?" he gasped. "Where?"

"Over there," she said, pointing.

Johnny was far too flustered to say "Pleased to meet you." He twirled around again and saw the warrior wraiths at the far side of the square. Among them was the very same female, Checheg, who had dueled with Mel in the upstairs hallway. She gripped her saber in the only hand she had left. Somehow, she had followed them halfway across the continent. With her were two other Steppe Warriors. And behind them came a rank of ghostly thugs—surly hatchet men who looked eager to use the bloody weapons in their hands.

"Not good, Sparks," Johnny moaned to his friend. "Now we're really in a pickle!"

CHAPTER 23

"YOU HAVE TO RUN," Betty Mongke whispered to the two kids, as one of the Steppe Warriors swaggered toward them. "Go into the laundry over there. Out through the back. Go right. To the golden ginseng on General Tang Boulevard. Then left."

Johnny heard Su Li's reedy voice behind them. "You are not alone. Ask us to fight."

Johnny and Betty Mongke turned around. Su Li and several of her ghostly companions had produced axes and swords of their own.

Of course, he thought. *How could he be so dumb?* If he asked, and the Jadetown ghosts agreed, they became real warriors with real weapons.

"Fight them for me!" he implored, looking right at Su Li. "Please fight them."

Every single ghost nodded and bowed. "To defend you and to avenge our friend Mongke Eng will be an honor," Su Li said.

"Johnny, Nina," whispered Betty Mongke. "Follow me when I tell you." In her right hand she held a broad, bloodied cleaver, just snatched from a butcher's stall a few feet away.

Most of the people in the square had melted away. Windows all around had cracked open and people were peeking out.

One of the Steppe Warriors came forward, leading his pony, stopping a good twenty paces before Johnny and his friends—right in the middle of a table full of colorful squashes.

"I am Unegan," he said, in a voice that sounded like a dozen hissing snakes. "You will come with us, boy. No harm will befall you or your friends. We only want you to take us to your sister."

"To kill her," Johnny snarled. "You're gonna use me for bait."

"The boy's right," Betty Mongke said, her voice simmering with anger. "No one can trust foul murderers like you."

Betty touched Johnny and Nina's shoulders, and drew in a deep breath. "Into the laundry. *Now!*"

Johnny and Nina dashed after her, dodging between abandoned stalls and carts. He could see the gaudy red-and-gold sign for "Wing's Fine Laundry." A clatter of ponies' hooves and throaty shouts of anger erupted in the square. Then came terrible screams and the clanging of metal on metal. The battle of the ghosts had begun.

Johnny, Nina, and Betty had almost made it to the laundry. Just as they were about to dive in through its front door, two hideous wraiths bearing axes popped out of the grimy window of the restaurant next door. It was hard to say who was more surprised—the living or the dead. For a few seconds they stared at each other, slack-jawed.

The first to collect her wits was Betty Mongke, who turned to Johnny and Nina. "Off with you now and may the sacred one protect you!"

Before Johnny could utter a peep, Betty shoved him and Nina in through the laundry's door, and charged the hatchet men.

With Nina right behind him, Johnny pushed his way through a forest of packed clothing racks. Somewhere in there a wool overcoat stripped away his camera bag. But he managed to hang onto his Zoom 4x5. Two scrawny, shirtless men hand-ironing trousers shouted at them as Johnny and Nina rushed out the back door.

They emerged into a dim, filthy alleyway. The smell of chemicals, rotten food, and ripe human odors assaulted their noses. The only light came from a ribbon of sky many stories overhead.

"She said 'right,'" Johnny panted. "Far as the golden ginseng. What's a ginseng?"

"A root kinda shaped like a deformed human figure," answered Nina, her eyes full of dread.

"Root," said Johnny. "Human shape. Got it. Now let's go." He grabbed Nina's hand and off they charged to the right, up the alley. They breathlessly hopped and skipped, trying to avoid stepping in mysterious seepages and decayed items of food. Johnny kept looking back over his shoulder. *Maybe we got away*, he thought hopefully. *Maybe this won't turn out to be a disaster after all.*

Then, right after they crossed a narrow street and pounded back into the alley, Nina caught a toe on a protruding cobblestone and sprawled face-first with a yelp of shock. Right into a puddle of unknown, slimy, green-colored crud.

"Nooo!" she howled, struggling to get back on her feet. She turned and glared at Johnny—as if this somehow was all his fault.

He glared right back and grumbled, "Don't look at me! You're the one who wanted to come!"

Before she could sputter a reply, he grabbed her hand again and hauled her away at an urgent trot. A few minutes later they saw a bright, busy street dead ahead. Maybe General Tang Boulevard. Johnny heaved a sigh of relief. *Almost there, almost safe.*

"BOY!"

Johnny stopped in his tracks, his blood turning to ice water. He pivoted around and saw the Steppe Warrior who had addressed him in the square. The wraith was forty paces behind them, legs spread, with an arrow nocked and aimed.

"You will come with me," the specter said.

Johnny gingerly took a step backward. He quickly glanced at his friend. "Run, Sparks. Now!"

The sodden, bedraggled Nina gave him a desolate, conflicted look.

"Go!" Johnny ordered.

With a grimace, Nina dashed off toward the busy main street.

Feeling a terrible dread, Johnny waited for the TWANG of the bowstring. But the ghost let Nina live. She had escaped.

"I can kill you whenever I want," the Steppe Warrior said, walking toward Johnny. "Come with me and I won't hurt you."

"Nuts to you!" Johnny spat and bolted for the street.

There was a loud *twang* and a ghostly arrow slashed through his pant leg, grazing the outside of his right calf. He felt a searing flash of pain, then heard the *zwwwing* of a sword coming out of a scabbard.

Johnny took off, half limping, half running. In a window up ahead he could see a giant ginseng root—shaped like a deformed human, just as Nina had described it.

In a wink, he figured out what he had to do. The instant his feet hit the boulevard's sidewalk, he darted to the right and squeezed his back against the brick wall of the Third Jadetown National Bank. He knew his pursuer would have seen which way he'd gone.

Sure enough, the bandy-legged specter burst out of the alley and cut right, without looking.

A mistake.

A *huge* mistake.

Johnny charged the specter the way he had seen cricket bowlers do it in newsreels, with a looping, powerful overhand pitch. But instead of grasping a cricket ball, he gripped the leather strap of his Zoom 4x5 and swung it up over his head—putting every drop of centrifugal force into it that his 75-pound body could provide.

The ghost's eyes snapped wide open. He put up his curved blade to parry the blow. It was too late for anything else.

The camera smashed through the Steppe Warrior's hands.

It broke his etheric fingers and wrist with a terrible *cruuunch*.

The sword went flying.

Then the sturdy metal box caught the warrior wraith full in the face, shattering a dozen bones—from the eyebrows down to the jaw.

Johnny landed on top of the Steppe Warrior, crushing him to the pavement. All around them, people scattered in every direction, screaming.

His heart pounding like a steam locomotive, his vision going red, Johnny pinned down the wounded ghost. He lifted up his heavy camera and smashed it down into the ghost's face again.

And again.

And again.

Livid with rage, he wanted to crush this Steppe Warrior into jelly.

He held the smashed, ruined camera high, for another blow, but oddly his arm was quaking, shaking.

Suddenly Johnny felt very, very tired. His calf was beginning to throb and burn where the arrow had sliced him. A dark bloodstain spread down his trouser leg.

He stood up all wobbly—still gripping his wrecked Zoom 4x5—and started to limp away, toward the grand entrance gate he and Nina had walked beneath two hours before. Odd, how the world was spinning around.

Just before crumpling to the sidewalk, Johnny thought he saw blue-clad cavalrymen galloping toward him.

CHAPTER 24

"THIS JOB IS *WAY* HARDER than I thought it would be."

Johnny was sitting up in the hotel bed in his pajamas—feeling washed-out and still a little shaky. They had cleaned his leg wound at the hospital, and stitched and dressed it with a big, uncomfortable bandage. But it continued to throb something awful. He didn't like pain. Pain hurt.

"I've got news for you, John, old man," said Uncle Louie, towering over the foot of the bed, arms crossed. "Jobs usually aren't that easy. That's why they call 'em *work*."

Uncle Louie still didn't look very happy about Nina and Johnny's Jadetown misadventure. But he and Mel had simply asked Johnny to think about what Lydia Graphic might have told him. That, Uncle Louie said, ought to be lecture enough. And it was. Johnny could almost hear his mom's voice telling him what a foolish thing it had been, going into Jadetown without the colonel. But Johnny knew that if a good story demanded it, he probably would risk his neck again someday. Any news photog would do the same thing.

"Hey, Johnny, there's a picture of you on the front page," Mel shouted from the sitting room. She came into the bedroom, holding up the new edition of Silver City's *Evening Standard*. Nina followed, hard on her heels.

"You're being bundled into the ambulance," continued Mel. "It's a swell shot."

Johnny grunted his displeasure as he peered at the photo. The only thing worse than not having his own pix on the front page was having a shot of *him* out cold and supine.

The big black headline proclaimed:

GHOSTLY BATTLE ROYAL IN JADETOWN!

Zenith Clarion Lensman Attacked by Marauding Steppe Warrior Ghosts. Flees with Friend and Defends Self. Fights Off Murderous Specter. Marketplace Turned Upside Down. Jadetown Etherists and Spooks on Patrol.

Two of the four photos showed the market looking as if a tornado had ripped through it—carts and stands tipped over, windows broken. Another showed Betty Mongke, her right arm in a sling, her other hand proudly showing off a battered cleaver. The last shot, at the bottom of the page, depicted Johnny on a stretcher, being put into an ambulance. He could only shake his head when he saw it.

Mel and Nina sat down on the edge of the bed. "What's the matter, Johnny?" Nina said, grabbing the paper from Mel. "This'll be great for your career."

"In case you hadn't noticed, I've had kind of a bad day," he whined. "Fighting hand to hand with an etheric killer. Smashing my favorite camera. Getting thirteen stitches. The nurse had to take my pants off. Cut the pant leg and yanked 'em right off. Pretty embarrassing. And I don't think having a front-page photo of me knocked senseless on a stretcher will exactly help my career."

Uncle Louie gave Johnny a troubled look. "There's something else. Something you don't know about yet."

A cold lump formed in the pit of Johnny's stomach. "Yeah? What?"

"Two telegrams came in after you went to bed last night," said Mel. "Both from Mr. Cargill."

Johnny gulped. "Uh-huh?"

"A judge has forbidden the *Clarion*, or any news outlet, from publishing our stories in the Plains Republic."

"Well, that stinks. Nobody at home's gonna see our stuff. So what's the chief doing about it?"

"I guess the *Clarion*'s attorneys are going to court to try and get the government's ban overturned," said Uncle Louie. "But there's no telling how long that'll take."

Mel and Uncle Louie and even Nina still looked pretty grim. That must mean the second item of news was even worse.

"And you know that Dame Honoria went to hide out on her island in Rotonesia," Mel said.

Johnny nodded. "Yeah. Gorton Island. Her favorite place in the world outside of Gilbeyshire."

Mel sighed. "She's vanished."

"You mean like *abducted?*" Johnny yelped. "*Dead maybe?*"

Uncle Louie jumped in. "We don't know what happened. Authorities searched all over the island. There wasn't anybody there. No living people. No ghosts. The police talked to folks on nearby islands, but no one knows a thing."

Johnny pulled himself bolt upright. "Then we have to forget about Mrs. Deng's murder in Tor Chan. We've got to go to Gorton Island and figure out what happened to Dame Honoria. If she's alive, we've got to rescue her."

"No disagreement here," Mel said.

"But we can't leave for a few days," said Uncle Louie. "Nina and I need some training at the Zephyr Lines base. And, of course, our news photographer here has to heal up a little and get himself a new camera."

"And I'm going to talk with Betty Mongke," Mel added. "After all, we came to Silver City to report on her father's murder. She might have some good info for us. If you feel up to it, Johnny, you ought to come with me tomorrow and take a few pictures."

"So long as I can get that new camera," said Johnny. "'Cause no sore leg's going to keep me off the job."

CHAPTER 25

WEDNESDAY, OCTOBER 23, 1935
SILVER CITY

MONGKE ENG'S DAUGHTER lived in a cramped, dingy Jadetown apartment three flights up. In a corner near a window sat a painter's easel, which held an unfinished landscape of rocky outcroppings and gnarly evergreens.

When Johnny and Mel arrived, Betty Mongke greeted them warmly. With the arm that wasn't in a sling, she motioned them toward her dilapidated kitchen table and mismatched chairs. "Can I offer you some tea?"

"Yes, please," said Mel, sitting down on a spindly chair that swayed and creaked audibly.

"You don't have a root beer, do you?" Johnny asked, delicately lowering himself onto his chair. His leg was still plenty sore and it had not been easy getting up those stairs. But no way was he going to miss taking photos of Betty to go with Mel's story.

"Orange soda okay?" asked Betty.

"You betcha." Johnny liked orange soda almost as much as root beer.

Their hostess shouted a few sharp words in Jade tongue and the specter of an old woman floated through the door of what must have been the bedroom. The ghost set about preparing tea, then fetched an orange soda from the refrigerator, opening the bottle and setting it on the counter.

"Mei Ling kept house and cooked for Father," Betty explained. "He found her on a trip to the Jade Kingdom, after Mother died."

Betty glanced over her shoulder at the ghost and sighed. Then she whispered, "I think Mei Ling fell in love with him a little. Of course, though he was fond of her, he had no romantic feelings. Still, Father's death devastated the poor thing. I hope she'll be all right."

After serving the drinks, Mei Ling bowed deeply, put the tray back on the counter, and disappeared into the kitchen wall.

"I knew about the murders, of course," Betty said. "But I had no idea that Father was in such danger. If my sisters and I had realized, we would have taken him to a safe place."

After a few sips of tea, the artist pushed back her chair and went over to a bookshelf next to her easel. From between two heavy volumes she extracted a battered brown envelope and a cardboard tube. She set the items on the table in front of Mel.

"The day Father died," she said, "some Steppe Warriors broke into his apartment. He lived above a grocery store several blocks from here. They set the place on fire. Most of the building burned. A tenant, a crippled woman, died. Almost all of Father's papers and research went up in smoke."

"I don't know if you're aware of it," said Mel, "but I was attacked by a Steppe Warrior, a female, in my own bedroom."

"Oh yes," answered Betty. "It was in all the papers."

"Johnny tells me she was here in Jadetown yesterday. Back in Zenith she said that they were following the orders of a khan, a leader of some sort. Did your father know anything about that?"

Betty shook her head. "If he did, he never mentioned it. All he ever said is that no one in three centuries had been powerful enough to unite the Steppe clans as khan."

"So what're these?" Johnny tapped a finger on the brown envelope and the cardboard tube.

Betty allowed herself a little smile. "Father was a clever man. He saw a pattern in the murders and he knew to take precautions. So he gathered up certain material—"

She opened the big brown envelope first and spilled the contents out onto the table. There was a sheaf of handwritten papers crawling with equations, a carbon copy of a typewritten article, a single issue of *The Annals of the Oskar Hausenhofer Gesellschaft*, a small white envelope, and a color postcard showing one of Jade-town's great ceremonial gates.

"—and he told Mei Ling that if anything unusual occurred, she was to get this envelope and this tube out of the house and safely to me. When the Steppe Warriors came, Mei Ling slipped away and brought them here. Read this first." She picked up the post-card and handed it to Mel.

On the back of the card Johnny could see the cramped, spidery handwriting of an old man. Mel read it out loud:

"'Betty, if you are reading this, something bad has happened. Mei Ling brings you papers of mine that reveal a terrible danger from the ether. And I am partly to blame. Tell no one. Hold this envelope until you are able to safely convey it to young Melanie Graphic, the daughter of my friends William and Lydia Graphic. I love you, my precious little girl.'"

Betty sighed and dabbed at the tears forming in the corners of her eyes with a paper napkin.

Mel riffled through the first handwritten sheets. "Holy cow!

These are Mongke's advanced notes and equations for the creation of an etheric bomb."

Betty looked puzzled, but didn't say anything.

"Your father didn't come up with the idea, though," Mel continued. "Here he credits someone else with putting him on the path, with providing the original science."

"Who, then?" asked Johnny.

Mel shook her head in astonishment. "Mom and Dad."

Johnny's jaw dropped. This news defied belief. "They thought it up? They figured out how to create a bomb?"

"It's based on their theories of etheric lighting in solid matter. Stuff they came up with for their mining and medical work. Mongke says here he couldn't have done it without them. The three of them thought it up at the big etherists' conference in Neuport in 1929. And then Mongke worked out the details."

Betty held up her hand, as if she were a student in a classroom. "Forgive me, but can you tell me what this is? This etheric bomb?"

Mel explained, and Betty's look turned to horror.

Johnny still found it too incredible to accept. "But Mom and Pop wouldn't hurt a fly. Why would they do that? Create an explosive so powerful, so destructive? It's just not like them."

"Maybe they didn't think it would actually work," Mel speculated. "Maybe they figured it'd be a new source of energy, something beneficial. Maybe it was just a big puzzle for them, something scientifically challenging."

Johnny grabbed the smaller white envelope with Mel's name scrawled on it. Betty handed him a kitchen knife and he zipped it open. Out came a piece of blue stationery, which he unfolded and started to hand to his sister.

"You read it," said Mel.

"Okay, this is what he says," Johnny began. "'My dear Melanie… If you have received this note, then I am no longer among the living. It was my hope to discover what happened to your parents and, if they were alive, to rescue them. Word came from the Contessa di Altamonta, just months ago. And you will see her evidence with your own eyes. I am sure you will do the right thing. With deep affection, Mongke Eng.'"

"The contessa?" exclaimed Mel. "What does she have to do with this?"

Betty Mongke looked baffled. "Who is she?"

"She's a dead artist and a noblewoman. My mother befriended her many years ago. But we haven't heard from her in a long time. It's kind of strange that your dad was in touch with her."

"We better see what's in the tube, Mel," said Johnny, suddenly very excited.

Mel nodded and reached into it, pulling out a piece of heavy paper. She uncurled it and scrutinized it closely. "I don't understand," she said. Then she held up the paper for Johnny and Betty to see.

The pencil drawing—nearly as sharp and detailed as one of Johnny's press photos—showed a man and two women. The man had a bushy beard. He and the woman to his right wore tattered winter clothing, and appeared gaunt and exhausted. The second woman was quite pretty and wrapped in a fine fur coat. They were all standing before a yurt. Next to them, on its haunches, sat a giant ice wolf, almost the size of a horse.

Johnny suspected that the location was Okkatek Island, the only habitat of the ice wolf. And the animal must have been a ghost, because the actual species had become extinct over a century earlier.

"That's Mom and Dad for sure," gulped Mel. "I don't know who that other woman is. The signature on the drawing is the contessa's. I know that handwriting from her painting I have in my bedroom." She paused for a few seconds. "But this is odd. The date on this drawing is 1935. *It was made this year.*"

Johnny felt as if he were about to explode. "Do you think it means they're alive, Mel?"

"I don't know. But it means that as soon as we've rescued Dame Honoria, we have to find the contessa. We have to learn what she knows."

"Why didn't she just come to us straightaway? Why did she go to Betty's father?"

"Don't know," Mel replied. "Mom always said how shy she was. Super hard to get in touch with. But at some point we have to try and track her down."

Johnny nodded emphatically. Suddenly the whole world had shifted. There was now a real possibility that he and Mel might get their parents back. And that was the best news they'd had in five years.

"I knew they were still alive," he said with a huge smile. "*I just knew it!*"

CHAPTER 26

FORMERLY A RUBBER PLANTATION, Gorton Island was Dame Honoria's most private refuge. The jungle isle had belonged originally to her father, Sir Roderick Gorton. It was situated some dozens of miles across the Straits of Biru Gelombang from the northern coast of Rotonesia.

Sitting on her screened front verandah, which overlooked a white sand beach, Dame Honoria and the dead novelist Sir Chauncey Holyfield were enjoying a rare moment of silence. For the first time in weeks she felt able to relax. A warm, gentle breeze ruffled the comfortable old silk bag dress she had on. Her sandals kicked off, she wriggled her bare toes with delight. The view across the Straits was especially glorious today.

"Came here first as a little girl, Chauncey," she said, sighing with pleasure. "As a young mother, I watched my sweetums, my Percy, play out there on the beach."

"And now," said Sir Chauncey, "Gorton Island is your hidey hole. A place to escape to, a place where you can unwind from the pressures of celebrity."

"And a refuge from etheric assassins, I should hope. Ten days now, since my narrow squeak with the Neuport gangster ghost and his machine gun."

"Glad that you survived, old girl," observed the deceased novelist. "No one else I trust to take the red pencil to my scrawlings." As he spoke, Holyfield's ruddy face and several chins jiggled, and his mutton-chop whiskers bobbed up and down.

"Excuse me, ma'am, sir."

Dame Honoria and Holyfield twisted around.

Standing by one of the mahogany pillars that supported the verandah, a specter regarded them. He wore a safari jacket with many pockets, a pith helmet, jodhpurs, and riding boots. Above his left ear was a deep chasm, with skull bone and brain still visible.

"Ozzie Eccleston," Dame Honoria said. "Where in the devil have you been?"

He warily smiled at one corner of his mouth. "Well, you know—"

"I'd like you to meet my colleague, Sir Chauncey Holyfield."

"Good to meet you, Sir Chauncey," the weasel-faced wraith said.

"Likewise, I'm sure," replied the novelist, who didn't sound as if he meant it.

"We're working on the final draft of Chauncey's new novel, *Beatrice Periwinkle*," explained Dame Honoria.

"One of Sir Chauncey's scientific romances?"

Dame Honoria nodded. "Indeed, a time-travel adventure set in the days of the Great War. Young Beatrice Periwinkle is blessed with—"

"Always thought time travel a ridiculous notion, quite impossible." Ozzie sneered. "Who would believe it?"

"About a million readers who put down ten shillings every time one of my new books comes out," replied Sir Chauncey with a self-satisfied smirk.

"Ozzie, how often need I tell you?" Dame Honoria scolded. "*Niceties* must be observed. That was always your weakness. Daddy said that many times. You still blurt out whatever is on your mind. Telling that laborer he was a terrible, lazy fellow and sacking him on the spot." She scowled. "I witnessed it. Made quite an impression on a ten-year-old girl."

"Blighter *was* dreadfully quick with a machete," the wraith said, gently scratching at his wound.

"Well, do try to be more cordial," Dame Honoria pleaded for the hundredth time.

"Of course, ma'am," said Ozzie. "May I inquire about your recent doings? I've heard that things have gone rather badly for the Gesellschaft."

Dame Honoria turned her gaze back to the ocean and darkening sky for half a moment. "Yes, Ozzie. I intended to brief you with regard to the murders. We may need to institute new security measures."

When she finished recounting her narrow escape from the Neuport assassin, Ozzie harumphed. "The incident ought not to have been such a close call."

"I have great confidence," Dame Honoria said, "that you and our other ghosts will keep me quite safe."

Ozzie offered his employer an odd sort of smile. "You can count on us, Dame Honoria. I promise we'll take care of you."

A DEEP, DREAMLESS SLUMBER claimed Dame Honoria the very instant her head touched the pillow that night. Eight hours later, she came up out of the blackness to the brilliant light of a fine tropical morning.

She felt bracingly, wonderfully good. Rested, finally, after many days of aeroboats and trains and omnibuses and hotels. People who thought banging around the globe on flying boats was a glamorous occupation had clearly never been jammed into narrow, lumpy seats amid the din of roaring engines for days on end.

Dame Honoria pushed herself up from her bed, parted the mosquito netting, and hopped onto the rattan floor mat. She threw on her flowered silk robe and slipped on the old teak sandals that felt so comfortable under her feet. But instead of moving out into the hallway, she stood there stock-still.

She glanced at the clock on her dresser. "Peculiar, twenty minutes after eight." She sniffed again. "I know I distinctly asked for *bubur ayam* at eight."

There should have been an aroma of curry and chicken wafting up the stairs. Bubur ayam was her favorite island breakfast—thick rice porridge, shredded chicken with curry, fried green onion, and pomegranate.

Her ghost maid, Tala, should have been waiting outside her door—but was nowhere to be seen.

"Tala," she bellowed, "where are you?"

Something else was peculiar—the birds were not calling. It was weirdly silent outside.

Dame Honoria went slowly into the hallway, past a painting of Wickenham, her estate back in Gilbeyshire, where Lydia Graphic had given birth to Johnny. The canvas was by the ghost artist Maria Ghelarducci, the Contessa di Altamonta—an old, old friend who had lately vanished from view.

Dame Honoria approached the top of the stairs and peered down them.

"Ming Ho?" she said, her sonorous voice slightly louder than usual. "Tala? Ming Ho? Ozzie?"

Not a peep came from below.

"Ozzie!" she shouted. "Tala!"

Again, no one answered.

"Chauncey!"

Almost right at her feet, the ghost novelist popped up through the hallway floor, his mutton-chop whiskers aquiver. The look on his face—the pure terror in his eyes—made her heart catch and fall.

"They're here, Honoria!" he whispered. "I saw what they did to her. For heaven's sake, run! Hide! *Save yourself!*"

And before she could say a word, the ghost author shot through the ceiling and vanished without a by-your-leave. So much, she thought, for the fortitude of writers.

She trod deliberately down the stairs and peeked into the parlor and dining room. In the library the sturdy brown cardboard box containing the manuscript of *Beatrice Periwinkle* sat on her desk. She had a terrible premonition that it would be quite some time before she would again set to work on Sir Chauncey's tale.

Dame Honoria turned on her heel, walked toward the back door that led to the kitchen shack, then stepped out into dappled sunlight beneath the palms. She saw some vague figures moving about in the bushes. Wraiths, by the way they blended into the greenery.

"Who are you?" she demanded. Of course, she had a strong suspicion.

None of them replied.

"What do you want?"

At that the phalanx of ghosts came forward, almost but not quite transparent in the tropical humidity. They had been short, bandy-legged men, with flat, hard faces and narrow eyes that were impossible to read. They wore wool or leather tunics. Each of their heads was crowned with a pointed leather helmet. A few held bows. Others gripped short swords. From somewhere out of sight came the muffled sounds of horses snuffling and tramping the sand.

The rank of Steppe Warriors parted and a remarkable specter strode through, no taller than the rest, but somehow more powerful and more dangerous. He regarded Dame Honoria with empty, bleeding eye sockets. He had one hand behind his back.

Another ghost emerged from the jungle and the warriors parted for him, as well.

Ozzie Eccleston!

For a few brief, hopeful seconds, Dame Honoria thought that he had come to rescue her. But then she read the expression on his face. Grinning and self-satisfied. The very picture of a traitor.

"What do you *want?*" the etherist asked, focusing her full attention on the eyeless Steppe Warrior.

With a flourish, the horse soldier revealed the object that he had been hiding behind his back—the head of a ghost, a young native woman.

Looking equally embarrassed and despondent, the beheaded maid blinked at her mistress and said, "So sorry, ma'am."

"Oh, Tala," Dame Honoria sighed.

CHAPTER 27

THURSDAY, OCTOBER 24, 1935

AIRBORNE OVER THE PLAINS REPUBLIC

THE COMO EAGLE LANDED in the Orchid Isles late in the afternoon, after the long flight from Silver City. Johnny, Mel, Nina, and Uncle Louie soon found themselves in another handsomely decorated hotel suite. When he wasn't flying for Zephyr Lines, Danny lived in downtown Maholaihi, the island nation's capital.

Right after breakfast the next morning, Danny drove Mel and Johnny to a sprawling stuccoed house in one of the mountainside suburbs. The home was surrounded by gorgeous flowering shrubs and palm trees. Another member of the Hausenhofer Gesellschaft had been murdered here and Mr. Cargill wanted a story about the despicable deed.

Lani Muldoon, the new widow, greeted them at the front door. She was a short woman, nearly as wide as she was tall, with the dark, round face of a native islander.

Two ghost servants had the most to say about the murder of Mr. Muldoon. They had seen Steppe Warriors float through the front door late one evening, as the master dozed in his easy chair in the living room. They had seen arrows fly across the room, briefly turning B. K. Muldoon into a human pincushion. The spectral assassins darted out of the house and disappeared.

Mel took copious notes and Johnny shot several pictures of Mrs. Muldoon.

Then the widow took them to her husband's cramped office at the back of the house. Mel noticed almost immediately that his complete collection of *The Annals of the Hausenhofer Gesellschaft* was missing the number that contained a certain article by Mongke Eng—the same number missing from the libraries of other murdered Gesellschaft members.

As they were leaving, one of the ghost servants pulled Johnny aside. An old man with a bent back and stark white hair, he had on a kind of colored skirt pulled tightly around his skinny waist.

"Word among the spooks," he told Johnny, "is that the night watchers chased those murdering Steppe Warriors right off the island. I even heard a rumor that they captured a few of them."

"Tell me," Johnny asked, "who are the night watchers and how do we find them?"

The old man explained that the night watchers were primeval specters who had died on the island's ancient battlefields. They protected the Orchid Isles from interlopers living and dead, having received their powers from a hundred generations of island shamans.

"But take care, young sir," the ghost said ominously. "When you find a night watcher—or he finds you—don't look him in the eye. If you do, you'll become his slave forever."

"Silly superstition, is what that is," sniffed Mel, who had been listening in. "Now please tell us where to locate them."

Though looking very uneasy about it, the old man did just that.

EVEN DANNY SEEMED JITTERY about hiking into Awawa 'Ele'ele, the place the old ghost told them to go to. The name meant Black Valley.

"When I was little my granny warned me if I didn't behave, the night watchers would come and take me," he told Mel, Nina, and Johnny on their drive up into the backcountry. "And believe me, I behaved."

Wow, thought Johnny, sitting in the back seat of Danny's little sedan with Nina. If Danny was scared of them, then these specters must be pretty bad. But Mel was absolutely right to want to talk with them.

The car slowly climbed up a single-lane, dirt track on the north side of one of the island's interior mountains. Thick, green vegetation crowded in on all sides. The shade was so heavy, it almost felt like night. Suddenly, the road ended in a muddy clearing in the middle of the jungle, with just enough room to get Danny's car turned around. From here they had to hike a good two miles.

The undergrowth opened up as they entered Awawa 'Ele'ele, as if the plants were reluctant to flourish there. Everything looked stunted and deformed. *But at least we can see something now*, thought Johnny.

And, as he soon found out, something saw them, as well.

In a few winks of the eye, a troop of warrior wraiths surrounded the four hikers. Of course, Nina and Danny didn't realize it, until Johnny and Mel grabbed them and pulled them in close.

Johnny sure wished the colonel and his boys had come, but Mrs. Muldoon's servant had emphatically warned against it. Seeing alien ghost soldiers, the night watchers would attack mercilessly.

These island specters were all *huge*, wearing the same kind of wraparound skirt that the ghost servant had on. Their faces and upper bodies were covered with black, swirling, snake-like tattoos. And they had bones stuck through their ears and noses.

Now was the moment when Mel and Johnny had to test that old wife's tale. *Did looking into the eyes of night watchers actually enslave you to them?*

Not so far, thought Johnny, as Mel began to speak.

"We're peaceful visitors," she said, her voice trembling slightly. "We've come because of your recent fight with the Steppe Warriors who killed a man down in the city."

The night watchers—about thirty of them—crowded in closer, maces and slings and Stone-Age axes in their hands. One of them, the fiercest looking of all, came right up to Mel and glared down at her. Johnny had never thought that tattoos could look dangerous, but now he was reconsidering that opinion.

"What do you want?" the ghost rumbled.

"We've been told that you captured some Steppe Warriors," answered Mel. "They've been killing my friends around the world. If you have prisoners, I need to ask them some questions."

"Why should we help you?" the night watcher responded. His voice sounded like a tall elm groaning in the wind.

Usually Mel could answer tough questions pretty quickly. But her answers often tended to be kind of namby-pamby—diplomatic and reasonable and boring. And Johnny figured that diplomatic and reasonable and boring wouldn't wash with tough guys like these. So just as his sister was about to say something undoubtedly quite sensible and polite, he leapt in.

"So that we may revenge ourselves upon them!" he growled, as fiercely as a twelve-and-a-half-year-old boy could possibly growl. "So that we may destroy them and crush them into the earth!"

Mel looked appalled and Nina flabbergasted.

But the fearsome night watcher actually smiled, showing filthy, crooked teeth. He nodded to two of his compatriots. And simultaneously they reached into the primitive bags hanging across their chests and withdrew three objects.

Three desperate-looking and suddenly screaming bodyless heads. Three decapitated Steppe Warriors, dangling from their pigtails.

By the time Mel had finished interrogating them, she and Johnny had some answers.

And they didn't like them one bit.

CHAPTER 28

AS BAO FLEW from Paloa Atoll to the second island with her friend Evvie, she was already beginning to have doubts about getting blown up. All her friend would talk about as they soared over the vast ocean was how excited he was that *finally* he would cease to exist altogether. "Oblivion sounds lovely, old girl, doesn't it?" he said, as they zoomed along among a great flock of specters.

But Bao wasn't so sure. Deep in her heart, which hadn't beat in centuries, she had decided that she wasn't quite ready to leave the earth for good. The little girl was nothing if not a hopeful ghost. Perhaps her lot in life—well, actually her lot in death—would improve some day.

So she found herself edging away as, one by one, the thousands of ghosts who had come to the second island entered into the tin hut from which none of them emerged. Including Evvie. Finally there were only a few ghosts left outside, roaming around the island. She saw the khan and some of the other humans come in and out of the tin hut, again and again, carrying objects and devices that she didn't recognize.

And that is how she herself became one of the wandering wraiths. Nowhere to go, nothing to do. Until she decided to explore the many caves that wormed their ways through the island's rock mountains. At least it relieved the boredom.

One morning as she strolled through a stone formation and came into a black tunnel lit only by her gentle green glow, the futility of this whole adventure struck her like a blow. To come all this way! To make a new friend! And to lose him so soon! To be all alone again!

Bao squatted down on her haunches and started to sob and sniffle and rub out tears that didn't exist.

Then, from out of nowhere, came a voice. A living person's voice. An old woman's voice.

"Hullo? Who's there?"

Bao whimpered in reply.

"Can you see me?" the voice said. "Can you see my light?"

Bao didn't say anything, but sniffled again.

"Come out please. I won't hurt you, you know. If you're lost I can help."

The voice came from the front of the tunnel, somewhere around a bend in the stone passage. Bao very nearly nipped into the pink rock. Because living people who could see her had never talked to her, had always seemed afraid of her. She could no longer stand the horrified looks on their faces when they came upon her. But this time she stayed.

She could hear the shuffle of heavy feet coming her way. Then a dim orange light flickered around the bend in the tunnel and there she was, an old woman in a dirty gown of some kind, her mousy hair grimy and tangled. She had a long, gloomy face and dark circles under her eyes.

"I don't know what to do, Grandmother," Bao blurted out as she stood up.

The old woman edged closer and held her lamp up to the little ghost. "My dear, what's your name?"

"Bao."

"And I'm called Dame Honoria," the old woman said. "Little one, how did you come to be here?"

"I came with my friend Evvie from the first island. We flew over the water."

"What do you mean, 'first island'?"

"Where they made the first bomb."

The old woman's face looked shocked, baffled. "What kind of bomb?"

"A bomb with ghosts inside it," Bao answered. "The thing that truly kills them."

The old woman seemed as if she had suddenly been transported somewhere else, her mind apparently churning—as though Bao weren't even there. After a moment, she returned her attention to the little girl ghost. "My dear, did they explode the first bomb?"

For the first time since she had become a ghost, Bao felt a connection with a living human. She felt that, somehow, she could trust this person.

"I do not know, Grandmother. They brought us here, for the second bomb. I thought I wanted to go into the bomb, to truly die. But I was afraid to. My friend Evvie went into it, and I miss him."

Bao wobbled closer, gazing up—her chin quivering. The old woman was by no means tall, but she towered over the diminutive specter.

Bao tried to take the old woman's hand, but her fingers passed right through the living flesh and bones—as if through fog. The girl winced and began to cry again, as a profound sadness filled every part of her.

"I want…"

Sob.

"…to hold…"

Sniff.

"…your hand…"

Sigh.

"…Grandmother…"

Sob.

"…but I cannot."

Bao didn't need to, but she dragged her sleeve across her nose—just as a real little girl with a real runny nose would do.

"You can hold my hand, if you are willing to work," said Dame Honoria. "Are you afraid of working?"

Bao vigorously shook her head. "When I was alive I carried water. I helped with the food."

"Will you help me, then?"

"Yes, Grandmother," Bao said, "I will. I will help you."

The old woman reached down and took the little ghost's hand. That warm, solid flesh felt wonderful—the most wonderful thing Bao had known in many a long century.

CHAPTER 29

OZZIE GRASPED DAME HONORIA firmly by the left elbow as they crunched up the old shell road, past corrugated tin buildings in various states of decrepitude. Four spectral guards trudged behind the unhappy couple, swords drawn—as if the famous suffragist might scamper off into the jungle. Her scampering days, she regretted, were far behind her.

As they marched along, Dame Honoria ominously noted that the profusion of ghosts that had greeted her arrival on Old Number One was no longer profuse. A handful of wraiths were mooning about, looking typically ghostly and gloomy. But most of those thousands of specters had vanished. Now she understood why.

When she had discovered Bao in the tunnel, and heard the little ghost's story, all the pieces began to click into place. Will and Lydia Graphic, along with Mongke Eng, had come up with a notion of etheric power—how ghosts' "bodies" might be converted into energy in the physical realm. She knew that the three of them had worked on this theory purely as an intellectual exercise, as scientists often do.

Still, it could explain why Mongke Eng died with a spear in his chest. Why the others were killed. Someone was trying to build an etheric bomb, and they were murdering outsiders who might understand the science. *But why then*, Dame Honoria wondered, *am I still alive and kicking? Couldn't they simply have done me in back on Gorton Island?*

"So the etheric bomb exists, then, Ozzie?" she asked offhandedly, as they passed under some palms that arched over the road.

"Absolutely, of course it—"

Ozzie instantly looked mortified, and muttered a profanity. "Just shut up, you miserable old cow," he snapped. "You're to be told nothing until the khan himself informs you."

"I'm to see the khan then," sniffed Dame Honoria. "How grand."

Ozzie looked as if he wanted to slap her.

What a horrendous situation, thought Dame Honoria. Ozzie had confirmed the little girl's story. The bomb existed—and apparently more than one. But how in the world could she, a captive old woman, throw a wrench in the works? How could she prevent this horror from proceeding?

And to think that this morning had started off so encouragingly, with the unexpected appearance of one of her red-leather suitcases on the cave floor near her cot. She hadn't even had a chance to unpack it back on Gorton Island before Ozzie and his friends had hustled her off to Old Number One.

When she had popped the suitcase open, all her things were there. Her Gorton's toothpaste and toothbrush. Her Gorton's aspirin and iodine. Her Gorton's vanishing cream and makeup. Her unmentionables. Even her necklace with the big black diamond, cozy in its pigskin case.

At least Ozzie had done her one good deed, providing her with a few small comforts.

Another ten minutes of sweaty trudging brought them up to the general offices of her father's failed cassava operation. It was a long, low structure built of weathered teak logs, with a canted metal roof that provided ample shade. It showed decades of abandonment in its broken windows, rotted front staircase, and sagging foundation. Out in front of it, more Steppe Warriors and other unsavory-looking wraiths were lounging about.

"In you go," Ozzie commanded.

Dame Honoria carefully picked her way up the staircase. Once inside, amid the rotting walls and dank aroma of decay, she experienced a rush of memories. The days she'd spent in here as a young girl came flooding back. Running up and down the hallways. Dragooning favorite employees to come and play tea party with her. Or hide and seek. Or dollhouse. Happy days.

"Remember where the old man's office was?" asked Ozzie.

"Of course I know where Papa's office was. I'm not off to the races quite yet."

Dame Honoria sniffed and took a crisp left at the first turning in the main hallway. The floor was filthy with years of grime, guano, and the bones of small animals. Some of the old paintings remained on the walls—hanging at odd angles, moldering, but yet viewable. Scenes from the estate in Gilbeyshire. Papa's favorite race horse. The old portrait of a young Honoria, gripping her Sweet Sally doll like grim death.

Passing one of the doors, she heard odd groaning sounds. Before Ozzie could stop her, she pushed it open and briefly saw two men and a woman—not ghosts, but alive—lying on the filthy floor, bound and gagged. They were wearing white laboratory coats. Three pairs of desperate eyes widened when they saw her.

Ozzie dragged Dame Honoria aside and slammed the door shut. He herded her down the hallway, toward the last door on the left.

"Who are those people?" she demanded. "And why are they being held like that?"

He smirked. "None of your business. Now into Papa's office with you."

He gave her a mighty shove and in she staggered, barely avoiding a tumble. The door slammed shut behind her.

But once inside, she felt her outrage ebb away. For here was another dear memory—her father's handsome old desk. It had been made from the ash timbers of a whaler that wrecked up on Old Number One's rocky northern shore. *If I get out of this alive*, she thought, *I shall come back and reclaim this desk and—*

The door to the adjoining room creaked open, and a trim young woman in khaki safari clothes came in. Not a ghost, but a living person. Her face was a perfect oval and her hair, gathered on top in a bun, was the lightest and purest of blondes. She had bright green eyes and an oval face with a flawless complexion. Pretty in a way. *She looks oddly familiar*, thought Dame Honoria, *though I'm dashed if I can recall from where. Is she the khan?*

Then a gloomy figure of a man, also dressed in safari togs, stepped in after the young woman. He had a kind of grim intensity about his eyes, which peered out from beneath a pith helmet. He removed it and regarded Dame Honoria.

He was not a ghost, but a strange-looking creature nonetheless. Thick, dark, tangled hair clung to his head. Dark circles framed his burning eyes. He was somehow ungainly—his body at odds with itself, as if it couldn't quite decide what it wanted to be, how it wanted to move. Dame Honoria blinked at him. A dank, earthy smell filled her nostrils.

The bizarre personage surveyed her and offered a wan smile. "It's been a long time, hasn't it?" he said.

Recognizing the very familiar voice, she gasped and shuffled a few steps closer, for a better look.

"Percy? Sweetums? Is that you?"

CHAPTER 30

THE COMO EAGLE lifted neatly up off the aquamarine waters of Majuro Island just after sunrise, its four 1,200-horsepower engines roaring. The morning had been perfectly clear, with the dark blue sky retreating west. Johnny and his traveling companions had spent the night on Majuro, after a grueling flight from the Orchid Isles. And it was twenty-six hundred miles to Landfall Island, the Eagle's next stop. Fourteen or so hours of cruising along, two miles above the waves.

Half an hour before takeoff Johnny had stepped onto the Eagle's sea wing and entered through the cabin door. His photographer's backpack hung over his shoulder. Inside the backpack was the brand new Zoom press camera that Uncle Louie had bought for him in Silver City. It was awfully nice, but he missed his old, smashed-up Zoom 4x5. He had taken a lot of swell pictures with that camera. And it had saved his life.

For the takeoff, Danny had allowed Johnny to come up and sit on the flight deck in the empty seat next to Nina. His honorary cousin was happily running the radio gear—twirling dials and sounding very official as she talked to the Majuro control tower. Johnny wasn't about to let Sparks get a swollen head or anything, but he was impressed. It looked a lot more complicated than taking pictures. Nina was smart all right. But Johnny bet she wouldn't have the sneakiness to do some of the things he had done—like ambush those lazy sewermen and take their picture.

Uncle Louie handled the takeoff. And as far as Johnny could tell, he did it perfectly. Danny didn't say anything, but he nodded his head in approval. Uncle Louie took the Eagle up to a cruising altitude of ten thousand feet, as Majuro faded away behind them. Then he handed the controls to Danny and went back to the navigator's desk, next to Johnny's seat.

"I'm going to figure out our bearings and align the magnetic compass on the south-by-southwest line," he explained to Johnny. "Then I double-check things with the RDF, the radio direction finder. When you take an aeroboat across a huge ocean like this, your navigation is just as vital as the airworthiness of your ship. Get lost out here, and you're as good as dead. When I finish, Danny'll set the autopilot and let go of the yoke. At this point, flying a big aeroboat is easier than driving an automobile. The aircraft flies itself."

After a half hour with the pilots and Sparks, Johnny started to get bored and excused himself. He climbed back down into the passenger cabin and pulled the newest issue of the *Captain Justice Adventures* magazine out of his backpack. Mel was in the rear of the cabin, reading some etheristic journal.

From his starboard window seat Johnny caught a clear view of the ghost troopers of the First Zenith Cavalry Brigade galloping along just outside, whooping and hollering at the glorious new day.

He had never seen the boys look happier.

He planned to spend most of the flight reading his magazine. The picture on the cover was splendid. It showed Captain Justice—in his red cape and streamlined helmet—swinging on a jungle vine, about to knock the stuffing out of the Pirate King of Paranga. More than ever, Johnny felt a kinship with the captain, who had dedicated his life to the battle against dark conspiracies.

It kind of irritated Johnny that they had been forced to stay in the Orchid Isles for three whole days. He was terrifically anxious to find Dame Honoria and then start the new hunt for his long-lost parents. But one of the Como Eagle's engines had developed a problem and needed a new part, which had to be flown in from La Concha.

So after he and Mel had sent off their story and pictures on the ghostly murder of B. K. Muldoon, they had more than enough time for some sight-seeing.

They had spent the next day at Volcano Royal Park on one of the outlying islands. Danny had flown everyone over in a float-plane he'd borrowed and had given them the full tour. The next morning, he had taken Johnny and Mel for an audience with his distant cousin, the Queen of the Orchid Isles. She was a tiny woman, brown as a nut, with an infectious laugh. A passionate reader of mystery novels, she wanted to know all about their investigations into the etherist murders.

That afternoon Mel and Danny had gone off on their own, on a drive all around the island. They'd offered to take Johnny, Nina, and Uncle Louie along. Johnny almost said okay, but Uncle Louie signaled to him that he ought to say no thanks. That's when Johnny realized that his sister and the pilot might want a little time alone. Uncle Louie was pretty sharp about things like that.

Instead, Johnny and Nina had taken a long walk on one of the beaches—wishing that they'd brought swimming garments. The blue-green surf had sure looked warm and delightful. They had eaten a late lunch at a little grass-shack café beneath the palms: grilled reef fish, steamed rice, papaya custard, and some fruit punch. The grub was delicious.

But back at the hotel Johnny had found a telegram from Mr. Cargill that darkened his mood. Rumors had started floating around Capital City, the chief wrote, that several Army and Air Corps generals had flown west on a secret mission involving a powerful new weapon. The Ministry of War dismissed these tales as "pure balderdash and tittle-tattle." Pieces of a very large game seemed to be in motion. Johnny, with his natural-born instinct for the news, could feel it in his bones.

This, and what they had learned from the bodyless Steppe Warriors—still captives of the fearsome night watchers—gave him a wrenching feeling in his gut.

Now, cruising ten thousand feet above the Greater Ocean, Johnny was able to forget those disturbing thoughts, as he immersed himself in Captain Justice's adventure among the pirates of Paranga.

When he eventually took a break and peered out his porthole window, he could see the colonel still galloping along, as other troopers kept pace farther out. In the far distance Johnny spotted a tiny island. It had to be Paloa Atoll. He had noticed it on Uncle Louie's navigation chart. One of the few bits of land they would come close to all day. It was marked "uninhabited."

Just then, out on one of those tiny islets, a second sun—a dazzling green sun—burst into existence.

It blazed so intensely so quickly that its all-consuming brilliance blotted out everything that Johnny could see.

The sky.

The ocean.

The ghost troopers.

The broad wing of the aeroboat.

Everything.

Johnny didn't have time to shout a single syllable before the irresistible green light flooded and overwhelmed his eyes.

CHAPTER 31

NEXT THING JOHNNY KNEW, at least two people were screaming.

And one of them was him.

Because suddenly, he couldn't see a blasted thing!

He rubbed his eyes with his knuckles and blinked a few times. All he saw was a dazzling white wall of blankness starting to go grayish-black. He looked out the porthole. Same thing. *Nothing!*

Then he heard the voices more clearly.

"What was that? What happened?" That was Mel shouting.

Through the open flight deck door, Johnny faintly caught Uncle Louie's powerful voice. "Are you okay, Dan? Are you okay?"

Then someone else yelled from the flight deck. "I can't see! I can't see!"

Uh-oh, Danny was in trouble, too.

Someone grabbed Johnny by the shoulders and he jumped up, ready to fight.

"Johnny, it's me. It's Mel."

He quit struggling and blinked and blinked. Nothing. Nothing!

"Mel, I can't see. That light, it blinded me."

He just kept blinking at an ever-darkening fog. *Don't bawl,* he told himself. *Don't cry. News photographers* do not *cry.*

Mel plopped down next to him and snaked an arm around him. He'd never admit it, of course, but at that moment it felt good to have his big sister there. However, the next thing she uttered shattered his brief composure.

"*Oh my gosh!*" she exclaimed with a tone of horror. "*Oh no!*"

"What is it?" Johnny pleaded. What a horrible mess to be in, not able to see things.

"I'm looking through the porthole, Johnny." Mel's voice was shaking. "There's a huge, huge, dark gray cloud out there. It has a column on the bottom. And the top of it is starting to spread out. It's kind of making a giant cap."

She paused for a few seconds.

"Like a giant mushroom, Johnny. A mushroom cloud."

Johnny's response surprised even himself—given the fix they were in.

"We've gotta get some pictures of it, Sis. This is *massive* news."

Mel gave a little hysterical laugh. "How can you take a picture without seeing?"

"You've gotta help me, Mel," Johnny said as calmly as he could. "The camera's in the overhead compartment. I'll tell you how to set it up and aim it."

Johnny felt her get up and heard her rummaging through the compartment above his head.

"Okay," she said a moment later, "got it. Now what do I do?"

"Pull out the old film holder and put in a fresh one," he directed. "You know how it works. You've seen me do it a million times."

He listened carefully. The noises the camera made as Mel followed his instructions sounded okay. "Let me have it," he said, taking the big camera from her. He felt the back of the camera, and yeah, she had gotten the film holder in correctly. He pulled out the dark slide, flipped down the front, opened the bellows, and handed the camera back to her. "Now put the focus on infinity. Set the aperture to f/8 and the shutter speed to 1/250."

Mel placed the camera in his hands and helped him aim it out the porthole. Just holding it made him feel better.

He took four shots. That should be good. The sound of the shutter clicking was music to his ears.

"What's the cloud doing, Mel?"

"It seems to have stopped growing in height. Must be thirty thousand feet tall. But it's still spreading out."

"What do you think it is?"

"I'd like to think it was a volcano going off. Or a meteor strike. But..."

"But what?"

"I hate to say it, Johnny, but it has shades of green in it. The color that ghosts give off in the dark. A volcano or a meteor would just be gray or black. It could confirm what the Steppe Warriors in the Orchid Isles told us. It could be the etheric bomb."

Johnny's first thought was: *Here I am, a news photog and I can't even see the biggest news story of my life!* His second thought was that the world had just started down a very dangerous path.

"Excuse me, ma'am, for interrupting!" said a thin but powerfully urgent voice.

Mel and Johnny both twisted around.

"Colonel, you're all right," said Mel.

"Never better, ma'am," the ghost replied.

"And the lads?"

"They're fine, too. But we haven't time for chitchat, I'm afraid."

"What do you mean, Colonel?"

"From my vantage point outside I noticed that the explosion

has sent out a substantial shockwave," the old cavalryman explained. "It's coming like a giant tidal wave and tempest. Mr. Hofstedter and the other gentleman would be well advised to turn the ship about and flee. At highest feasible speed."

"I've gotta tell Danny and Uncle Louie," Mel said. Johnny heard her scrambling up the flight deck ladder.

Just about the time she returned, he felt the big aeroboat begin to tilt and turn onto its new course.

"How are they up there?" he asked.

Mel sounded breathless. "Danny's been blinded, too. Whacked his head. He's a little dizzy. Uncle Louie's in the pilot's spot now and Nina's in the co-pilot's seat." She paused for a second. "Do you think she's really up to flying this aeroboat?"

Wow, Johnny thought, that would be quite a story for Nina to tell once she got back to Grover Falkland Junior High. "Don't forget, Sis, she's flown solo," he said. "If any kid can do it, it's Sparks."

"Excuse me, ma'am."

"Yes, Colonel."

"I would like to propose making a reconnaissance of the phenomenon with a couple of the lads, then we will follow you to Landfall Island. Lieutenant Finn and the rest of the brigade will continue to fly escort."

"A sensible idea, Colonel," she said. "We need to know what we're up against. But if you come under any serious threat, you're to turn tail and report to me at Landfall Island. That is a direct order. No heroics, please. I will not risk losing you. Understood?"

"Yes, ma'am," the ghost colonel answered. "Understood."

"DO YOU THINK I'll ever see again?" Johnny asked tremulously. Not much scared him, but never again taking a picture most definitely did.

Mel was sitting next to him. "Absolutely. I've read about soldiers in the war, exposed to bomb bursts, who went temporarily blind. They call it flash blindness. Usually there's a prompt recovery. In fact, I—"

There was another bellow from the flight deck. Uncle Louie again. But Johnny couldn't make out what he'd said.

"I better go up there and see what's happening," Mel said. "You just sit tight and I'll be right back."

A minute after she left, something hugely powerful slammed into the Como Eagle from behind, ramming Johnny brutally into the back of his seat. He gasped in shock and held onto the arms of the seat with grim determination.

The shockwave—and it had to be a shockwave—passed and the Como Eagle continued to fly roughly along. It hadn't crashed. At least not just yet.

A few minutes later, Mel still hadn't returned. *If I'm going to die*, Johnny decided, *I'm sure as heck not going to be all alone, stuck back here in the passenger cabin.*

He unstrapped his seatbelt. Everything was still black. He began groping his way forward to the steep, narrow steps that led up to the Eagle's flight deck. He went slowly, grabbing the tops of seats as he inched along. But it wasn't easy, with the aircraft bouncing and jouncing. He suddenly had a lot more sympathy for the blind people he'd seen on the streets of Zenith, walking very carefully, tap-tap-tapping with their red-and-white canes.

Johnny needed to stop at one point to try and calm himself down. His heart was rushing and he was almost hyperventilating. There'd be time later, he told himself, to think about being blind the rest of his life. But it was hard to push the terrible thought out of his head, even while facing the prospect of a very premature death out in the vastness of the Greater Ocean.

He took a deep gulp and shuffled forward. As soon as he got a grip on the railing of the flight deck stairs, he climbed up it.

CHAPTER 32

"JOHNNY!" MEL HOLLERED from out of the blackness. "What're you doing up here?"

Holding onto the door frame at the back of the flight deck, Johnny started to explain. But a pair of hands rudely grabbed him and manhandled him into one of the spare seats. He could feel someone—almost certainly Mel—strap him in.

"Stay here," barked his sister into his left ear, sounding quite angry. "Don't you *dare* move."

"How's Danny?" he asked.

"Still woozy," she answered. "Still blinded. I got him into one of the other seats. Here are some headphones, so you can hear what's going on."

Mel jammed flight-deck headphones over Johnny's ears. He was about to thank her when another huge shockwave hit the Como Eagle.

The big flying boat almost tipped over onto its side, port wing down.

But somehow the aeroboat regained its equilibrium.

Over the headphones Johnny could hear every word Uncle Louie and Nina said. They both sounded tinny and disembodied, though—more like someone on the radio than people sitting just ten feet away.

"Nina, kiddo," Johnny's uncle said breathlessly, "just keep doing whatever I do. I push down on the yoke, you push down. We're gonna add your muscle power to mine. Now watch the horizon and call out the altitude. Got it?"

"Got it, Louie!" came Nina's response.

Johnny could hear the fear in his friend's voice. But if any kid had guts and fortitude, it was Nina Bain.

A bunch of memories flooded through his mind. He thought about all the fun he and Sparks had had together. All the things they'd learned. All the people they had gotten to know. All the years that should have been ahead of them. He felt awfully scared that it might soon be over—that neither of them would survive to become teenagers.

As the next blast of turbulence struck, every rivet and weld in the Eagle groaned and screamed. But the big aeroboat held together, surfing a turbulent hurricane of wind for what seemed like an eternity.

One encouraging thought popped into Johnny's head. According to Uncle Louie, there was no tougher old bird in the aeroboat world than the Como Eagle. He'd said that every pilot who knew her loved flying her.

In a severe test of its ruggedness, the aircraft then had to cope with cascades of wind that slammed it up, down, and sideways. As if that weren't enough, another shockwave stubbornly tried again to tip one wing up, the other down.

Johnny could feel it, sense it.

Two, three times the Como Eagle nearly went over sideways, toward certain doom. But each time Nina and Uncle Louie righted it, managing to straighten the wings.

Suddenly out of the static-filled silence of the headphones there came a startling announcement from Nina.

"Louie, we're up at eighteen thousand two hundred feet," she said, sounding quite startled. "The shockwaves have lifted us up nearly a mile and a half."

Of course, Johnny thought. That explained why he felt so breathless. It wasn't just being scared. The air was actually thinner up here, making it harder to breathe.

Then, quite unexpectedly—

WHAMMMM!

Another wave of tumult slammed into the Eagle, tipping the back of the aircraft down, its nose up. Johnny felt as if he were riding a bucking bronco.

As suddenly as it had arrived, what proved to be the last shock-wave passed by, leaving them in calmer air.

But Johnny could sense the Eagle wobbling and he didn't like it. His next thought was interrupted practically before it began.

"Hold on, kiddo!" Uncle Louie screamed to Nina over the headphones. "We're stalling!"

Johnny had heard enough about flying from his uncle and Nina to know that your aircraft stalls because you lose lift. And you lose lift because of low airspeed or bad angle of attack—the angle of the wings hitting the air.

"Push the yoke forward, Nina," Uncle Louie commanded. "Hard as you can. Gotta dive fierce and fast to get our airspeed back."

"*Yessir, Louie,*" she yelled back.

Johnny worried that eighteen thousand feet wouldn't give them enough altitude to get their flying boat horizontal—without tearing it apart. But he knew that this wasn't the moment to ask Uncle Louie for reassurances.

As they plummeted downward, Nina called out the altitude, one reading after another.

"Thirteen thousand feet."

There was a pause for a number of seconds.

"Eleven thousand. Airspeed up to one-fifty."

Nina was breathing so hard, Johnny could hear her inhalations and exhalations over the noisy headphones. Come to think of it, he was breathing hard, too.

"Nine thousand five hundred, Louie," she said. "Airspeed one seven five."

Gravity squeezed Johnny back into his seat. It was hard even to move.

"Now start pulling your yoke back, kiddo," Uncle Louie yelled to Nina.

"We're at seventy-five hundred feet," she shouted back.

"Get up, nose!" the big man urged the aeroboat. "*Get the heck up!*"

Johnny could hear the airframe groaning in protest. And all of a sudden, he realized that he was quaking almost uncontrollably, his clothes drenched with sweat. Not for the first time, a vexing thought popped into his head: *If I die, will I become a ghost? If I do become a ghost, what will it be like?*

"Five thousand feet," was Nina's next jittery announcement.

"I need your nose higher, Eagle," Uncle Louie shouted. "Come on now!"

Suddenly, Nina screamed, *"I see some horizon!"*

Johnny could sense the big flying boat leveling off from its dive, becoming more horizontal than vertical.

"Fifteen hundred feet, Louie," exclaimed Nina. "We're pulling out!"

Some long seconds later she reported again. "Five hundred feet.

I can see the foam on the wave tops."

There was a brief pause. *"Sixty feet!"*

"We've got her!" Uncle Louie yelled as the Eagle went perfectly horizontal. "We've got her! Practically right on top of the waves! Great job, Nina!"

"We made it!" Nina screamed.

"I'm taking her back up," Uncle Louie said, sounding fantastically relieved.

"Apart from the threat of instantaneous death," Nina proclaimed with a quaking voice, "this was the most amazing thing I have ever done."

"Maybe so," Uncle Louie responded. "But let's not do it again anytime soon, okay?"

CHAPTER 33

COLONEL MACFARLANE, Corporal Schecter, and Private Underwood flew straight toward the great, roiling mushroom cloud—galloping flat-out. It loomed taller and taller, darker and darker with every approaching mile.

Just as he was a practical and down-to-earth ghost, the colonel had been a practical and down-to-earth military man. He had never come up against anything he couldn't explain rationally, scientifically. That is, until one day over seven decades ago. The day he found himself standing over his own dead body on the battlefield at Digsby's Run that summer of 1862.

Those bucolic fields and woods—deep in the heart of the Old Dominion—had run red with rivers of blood. The air had been filled with the screams and moans of the dying and the wounded.

The colonel suddenly could see dozens of semi-transparent soldiers all over the battleground, stunned by their transformation into ghosts. Free-Staters and Dominionists both. Blue and butternut. Joined in the fraternity of death.

A number of horses became ghosts, as well. Most of them, not unreasonably, bolted away in pure terror. But one of them, a chestnut bay, came up to the colonel, as if looking for some kind of reassurance. Not knowing his name, the colonel gave him a new one. Buck. They had been together ever since.

Just as he had during his life, Horace MacFarlane still held to the notion that ghosts and the ether were nothing supernatural. Rather, they were phenomena that science would one day explain. He had never been one to believe in paradise or heaven or whatnot after death. Not a religious bone in his body. Scientists such as Melanie Graphic would, he believed, some day come up with the answers.

But now, soaring over the tempestuous ocean, toward that vast mushroom cloud, the colonel had little thought of delving into those deep waters of philosophy and science. No more than he planned to delve into the deep waters that churned below him.

The mission would only be for reconnaissance: What kind of damage had been done by the explosion? What could they find out about this remarkable occurrence?

The three ghost troopers could feel the mushroom cloud's furious winds, pulling them, shoving them. As this gigantic monstrosity roiled and churned, it ignited tremendous flashes of green lightning, with thunder that nearly deafened the colonel.

The buffeting gales made jockeying the horses terrifically hard. The three ghost soldiers jigged and jagged, up and down and sideways. It was almost a miracle that they could stay together.

Then they began to feel the nicks and impacts of minute debris and pulverized minerals on their skin. As if they were out in a sandstorm.

Horace MacFarlane gripped his reins tightly, wrapping them around both hands. He urged Buck forward through the whirlwind.

"*Je-hos-o-phat!*" hollered Schecter, staring goggle-eyed off to his right. He pointed urgently, jabbing with his right index finger.

"Take a gander at that thing!"

The other two ghosts swiveled their heads and gaped in horror.

It wasn't actually a gargantuan gray-green hand swinging up from the east-northeast. But it looked eerily like one, slowly clenching itself into a fist the size of a small mountain.

Boiling and churning like Hades itself—if you believed in such places.

Coming right at them.

A lot faster than any ghost horse could fly.

"Out of here now!" the colonel shouted, bringing Buck to a juddering halt. The chestnut bay pivoted and galloped headlong in the opposite direction. Over his shoulder, Horace MacFarlane could see Schecter and Underwood banging along behind him, hell-bent for leather.

Suddenly, the dark green gale slammed into the colonel and Buck, knocking them derriere over teakettle. They tumbled down through the tempest, pushed by the giant hand, spinning and rolling so violently that the colonel couldn't tell up from down.

The only thing that kept him and the horse from being smashed apart and losing one another was having the reins wrapped around his hand. Dismounted but tethered to Buck, the colonel kept bashing into horse and saddle. Even worse, when they flew apart, his arm felt as if it were going to get torn out of its socket.

But that was nothing compared to hitting the churning ocean.

It was a terrific electric jolt. His whole etheric body burned with pain. As ghost and horse slowly sank into the inky depths, the colonel screamed in agony. His muscles, his bones, his sinews, all on fire.

He thought it a pure misery that he hadn't the ability to lose consciousness.

When the pain finally ebbed away, all he could see in the blackness was the faint green luminescence of his body and Buck's—the gentle glow that every ghost gives off in the dark. They were resting on the ocean floor, on fine gray gravel. Several times, bizarre fishes with extravagant fins and needle-sharp teeth swam right through them.

"It'll be fine, Buck," the colonel said, patting his horse on the neck and flank. "It'll be just fine. We'll swim on out of here and get back to the commander. After we find Schecter and Underwood."

Just at that moment, the first miniscule voice popped into his head: "Help me."

Then another, different voice: "Where am I?"

And another: "It hurts, oh it hurts."

And another: "Awful, awful, awful—"

Then dozens, hundreds, thousands of voices.

As if they were coming down on him like raindrops.

Voices in his head?

Had he gone insane?

Huddling beside Buck, he put his hands up to his ears, trying to block out the agony in all those voices. But he couldn't make them stop.

To a horse it would have merely sounded like a lot of human jibber-jabbering. But Buck gently nudged the colonel's shoulder. As if he sensed that something was very, *very* wrong.

CHAPTER 34

WEDNESDAY, OCTOBER 30, 1935

LANDFALL ISLAND

JOHNNY DIDN'T SLEEP VERY WELL on the aeroboat that night, as it rocked in gentle seas, adrift. But then, no one did.

The Como Eagle had ended up dead in the water. The explosion's shockwaves had blown them far off course, and they had to fly many extra miles to get back on their flight path. For all intents and purposes, they were out of fuel. And without fuel, the engines couldn't run. And without the engines running, the air conditioning system would not work. And without the air conditioning, the temperature inside the aeroboat climbed up above one hundred stifling degrees.

Johnny, though, didn't lose sleep because of the heat and humidity. All through the night, stretched out in his narrow bunk, he kept opening his eyes—again and again and again. Hoping *this time* to see the dim lightbulb that he knew was burning in the sleeper compartment. But all his damaged eyes could sense was inky, stubborn blackness. No matter how much he blinked, no matter how much he rubbed them. He felt more and more afraid as the hours crept by.

Their destination, Landfall Island, was only a few dozen miles away. The minute they splashed down, Nina called on the radio and arranged for a sea-going tug to come and tow the flying boat into port.

An hour or so after breakfast, Johnny—sitting in his customary window seat—could hear Uncle Louie walking around on the top of the aircraft. His uncle was waiting to shoot off a flare as soon as the tugboat came into view. Mel tapped away on her typewriter in the back of the cabin. And Nina still seemed a little giddy over how she and Uncle Louie had saved the day. Not that Johnny blamed her. It had been a brilliant act of heroism.

The best news of the young day was that Danny had gone to sleep seeing only vague, fuzzy forms, but when he woke up, his vision was almost back to normal. Everyone congratulated him—Johnny, most heartily, because he knew just what Danny had been through. All the while, Johnny kept worrying that he might be one of those occasional victims of flash blindness who never got his sight back.

He couldn't do anything but sit in his window seat in the sweltering heat. Couldn't do anything to help Mel, who was typing her story. Couldn't even dig into his *Captain Justice Adventures* magazine. Nina offered to read it to him, but he had sulkily told her *no thanks*.

Johnny's whole life seemed as if it had ended practically before it began. He felt as low as he ever had since his mom and pop disappeared.

He tried not to think too much about his parents. But now that there was a tiny scrap of hope that they might be out there somewhere, still alive, they had been showing up in every dream, in every daydream.

It had been his pop who had ignited his passion for photography. Johnny could still almost see his old man, grinning broadly, handing him the gift-wrapped package on his sixth birthday.

Will Graphic had been a short, slender fellow with a thick head of sandy hair, smiling blue eyes, and a kindly, freckled face. His voice was a smooth, rich baritone. No one ever had a better father. And everyone adored Will Graphic. No wonder his ghosts would do anything for him. Even trek deep into the earth to hunt for iron and copper that could be mined.

Remembering that morning of six-and-a-half years ago as if it were yesterday, Johnny could almost hear his pop saying something like, "Here you go, sport. I bet you'll have a barrel of fun with this item."

As any typical six-year-old would, Johnny had ripped off the gift wrapping in a rush. The box inside was yellow and black, and the glorious printing on it said:

YOU PUSH THE SHUTTER!
THEN LEAVE IT TO US!
POLDARK SNAP-RITE CAMERA™

A picture on the package showed a black box camera with a single button on the top, a knob on the side, two glass lenses, and a glass viewer that the photographer looked down through.

The Snap-Rite was a simple, cheap camera that took fuzzy pictures, but still Johnny had filled up photo album after photo album.

Then Mom and Pop had left for Okkatek Island. They were to be away for only a month.

Soon after Johnny's parents disappeared, Louie Hofstedter and

Nina Bain had come to live in the big brick house. Johnny and his uncle finished the darkroom that Pop had started. Uncle Louie bought his nephew a good folding rollfilm camera. And the dream of becoming a news photog had taken hold.

But now, slouched in his aeroboat seat, in the oppressive heat, Johnny wondered if that dream had died. He knew there were lots of twelve-and-a-half-year-olds all over the world who had it worse than he did. Hadn't enough to eat. Hadn't the chance to go to school. Hadn't anyone to take care of them. Hadn't good health.

So, he thought—sitting up straighter, turning up the corners of his mouth—*I'd darned well better stop feeling so sorry for myself.* No one gets anywhere with an attitude like that.

He took a deep breath, twisted around, and shouted, "Hey, Sparks. If you wanna read me that story, that'd be swell."

A moment later he heard a shout from the top of the flying boat.

"I see 'em," Uncle Louie hollered. "I see the tugboat."

Johnny heard the *whooosh* of the flare as it shot up into the sky.

AS SOON AS THE TUGBOAT nudged the Como Eagle into the dock in Landfall Harbor, Nina led Johnny off the flying boat. The bureau chief of the local World Press Association office was there to meet them. His name was Tangie Farhar and he had a high, squeaky voice. Johnny wished he could see him. He imagined him being short and fat, wearing a funny hat, like the movie comedian Stanley Sterling. The fellow took several pictures of the exhausted adventurers. Then they piled into a decrepit-sounding convertible and rattled off into town. Danny had stayed with the flying boat, to do an inspection and get her ready for the next leg of their journey.

"So what happened out there?" Tangie asked along the way.

"Why the delay?"

As Johnny and the others told their tale to Tangie—who was, in fact, the entire staff of the WPA Bureau on Landfall Island—the automobile went faster and faster.

"I can barely wait to get Johnny's film processed and Mel's story out on the wire," Tangie shouted over the brisk breeze. "But how about we take this young man to the doctor first?"

Johnny didn't know what to expect, though he hoped the physician would have some kind of cure. Unfortunately, the saw-bones echoed what Mel had said the day before. Flash blindness resolves spontaneously, *usually*. Johnny could only wait. There was nothing that medicine could do.

Their next stop was the WPA office. They trod up a set of outside stairs into a room that was cacophonous with the sound of teletypewriting relay machines rattling and banging away.

"Story first?" asked Tangie. "Or photos?"

"Photos," said Johnny. "Absolutely."

"Photos," his sister agreed.

"Mel, give him the film holders," said Johnny.

Fifteen minutes later the rotary door of the darkroom squawked loudly as it opened. Johnny recognized the sound from the *Clarion* photo department. Tangie's feet shuffled across the room. Johnny waited with bated breath.

"Sorry, friends," sighed Tangie. "The negatives are fogged. Blanked out. Nothing on 'em. No mushroom cloud. Zippo."

CHAPTER 35

JOHNNY SAT WITH MEL as she worked on the final draft of her article on the etheric bomb. She read out loud after she finished each paragraph and he told her what he thought sounded good, or how she ought to change it.

Normally, Johnny would have loved telling his sister what to do. What kid brother wouldn't? But he was still blind and there were no pictures of the mushroom cloud. Something about the explosion—like x-rays—had ruined his film. What a mess.

Still, he made sure Mel followed the "inverted pyramid" technique of news writing—putting the really important stuff at the beginning, the less important facts later on. They both interviewed Uncle Louie, Nina, and Danny about the crisis in the cockpit. It was a spine-tingling tale, worthy of any front page anywhere.

But right in the middle of Nina's interview, something very peculiar happened in Johnny's unseeing eyes.

Ever since the bomb exploded, he had, for practical purposes, been watching an ebony cat in an unlit coal mine at midnight. Only inky blackness. But now, sitting there carefully listening to Nina, he saw some flashes—glitters of green off to his right.

Then, as he turned in that direction, a human figure took shape, also in green. A stout man in a uniform with a bushy beard. Lieutenant Finn! The colonel's second in command, standing at ease at the other end of the room.

Johnny was dumbfounded. Was he just imagining it or could he really see the ghost soldier? And if he could, how was it that he could see someone who was dead, but no one who was alive? How could he see something ethereal, but nothing solid?

Mel's voice cut in on his reverie. "Johnny, what is it? Are you okay?"

He fluttered his eyelids a few times, and Finn was still visible, suddenly looking at Johnny with a curious expression.

"I can see Lieutenant Finn," he said. "Nothing else, though."

Johnny could almost feel everyone in the room staring at him.

"You're sure that all you're seeing is Finn?" asked Mel.

"Uh-huh, that's right."

"Lieutenant Finn, please make a gesture of some kind at Johnny."

"Yes, ma'am," the lieutenant answered.

Johnny stared at Finn. "He saluted us, Mel," he said, as the first grin in many a long hour broke out on his face.

Someone grabbed him and hugged him. It had to be Mel.

"This is good," she said. "This is very good."

"Now he's giving me the A-OK sign."

"But you can't see anything else?"

"That's right."

"Hmmm..." Mel muttered. "That seems kind of strange. It could mean your regular vision's on the way back. But I've never heard of anything like this happening before, when someone with etheristic sight goes blind. I guess we'll just have to wait and see."

A bit after three in the afternoon, Tangie typed Mel and Johnny's finished story into one of his teletypewriters. Mel insisted that Johnny share the byline with her. It was thrilling to know that their report would travel halfway around the globe in a matter of moments—to the headquarters of the World Press Association in Neuport. And from there it would go to hundreds of newspapers and radio stations all over the world.

An hour and a half later everyone was sitting directly under the WPA office, on benches at a plank table in Theodore's Island Café. Dinner was Theodore's chicken gumbo, fried seaweed, pineapple slices, and coconut cream pie. Johnny managed to eat his food without any help. It intrigued him that the flavors tasted more intense without his eyesight.

And he had to admit, it was nice to see somebody, *anybody*—even if they were just the ghosts of Lieutenant Finn and a few of the troopers.

ONE OF THE TELETYPEWRITING machines was rattling madly away upstairs, as everyone filed back into the office. The teletypewriter finally dinged, indicating that the transmission was complete. Johnny heard the rip of paper being torn out of the machine. There was a pause and Tangie announced, "Home office in Neuport didn't make many edits in your story. Good job, you two."

Just then, another teletypewriter clattered to life. A short time later another piece of paper was ripped out.

"A message from a Mr. Carlton Cargill?" Tangie said.

"The editor at the *Zenith Clarion*," said Uncle Louie. "Let me look at it." There was a pause. "Dogs in dishwater! More bad news."

"What is it, Uncle Louie?" asked Johnny.

"Mr. Cargill's gotten word that the Ministry of War knows

we're here. They've arranged for a special team of agents to fly in tomorrow morning and grab us all."

"You mean, like kidnap us?" Johnny asked, incredulous.

"That's what Mr. Cargill says. Haul us back home in chains. If it's true—and we've gotta assume it is—we have to make some tough choices. Do we stick around until morning, and chance getting in a dust-up with these people? Or do we make a run for it in the dark tonight?"

"Absolutely no way," Danny said firmly. "Remember our little escapade up over the Treport River? No more of that, thanks very much. That bird's not flying in the dark!"

"Okay then, Dan," Uncle Louie agreed. "Fair enough. We can hide out here. But the problem is we can't hide the Eagle. How do you conceal a big four-engine flying boat? They'll take her or disable her and we'll end up stranded on this island. It'll all be over."

Tangie cleared his throat. "Umm, sorry to contradict, Mr. Hofstedter, but *yes*, you can hide her. We can ferry your aircraft a few miles up the coast and anchor in my private lagoon overnight. I have spare bedrooms and a nice sofa. You can fly out at first light."

"That's a super idea," Johnny exclaimed.

"Gotta admit that I like it, too," said Uncle Louie. "How's the gas, Dan? The food and water?"

"Clever me," the pilot boasted. "I had her fueled up as soon as we arrived. The local market delivered food and other supplies just before I hiked over here. Filled up the fresh water tank. Kinda wondered if this might happen. Half the time we seem to be making narrow escapes."

"But what about that charming guesthouse where we're supposed to stay?" asked Nina, sounding disappointed. "The comfy beds with down pillows? Cakes and eggs and ham and delectable tropical fruits for breakfast? Sunrise over the scenic lagoon?"

"Sorry, kiddo," Uncle Louie laughed. "We all gotta make sacrifices."

Suddenly Johnny let out a gasp of surprise. Something was happening. Something perhaps very good. He rubbed his eyes with his knuckles.

It looked a lot to him like it did when the rising sun slowly lit up his darkened bedroom early in the morning. And it was revealing the real world, not just the ether.

"Johnny, are you all right?" Mel said.

He looked toward his sister's voice and felt a big smile creep across his face. "You were right, Mel. Seeing Finn was the beginning. I'm starting to see some regular light. I see the light bulbs, and the bright windows, and some people shapes."

"Great news, John!" boomed Uncle Louie.

Mel hugged her brother *again*, and Nina and his uncle slapped him on the back. Tangie ran downstairs for more root beer and something a little stronger for Danny, Uncle Louie, and himself. A toast and a celebration, he said, were most definitely in order.

JUST BEFORE THEY LEFT for the flying boat docks, Mel and Johnny stood with Lieutenant Finn on Landfall's dusty, rutted Main Street. His eyes finally working again, Johnny noticed that there wasn't much there—a few threadbare shops, saloons, offices, a bank, a police station, and lots of palm trees. It was weird, though, how he saw ghosts at first, when his peepers started coming back. Even Mel couldn't figure that one out.

"Commander Graphic," asked Lieutenant Finn, "what are your orders with regard to the colonel? No sign of him yet."

"I can't understand what could have delayed him," Mel said, with a clear tone of concern. "It's simply not like the colonel to be this late. I told him not to take any risks." She looked down and shook her head. "Maybe he misunderstood me. Maybe he and the men went ahead to Gorton Island and he's waiting for us there."

"Always a possibility, ma'am."

To Johnny it sounded as if both of them were trying to avoid mentioning the unmentionable. Who knows what that horrible explosion could have done? Even to a ghost.

"But let's leave a few men here, in case they show up after our departure," said Mel.

Johnny was uncomfortably warm, but he shivered nonetheless. He didn't want to think that he might never see Horace MacFarlane again.

CHAPTER 36

PETER SANTANGELO WATCHED Minister of Etheristics Hubert Scofield pace up and down alongside the broad oak table, twirling his gold-rimmed spectacles in his right hand. They were in a room many levels underground, in the bowels of the Ministry of War Building. This bare, windowless chamber had seen a thousand top-secret meetings since the Second Border War. It was a depressing place, especially in the middle of the night. Even more depressing than some of the places where Santangelo had recruited his ghost assassins.

Without warning the big double doors flew open and the minister of war trod into the room—red in the face, her silver hair plastered around her head like a helmet. Mabel Patterson threw her fur stole and white kid leather gloves down on the table. Looking slightly inebriated, she wobbled a bit. She was short and stooped at the shoulders.

Her assistant—a brigadier Army general in full dress uniform—tried to take her elbow. But she turned on him and snapped,

"Out." He nodded sharply, backed away, and closed the doors.

"Where were you?" said Scofield. "The report about the bomb came over the news wires hours ago. Had a devil of a time locating you."

She squinted at him, looking like a grumpy bulldog. "The opera. Tickets scarce as hens' teeth. Giacomo Paranelli himself singing King Renaldo. Afterwards to Mrs. Pillsbury's party. Then this news gets whispered in my ear. A splendid evening ruined. Those blasted Graphic brats!"

Scofield put on his spectacles and sat. "I am sorry."

The woman regarded Santangelo with an evil eye, and he felt his stomach flip-flop. She was one of the most dangerous politicians in Capital City. Rumor had it that the reason Mabel Patterson was chosen as minister of war was because one look at that scary face of hers was enough to stop an advancing army.

"Who is this, Hubert?"

"Peter Santangelo. He's been handling some of the, um, trickier aspects of the operation. He came here to tell us what he thinks has gone awry."

Mabel Patterson plopped down in her chair, opposite Santangelo and Scofield. "Tell you something, Hubert. Didn't take this affair seriously enough. Never *really* believed our so-called 'khan' would pull it off. I mean, a bomb made of ghosts? Really now. But the generals told me we had to have a piece of it, had to play his game in order to get the knowledge. So we put our scientists in there. Funded it. Helped eliminate that ratty little bunch of etherists he was so worried about, who might be able to peddle the information elsewhere. What's it you call them? The, um, Hammerschlager something or other."

"Hausenhofer Gesellschaft," said Scofield.

Patterson glared at Santangelo. "And this nincompoop here

fails to deal with the most dangerous opponents that we have, Melanie Graphic and that pipsqueak brother of hers. A seventeen-year-old girl and a twelve-year-old boy. Three chances to get rid of her, all flops. And their wretched newspaper articles, besides, creating unhelpful publicity about our little project. Do you have any idea of the mess you have made, Mr. Sat… Sat… Sat-in-cello? Any idea?"

Santangelo wasn't about to correct the minister of war's pronunciation of his name. And he hardly thought it his fault that his ghosts couldn't get to Miss Graphic. She had a blasted cavalry troop to protect her and was a decent swordswoman, to boot. Her brother, for his part, was certainly a feisty little fellow. He had underestimated them badly.

"I take all the blame," he gulped, nodding. Excuses would get him nowhere with Mabel Patterson.

"The bomb could make us the most powerful nation on earth," Patterson continued, bright red in the face. "The prime minister agrees. But why in Hades did Mr. Khan set off the device days early? Why didn't our people warn us?"

"Where, indeed, are our people?" sighed Scofield. "They've all vanished."

"No chance now to see the thingy go boom. In fact, the only people who apparently saw the explosion were the Graphic brats. And they send out the news worldwide. Could our luck be any worse? Couldn't the bomb have blown them up? Done something useful for us, at least?"

The war minister drummed her pink-enameled, highly manicured fingernails in a military cadence on the glossy oak. "Might it have been the business with Mrs. Rathbone? Maybe we angered the khan."

"Perhaps," said Scofield.

"The khan specifically asked that no one harm her."

"Ma'am," said Santangelo, screwing up his nerve, "that information got to me too late. I'd already given Mr. Canfield, the ghost gangster, his orders. To machine-gun the old lady in Neuport. Couldn't stop him."

Santangelo felt fortunate that the minister of war merely gave him a dirty look.

"And why is our khan so solicitous about an old, washed-up suffragist?" the war minister asked.

Scofield shrugged. "Not a clue."

"So what now, Hubert?"

"You're the one with an army and a secret service at your beck and call, Mabel. You tell me."

"We still have agents after the Graphics," she said. "We know they're going to Landfall Island and we will have a team there in about twelve hours. Grab them or kill them. And I told them to find out what they can about the bomb. The gizmo has massive destructive power. Maybe enough to level a city. If we had only a dozen of these things, we could—"

"Rule the world?" Scofield chuckled. "Let's not get ahead of ourselves, Mabel. Finally dealing with the Old Dominion would be quite enough, don't you think?"

"The voice of reason, as usual, Hubert."

"And one thing for sure—we have to get our scientists out. If we can find them. They know how to build the thing. And they can tell us if the khan has double-crossed us."

A look of apprehension clouded Mabel Patterson's face. "What if he's made another device, Hubert? One we don't know about?"

Scofield groaned. "I don't even want to think about it."

Santangelo felt that he had become invisible, as these two powerful people plotted their baleful schemes. And "invisible" was perfectly fine, as far as he was concerned.

"On the public side," the war minister continued, "my people will have a press conference later today. Our story: Have no idea what just happened in the Greater Ocean. Volcano or meteorite most likely. Tidal wave. Rumors of etheric bomb, ridiculous. You have the easy job, Hubert—waking up the prime minister and briefing him." She chuckled darkly.

The minister of etheristics groaned. "I was afraid you'd say that."

CHAPTER 37

THURSDAY, OCTOBER 31, 1935
GORTON ISLAND

FROM HIS WINDOW SEAT on the starboard side, Johnny watched through the porthole as the flying boat cruised up the western shore of Gorton Island. The aircraft circled around, and came back down the eastern side—a few hundred feet over the shoreline. Johnny took one aerial shot of the island, just in case he might need it for Mel's next story.

A dense canopy of palms and other trees hid almost everything from sight. The only landmarks Johnny could clearly make out were Dame Honoria's tin-roofed house and outbuildings, a clutch of decrepit barns, a brief stretch of white beach, and a substantial timber dock and boathouse. He didn't observe anything moving on the island. Not a single person or animal or wraith. Not even a bird or the ghost of a bird.

Half an hour later he and Uncle Louie were wrestling two black rubber dinghies out through the passenger door onto the sea wing. Together, they dropped them in the gently lapping emerald green water. Within minutes, Johnny, Uncle Louie, and Nina were paddling under the pounding mid-day sun, toward the dock, through a wide gap in the reef. Behind them in the second dinghy came Mel and Danny.

Even though Johnny knew that Dame Honoria had been taken from the island, he felt excited just being here—a place he had heard about all his life. Certainly they'd find some clues about her abduction and, with any luck, some idea of where to find her.

THE FIVE OF THEM and Lieutenant Finn were standing in Dame Honoria's library. They'd gone through every room in the house, with nary a sign of anyone living or dead. They found no one in the servants' huts, kitchen shack, or storage sheds. Troopers of the Zenith Brigade had fanned out across the island and con-firmed that it was utterly deserted.

Bookshelves covered two walls of the library. Big windows in the third wall looked out on the white sand beach. The fourth wall was covered with old photographs. Honoria as a girl with her father and mother, on her winter holidays on Gorton Island. Honoria as a young mother, with her glum-faced little lad Percy.

"What's this here?" Johnny asked, poking at the only item on the broad rosewood desk—a heavy brown cardboard box. He took the top off and peered inside. "Umm, '*Beatrice Periwinkle*. A Novel by Chauncey Holyfield.'"

"Let me see," Nina said, dashing over. She pulled out the first few pages of the manuscript, scanning through them rapidly, eyes wide as saucers. "This is the new Holyfield novel that Dame Hon-oria's working on."

Johnny knew that Nina was a huge Holyfield fan and would give anything to be among the first to read this new book. He was about to suggest that they bring it along when a papery, ghostly voice intruded.

"Excuse me."

Mel and Johnny turned around.

A weasel-faced wraith stood in the doorframe, peering at them with an air of superciliousness, arms crossed. He wore a khaki safari jacket, a pith helmet, jodhpurs, and riding boots. He held a riding crop in his right hand.

"Who are you?" asked Johnny.

"I believe I have the advantage of you, young sir," the ghost hissed, "as manager of this estate. Who are *you?*"

"You're Mr. Eccleston, aren't you?" said Mel.

Nina and Uncle Louie were old hands at observing one-sided conversations, and listened intently. Danny merely looked confused.

"What if I am?" the ghost snapped. "The question at hand is why are you trespassing here? This is a private island."

"We're friends of Dame Honoria," said Johnny, "and we've come to try to find out what happened to her."

"And to rescue her," added Mel.

The ghost sighed disgustedly. "I repeat myself: *Who are you people?*"

Johnny strode over to him and tried to strike a friendly chord. "My name is Johnny Graphic," he said. "This is my sister Mel. And the big fellow is my uncle, Louie Hofstedter. And that's his ward, Nina Bain. This is our pilot, Danny Kailolu. I've known Dame Honoria since I was little. I was born at her estate in Gilbeyshire. Believe it or not, she's my godmother."

Ozzie Eccleston's face underwent a remarkable transformation, going from utter vexation to pure obsequiousness in the matter of two or three seconds.

"Oh, *do* forgive me," he pleaded. "Master Graphic, Miss Graphic. Of course, I know who you are. Dame Honoria has mentioned you often. But so many officials, investigators, and curiosity seekers have visited since the abduction that I've become quite impatient with interlopers."

"So Dame Honoria was okay last time you saw her?" Johnny asked.

The ghost looked at him and grinned frighteningly. "She was indeed *okay*, as you *folks* like to put it." His chuckle was patronizing.

Uncle Louie couldn't contain himself. "Ask the palooka to just tell us what happened to her."

In response, Ozzie recounted a dramatic tale of how a platoon of Steppe Warriors appeared on the island on Dame Honoria's first morning back.

"She came downstairs, confronted them. Quite bravely, I thought. But they took her prisoner nonetheless. Alas, I had no weapon but this." He held up his riding crop and waggled it around. "And I would have gone after the blighters. *Indeed I would have!* But Dame Honoria shouted, 'It's hopeless, Ozzie. Save yourself.'"

"But what happened to Dame Honoria?" Johnny demanded, after reprising the story for Nina and Uncle Louie. "Where did they take her?"

"Until just yesterday," said the ghost, "I had no idea. But I had my suspicions. So I went looking. And I found her. They're holding our lady captive in a cave on Old Number One."

"Her father's tapioca plantation?" asked Mel.

"Cassava plantation, actually," Ozzie corrected her. "The cassava is made into a meal and tapioca beads manufactured therefrom."

Mel and Johnny told the others what Ozzie had said.

"Then we have to get her out of there," Uncle Louie replied.

"My feelings exactly," the ghost affirmed. "And I should be delighted to guide you."

Since it was already late in the day, everyone agreed that they should stay that night on Gorton Island and get an early start first thing in the morning. There was plenty of canned food in Dame Honoria's larder. And her beds looked far more comfortable than anything they'd slept in since the Orchid Isles. Certainly more comfortable than sleeping on the Eagle.

At about nine o'clock that evening Johnny was sliding off into dreamland in the grass-roofed guesthouse when he heard a terrible yelp from outside. He grabbed the flashlight on his bedstand and rushed out through the screen door.

There, sitting on the ground next to the rainwater shower, rubbing his left ankle, was Uncle Louie. He was in his boxer shorts and t-shirt. He grimaced and blinked up into the bright glare of Johnny's flashlight.

"Thought a shower sounded awful nice," Uncle Louie groaned. "Stepped in a hole just on the edge of the path there. Hurts like the deuce. You think Dame Honoria's got any ice around this place?"

"No electricity on the island," said Johnny, shaking his head. "So no freezer. We'll ask Ozzie if there's an icehouse. Here, let me see if I can help you."

He managed to get his uncle upright, and they went very slowly back to the guesthouse. The big man was barely able to put any weight on the ankle.

"You know what's funny, John?" he said. "I fly an aeroboat almost halfway across the world, save it from certain doom in an out-of-control dive, and then I go and cripple my ankle because of a hole in the ground."

MEL AND NINA tramped out the back door of the house shortly after dawn, following Ozzie Eccleston. Uncle Louie limped out next, his arm over Danny's shoulder. His ankle was pretty swollen and he winced at every hobbling step.

Johnny and Lieutenant Finn came out last and started to follow the others down to the dock. But Johnny noticed a strange-looking object obscured by the undergrowth next to the kitchen shack.

"I think I see something weird over there, Lieutenant Finn," he said.

He tiptoed up the shell path toward the rickety structure. Finn came after him.

Johnny gasped in horror when he saw what had caught his attention.

A pretty native face peered up from the ground, amid some flowered stems, wearing a look of utter desperation. The girl ghost had no body. Her lips were moving. But Johnny could only hear a whisper of a voice. He squatted down to get closer.

"My name is Tala," the ghost said urgently. "Mr. Eccleston betrayed Dame Honoria. He and those terrible ghost soldiers took her away. He's a villain! Don't trust him! Don't trust him!"

His stomach almost churning, Johnny nodded, stood, and turned to Lieutenant Finn with a scowl. "Sounds like our chum Ozzie may be leading us into a trap."

CHAPTER 38

FRIDAY, NOVEMBER 1, 1935

OLD NUMBER ONE

UNCLE LOUIE had rarely looked so frustrated. Never one to back away from a good fight for a good cause, the big man was now confined to his co-pilot's seat—sidelined by his badly sprained ankle. He reluctantly agreed that he couldn't go on the hunt for Dame Honoria on Old Number One. He'd be practically useless. He had to stay on the Como Eagle.

Danny couldn't leave the aeroboat, either. An important gauge on the control panel had stopped working and he—with some help from Louie—had to fix the thing. A quick escape from the island might depend on it.

The kids and the ghosts would have to search Old Number One on their own.

"All I ask of you characters," Uncle Louie admonished them, "is that you use your noggins. Think before you jump, okay? Don't try to be big heroes. Just figure out Dame Honoria's location and get her out. The lieutenant'll help you come up with the best strategy."

On the one-hour flight from Gorton Island to Old Number

One, Ozzie had spent time up on the flight deck, fascinated by the workings of the flying machine. Johnny kept "translating" the ghost's questions, and Danny explained everything he was doing and why.

Leaving Ozzie in the cockpit, Johnny returned to the passenger cabin, and had an urgent, whispered conference with his sister and Lieutenant Finn. They hatched a plan to deal with the traitorous ghost.

Within moments of beaching their dinghy on the southwestern shore of Old Number One, Johnny, Mel, and Nina headed inland through dense jungle, led by Ozzie. Lieutenant Finn and the depleted First Zenith Cavalry Brigade rode alongside them and out ahead. It wouldn't do for them to be flying up above the jungle, potentially visible to Dame Honoria's captors.

Leaves and branches and thorns grabbed at the three kids at every step. Johnny took the lead and had to slash at the undergrowth with a machete. Clouds of insects swarmed around, pestering and biting.

The worst stretch of their march inland was mushing through the swampy spots. Johnny's boots and socks quickly soaked through. When he felt a peculiar itch on his right shin, he lifted up his trouser leg and discovered a huge leech, half the size of his hand, enjoying lunch.

"*Oh man!*" he yelped.

Nina hurried forward and gave him a disgusted look. "Stop fussing, okay?" She bent over and gently pried the leech away from his shin. Then, probably for the only time in its life, the squishy black parasite went flying.

Mel was wearing her saber. Johnny wondered if maybe she was overdoing it. It sure did look silly, dangling on her hip. But who knew? It might come in handy.

After an hour of strenuous trudging, the group reached a jungle clearing near a large, wide bog. There they paused for water and food. Johnny was panting and exhausted. He had taken off his hat and was wiping his face with a handkerchief already damp with sweat.

"Hello," said a tiny voice.

Just at the edge of the clearing, not thirty feet away, stood a diminutive girl ghost in a dusty, dark shift and headdress.

Johnny tipped back his straw fedora and walked over to her. "Hi, there. What's your name?"

"Bao," she said. "Why are you here?"

"We're looking for a friend of ours."

Bao regarded the people and ghosts with a certain wariness. Her little black eyes paused ever so briefly on Ozzie. "Who?" she asked.

"A lady named Honoria Rathbone. We think she's being held prisoner here on the island."

"Are you her friends?"

"You betcha we are," said Johnny. "I was born in her house."

The little girl wraith crooked an index finger and motioned for Johnny to come closer. He listened carefully to what she had to say.

When she'd finished, he joined the others. "She doesn't know anything about Dame Honoria. She saw us arrive, and she was curious about the flying machine."

Johnny tried to look as casual as possible as he strolled up to Finn and spoke a few quiet words in the ghost's ear. The lieutenant listened attentively, his face expressionless. In turn, he gave a surreptitious nod to Corporal Marchiano, a small but muscular specter with piercing black eyes and a black beard.

Ozzie didn't seem to notice Marchiano coming up behind him.

Without warning, the ghost trooper locked him into a python-tight full nelson hold, Marchiano's hands gripping the back of Ozzie's neck.

"Nooo!" Ozzie howled, his pith helmet flying off. "*What are you doing?*" He struggled to get free, but Marchiano had the upper hand. Ozzie was going nowhere.

Johnny understood all too well that the only way to hold a ghost captive was to have another ghost restrain him. To prevent Ozzie from springing any ambush, someone would have to stay here and keep him out of action. And that someone was the corporal.

"The little girl ghost here says that you helped the Steppe Warriors abduct Dame Honoria," Johnny accused him. "She says that you're sure to betray us, too."

"Pish-posh," Ozzie said, his head bent at a very odd angle. "Whom do you trust? Someone who has given decades of service to the lady?" He forced a smile that no one could possibly believe. "Or a vile little guttersnipe?"

Johnny looked at Mel, who nodded.

"I think we trust the guttersnipe." he said. "And Tala—or at least Tala's head—told me the exact same thing this morning."

"There's been a dreadful misunderstanding!" wailed the captive ghost. "This miserable child is leading you into a terrible trap. I am first and foremost my mistress's loyal servant."

Johnny looked him in his weasel face. "We'll see what Dame Honoria has to say about that."

CHAPTER 39

LEAVING THE VILE OZZIE in Corporal Marchiano's firm grip, the three living people and the ghost troopers followed Bao. She promised to take them to Dame Honoria's cave, where she had left the old lady. A bit more than an hour later they arrived in the shadow of the coral hills that divided Old Number One. The razor-sharp, jagged stone formations were a good three hundred feet tall.

"Is Dame Honoria alright?" Mel had asked Bao along the way. "Have they hurt her?"

"I don't think so," answered Bao. "But a few days ago the man in the helmet—"

"Ozzie Eccleston?" Johnny prompted.

"Yes, him. He and some Steppe Warriors took her to see the khan."

"The khan!" blurted Johnny. "Their chief is here?"

"Yes, he is."

"Who is he? What's he like?"

Bao seemed puzzled, but tried to answer. "He is a man, not a ghost. But a strange-looking man, with scary eyes. He looks very strong."

Mel quickly translated for Nina, then turned back to the little girl. "What did Dame Honoria say about him, Bao?" Mel asked.

"Nothing. She would say nothing. She was quiet and sad. 'Grandmother,' I asked, 'what is the matter? Are you sick? Have they hurt you?' She said no. 'Then why do you seem so sad?' She would not say. And it is not like Grandmother to speak so little."

"That's for sure," said Johnny. "She's never at a loss for words."

Mel glared at her brother. "At least she's alive and unharmed."

As much as Johnny respected Dame Honoria, he thought that she talked way too much and tended to stick her nose in other people's business. So if she had clammed up, something bad must have happened.

"Do you know why the khan's here?" he asked.

"To make the second bomb," answered Bao, as if this ought to be quite obvious.

Johnny and Mel stopped in their tracks and stared in horror at the little girl ghost.

"*There's another bomb?*" Mel asked, looking appalled. "Have they finished it?"

"I do not know, Mel."

"Have you seen the bomb?" asked Johnny, thinking darkly about how the first one had blinded him.

"I am sorry, but I do not know what it looks like."

Johnny whistled and shook his head. The khan and his super bomb were only a mile or two away. Not exactly a reassuring thought.

As they rested at the base of the coral hills, Johnny pulled a yellowed map of Old Number One out of his camera pack and spread it on a rock shelf.

Mel took Bao gently by the elbow and led her to the map. "Now point out to us where everything is. Dame Honoria's cave, where they made the bomb, where the Steppe Warriors may be. Whatever you can think of."

Bao understood the map perfectly, having flown over the island many times. She showed them where everything was.

"Okay, now we need a plan," said Mel. "Lieutenant Finn, what do you think?"

The lieutenant leaned in over the map, jabbing at it with a bent index finger. "I think we ghosts ought to go on a double action, right through here."

Johnny and Mel agreed that Finn's tactic of a pincer movement—attacking from two sides at once—was the proper strategy. One group of troopers would strike from the back of Dame Honoria's cave, the other would advance from the front. The two units would hopefully overpower the Steppe Warrior guards and safely spirit the old lady away.

Johnny explained the plan to Nina, who said, "I'm no soldier, but it sounds good to me"

With her seal of approval, off they went.

IN THE HOURS since they'd set foot on Old Number One, Johnny had been painfully aware that the seventeen men and officers of the First Zenith Cavalry Brigade were scattered all to hell and gone. The colonel and two others had vanished in the roiling inferno of the etheric bomb. Four troopers remained on Landfall Island, waiting for the lost threesome. Two more remained with Uncle Louie and Danny, guarding the flying boat. Corporal Marchiano held the treacherous Ozzie Eccleston. That left just seven troopers and seven horses fit for action. Not a very big force, not even a platoon.

A bit after ten o'clock, beneath a clear sky and blistering sun, Lieutenant Finn led three mounted troopers straight into the solid pink stone that formed the coral hills. Bao guided them, sitting in front of Finn on his saddle. Simultaneously, Sergeant Clegg and his two men headed up the narrow path that divided the island's rocky spine—a stone-strewn track just barely passable for the living. Finn promised that he would send back a trooper in an hour or less to report on the mission's outcome.

But the hour passed, then another half hour, and no one showed up. No Zenith Trooper of any sort.

"I'm really afraid that something's gone wrong," said Johnny, his patience wearing thin. There'd been nothing to do but sit and wait and sweat. He wanted to get into action. "We have to go check things out."

In spite of being an accomplished hiker and outdoorswoman, Nina didn't look happy about trekking through the coral hills. She had examined the path and said it was terrible ground. But Mel agreed with her brother. It wasn't like Finn to not report back.

Nina, as usual, was right.

Johnny had never taken a harder, more arduous hike. The path wended through the coral hills for over a curving, twisting mile. Much of the way there was no flat surface to walk on. They all balanced precariously on angled rock after angled rock. It was a miracle that no one ended up with a sprained ankle like Uncle Louie's.

The trio stopped only to replenish their canteens at a freshwater spring, where Johnny also snapped a picture of the two girls. To add to the ordeal, the sun was beating down, with a searing, oven-like heat.

Finally emerging on the other side, the three peeked out through a jumble of rocks to survey the situation. They saw decrepit tin buildings, rusting farm equipment, palm trees, dense undergrowth, and a road covered with crushed seashells. A few ghosts wafted around aimlessly. From what Bao had said, the cave mouth to the northwest was where Dame Honoria would be.

"Do you see any of the troopers or Bao?" Nina asked.

"Nope, no one," Mel answered, peeping above some rocks, searching the sun-blasted landscape. "The place looks deserted. No guards in front of any of the buildings."

"No Steppe Warriors?"

"Don't see any."

The whole business was getting on Johnny's nerves. He was tired of waiting for others to act. He just wanted to find Dame Honoria and get the heck out of there. The sooner she was rescued, the sooner they could continue on their around-the-world newspaper assignment. And the sooner they could start investigating what had happened to their parents. But they wouldn't get anywhere unless they quit hiding. Like Uncle Louie always said, the best defense is a good offense.

"Why don't I run over there and check Dame Honoria's cave?" Johnny said. "It'll take me a few minutes, tops. Nobody'll see me."

Nina shook her head vigorously. "I think we ought to wait until dark before we go exploring. Too dangerous in the daylight."

In turn, Mel shook her head. "I don't think we can wait that long. But I'm the oldest, so I should go."

"Are you nuts, Sis?" Johnny sputtered. "If anyone gets caught, it oughta be me. They grab you, they get what they've been after all along."

"It's a bad idea for either of you," argued Nina. "You don't have any idea who might be sneaking around out there, or where Steppe Warriors might be lurking. Johnny's right, Mel, you're too important." Then she glared at Johnny. "As for you, I'd have hoped our little adventure in Jadetown would have made an impresssion. Recklessness is just dumb."

Johnny glared back at Nina. Who did she think she was? His mother?

"Some friend you are!" he snapped.

Eyes and mouth wide open, Nina looked as though he had slapped her in the face.

She was about to make a retort when Johnny abruptly barked, "*Gotta go!*"

And he spurted out from behind the sheltering rocks, into the open.

Feet pounding, legs pumping, he made for Dame Honoria's cave—gripping his camera pack for dear life.

CHAPTER 40

JOHNNY TOOK A HARD LEFT into the open cave mouth, past two rusted, gaping steel doors that drooped on their hinges. Deep shadows enveloped him, cutting ten degrees off the baking heat. He panted wildly, bending over and putting his hands on his knees.

Suddenly he heard rushing footsteps outside. He pivoted around with a fierce expression, ready to wallop whomever it was with his camera pack. And he almost did, too, until he realized his pursuer was none other than Nina.

She skidded to a stop, not quite seeing him in the dim light. The instant she did, she screeched and hopped backward. She glared at him. "Now you're going to smack me with your camera bag? *Some friend you are!*"

Having his own insult thrown back in his face stung considerably—and, Johnny had to admit, deservedly. "You shoulda stayed back with Mel, Sparks. Why'd you follow me?"

She frowned furiously at him. "I really have no idea. Temporary insanity, perhaps?"

He put up a single index finger. "Just a minute."

He quickly scanned the cave. It would be rotten luck if, while getting chewed out by Nina, he had a bunch of Steppe Warriors charge at him. But as far as he could see no one else was here. No Dame Honoria. No Steppe Warriors. No ghost troopers. No Bao.

"Jeez Louise," he sighed. "I know I open my trap before I think sometimes. But we're still pals, aren't we?"

She put her hands on her hips—never a good sign—and scrunched up her mouth. "A friend does not talk to a friend like that."

"Sparks, I thought you were on my side."

"I am on your side. But sometimes friends need to tell friends things that friends don't want to hear. Because they don't want their friends to get *exterminated*."

"Oh."

"Every time the young news photographer puts his skinny neck on the line—which is frighteningly often—his friends and relatives all hold their breaths and suffer heart attacks."

"Oh."

"Believe it or not, Miss Nina Bain would much prefer that Mister John Joshua Graphic doesn't end his very brief professional career *as an archery target*."

"Oh."

Johnny pushed up the brim of his straw fedora and tried to puzzle out what had just happened—but came to no immediate conclusions. Other than the fact that it was tough to win an argument with a girl.

"Well, you're here," he said, "so you might as well pitch in. No one's around, but let's have a look before we go back to Mel."

They quickly found the tattered cot and one of Dame Honoria's battered red valises. Johnny peeked inside it and discovered shampoo, mouthwash, aspirins, a toothbrush, and toothpaste. There were also a number of roomy female undergarments that he didn't care to examine. He assigned that task to Nina.

Sorting through the clothes, she found a small pigskin case at the bottom of the valise. She opened it and made a lengthy "oooooh" sound. Johnny recognized the object, having seen it back in Zenith not too long ago, at the party Mel and Uncle Louie had thrown for Dame Honoria.

"The Star of Gilbeyshire," Nina cooed. "One hundred and ninety-six wonderful carats of perfect black diamond. Pear cut. Nearly unbreakable titanium setting and necklace. Dame Honoria can't be far away because she would never leave it." She put the jewel back in its case.

"Why's it called 'star,' then, when it's shaped like a pear?" Johnny asked innocently.

"Well, what kind of name is The *Pear* of Gilbeyshire?" Nina jammed the pigskin case into her deepest jacket pocket.

They searched some more and found nothing but piles of moldering old junk. And no clues about what had happened earlier that day. They were getting ready to head back to Mel when Johnny heard a tiny voice saying, "Johnny? Nina?" He pointed his flashlight in the direction the voice came from.

There, slightly protruding from the cave wall to his left, was Bao—wide-eyed and looking frightened.

Johnny shouted her name and ran over to her, with Nina right behind.

He offered his hand to the little ghost. Bao reached out from the coral stone and took it. He gently pulled her out, then squatted down, facing her.

"Are you all right?" he asked.

"Yes, Johnny."

"Where are the men who came with you?"

"Grandmother was not here. We went looking for her, to the

places that I know about. We were attacked. I fell from the horse and ran away. I did not know what to do, so I came back here. I am sorry, Johnny. *I am so sorry.*" And she began to sob and quake.

Feeling a little embarrassed, Johnny set down his camera pack, put his arms around the diminutive ghost, and gave her a long, tight hug. "Umm, that's okay, Bao. Really. You couldn't help it. Don't worry, we'll figure out what to do."

Several moments later Johnny and Nina dashed out of the cave entrance, back toward their hiding place in the rocks. Bao flew along behind. Johnny almost overshot the gap in the coral stone where they had hidden.

"No," he groaned, when they nipped into the space. "*I don't believe it.*"

Mel had vanished.

CHAPTER 41

ON THE CHANCE that Mel had retreated back down the stony path, Johnny and Nina crept carefully in the same direction. It wouldn't do to sprain an ankle now. But Mel was nowhere to be seen.

"How long were we in that cave?" Johnny asked with exasperation.

"Long enough for Mel to get captured, I guess," Nina answered glumly, balancing delicately between two rocks.

The thing that Johnny feared most had happened. It was all his fault. He had stupidly run off to check out Dame Honoria's cave. And this was the result. If anything really bad happened to Mel, he would never forgive himself.

With uncanny clairvoyance, Nina said, "It's not your fault, Johnny. If we'd been there, they'd probably have caught us, too. And be logical. If they had killed Mel, her body would be there. There's still a chance she's alive, still a chance we can rescue her."

They paused to catch their breaths. Both took sips of water from Johnny's canteen and nibbled on the graham crackers they had requisitioned from Dame Honoria's larder. Floating up above, Bao kept watch.

Johnny tipped back his straw fedora, mopped his sweaty brow with his damp, red handkerchief, and broke the silence. "Hey, Sparks," he said quietly, "thanks for putting up with me."

"Aw, you're not so bad," Nina replied. "For a boy."

Johnny flashed her a grin. "Now listen. I have a plan. Tell me what you think of it. You too, Bao."

WHILE IT MIGHT HAVE MADE SENSE to wait until dark, and not gamble on being seen by Steppe Warriors, Johnny felt that time was of the essence. Now they had two to rescue. It might already be too late, but he and Nina had to assume that Mel and Dame Honoria were both still alive and unharmed.

First, they sent Bao out into the open, to check for ambushes and traps. The diminutive ghost returned a little while later, reporting that the way looked clear. Rather than darting along on the shell road, Johnny and Nina crept through the undergrowth. The going was definitely slow. But before long they arrived at a long tin shed, a few hundred yards from the main cluster of buildings. Bao said it was the hut where all the ghosts had disappeared.

"That's where they made the bomb," Johnny told Nina. "Where the ghosts vanished."

After Bao checked out the building, they tiptoed inside. The long room was almost empty, except for a few pieces of stainless steel tubing here and there, and a rusty folding chair. Empty metal brackets were screwed into the wooden floor.

I still have a job to do, thought Johnny, taking off his backpack and pulling out his Zoom press camera. He figured that using a flashbulb would be dangerous—some passing Steppe Warrior might notice it going off. So he kneeled down and set the camera on the seat of the folding chair. That enabled him to make a long, slow exposure of the room with natural light.

When he had finished, Bao tugged on his sleeve. "They came in here," she said, wearing a fierce scowl. "All the ghosts. They came into this place and never came out. I saw my friend Evvie come in and he never came out."

"Master Graphic!"

Adrenaline suddenly surging, Johnny pivoted toward the voice.

"Lieutenant Finn!" he gasped. Then a broad grin broke out on his face. "You scared the sap outta me. But am I happy to see you!"

The ginger-bearded specter strode toward them. "Pleased to find you well, young sir, young lady. And you, too, missy." He winked at Bao, who giggled. And though his gesture wouldn't be seen by her, he nodded companionably at Nina.

"Where are the boys, Lieutenant?" asked Johnny. "What in the devil happened?"

The ghost shook his head dejectedly. "Nothing good, alas. We met in the cave, as planned, all seven of us, along with Miss Bao. But no one was there. No Dame Honoria, no guards. So we aimed to sneak over this way. Well, they came down on us like wolves onto sheep. Dozens of them. Those Steppe Warrior fellows. The little lady here, she fell off the saddle in the midst of the fight. Glad she's all right. The rest of us scattered. Nothing else for it.

"As for the missing men, Master Graphic, I've located only a couple of them. The other four, including the sergeant—their wellbeing I cannot vouchsafe. Not hacked to pieces, I can only hope."

The horse soldier glanced from Johnny to Nina to Bao, looking suddenly puzzled and concerned. "If you'll pardon me, Master Johnny—where's Commander Graphic?"

THEY ALL WITHDREW to a spot in the jungle that Lieutenant Finn had specified that morning as a "rally point"—a place to meet, in case the troopers got separated.

One by one, the missing horse soldiers reappeared.

Sergeant Clegg, a string bean of a man with a prominent nose and bobbing Adam's apple, gave Johnny the most encouraging news. "I don't know for sure," he said, "but I have a notion where Commander Graphic and Dame Honoria might be."

Johnny's face brightened and for the first time in hours he started to feel as if this might all turn out okay. "That's fantastic! Where do you think they're holding them?"

"I suspect that they've been confined in the headquarters building of the old plantation, several hundred yards up that shell road. A few of the Steppe Warriors are lollygagging around outside by the front entrance, with a lot more inside. Thirty or forty of them. Makes sense to keep the ladies in such a place."

"Assuming they're there, how do we rescue Mel and Dame Honoria?" Johnny asked with urgency.

"A diversion might do the trick," suggested Lieutenant Finn, stepping up next to the sergeant. "I say Clegg and a couple of the boys stage a sneak attack on the fellows loitering outside the headquarters. Knock off a head or two. I'd bet my last paycheck that the other guards pile out of that place like angry fire ants, hot to chase after Clegg and his lads. With any luck, that'll even our odds in the event of a fight inside the building. Those of us who remain with you and the young ladies, well, we force our way in there and release our people."

"First, though," said Johnny, "I think we send in Bao to get the lay of the land and make sure that Mel and Dame Honoria haven't been moved somewhere else. Nobody would ever suspect her of being a spy."

CHAPTER 42

BAO POKED HER HEAD UP over the teak floorboards—just barely. Only her eyes, ears, and headdress showed. She surveyed the room.

Except for some crumbling furniture, nothing was here. Johnny and the ghost with the startling red beard had asked her to find where Grandmother and Mel were being kept. She had already slipped in and out of five different rooms. In one of them several Steppe Warriors were playing some kind of game with dried bones. The other chambers had been empty.

She was about to sink silently through the floorboards of the sixth room, when the door creaked open and two living people stepped in. Bao recognized them instantly. She had seen them back on the much smaller island, where they had made the first bomb. And she had seen them here. She ducked beneath the floorboards, scooted back to a wall, then floated up again. From that vantage point she peeked out through the rotting plaster.

The woman had golden hair that was crammed helter-skelter under some kind of leather helmet with earflaps. She was pretty, Bao supposed, but did not look kind. In fact, that hard, cruel face promised nothing good.

The other person was the khan—dark, hulking, brooding. Bao didn't often judge people just by appearances, but this man was not anyone she cared to ever see again. He looked even crueler than the woman, if that was possible.

Bao eavesdropped very carefully, in the event that Johnny and the ghost soldier with the red beard might want to know what this menacing pair had to say.

"Time for us to withdraw, Pamela," pronounced the khan in a hoarse, gritty voice. "We've accomplished everything here that we set out to. The second gizmo is ready. Burilgi and Checheg know how to set it off. Mummy shall be well looked after and find her way home. Temur and his Steppe Warriors will have their fun with those vile little creatures, Melanie and Johnny Graphic. Assuming we get hold of the boy, as well."

"Percy," the woman said with a tone of impatience, "why don't you just shoot Miss Graphic, so long as you have her in hand?"

The khan looked slightly hurt by the query. "Pamela, you know how I abhor the sight of blood. Temur will handle it when we're safely away."

The woman sighed, obviously disappointed. "Well then, I think I should prepare the floatplane. We oughtn't to dally."

The grim, hulking man nodded. "I have a few things here to finish up, my dear. Documents to destroy and whatnot. I shall join you as soon as I can. Fire up the engines the moment you see me paddling out."

"You really ought to come with me, Percy. Miss Graphic's Border War troopers could come back to bite us."

The khan took the woman's hand and looked as if he were trying to smile. But it seemed that his face didn't know how. "Most considerate, Pamela. But these files cannot fall into the wrong hands. I'll be just fine. You get the floatplane in order, and off we'll go to the mainland. We'll be back home before you can say 'Bob's your uncle.' And we can rest easy, knowing that our friends Burilgi and Checheg have safely departed and are even now arranging the next little blow-up."

As soon as the pair left, Bao sank once again through the teak flooring.

In the next room she went to, her headdress went up through the floor and bumped into something soft but solid. She heard a girl's muffled voice mutter, "What the—?"

Bao moved sideways and emerged partway through the teak. She looked up into Mel's startled face. Johnny's sister was sitting cross-legged and looked as though she had been through a terrible ordeal.

With a tone of urgency Bao whispered, "Quiet, Mel! Listen to me. Johnny sent me to find you. Your soldiers will be coming very soon."

Grandmother was lying on the floor a few feet away, snoring loudly. There were three other people there, as well, all of them wearing dirty white coats. Bao had seen them before, going in and out of the building where they made the bomb. Now they looked tired, hungry, scared—and curious about whom Mel was talking to.

"When are they coming?" asked Mel.

"Very soon. Best that you keep still for now. You do not want to alert the Steppe Warriors to our plan."

"Are Johnny and Nina all right?"

"They are fine, Mel."

Mel looked as if a weight had been taken off her shoulders.

Bao told her to wait a few moments, and the little ghost descended through the floor. When she popped back up through the teak, Lieutenant Finn was with her. The first thing he did was salute. Bao thought it a rather odd gesture, but these people seemed rather odd to begin with.

"Good to see you, Lieutenant," Mel whispered.

"Likewise, ma'am," he said, leaning toward her. "You all right?"

"Stiff and sore. Otherwise fine."

"And Dame Honoria?"

"Dozing at the moment, as you can see. But oddly subdued. Don't know why. She doesn't seem to be hurt."

"Who are these other three, ma'am?"

"Scientists, engineers of some kind. Had to have worked on the bomb. Rather close-mouthed about it, though."

The conversation was more than Bao could really understand, but she enjoyed being amid people again. Sometimes just the sound of friendly grown-ups talking—the way her parents and aunts and uncles used to do—was enough to make her happy. It didn't matter what they were saying.

"We have a plan to get you all out," Finn said. "It involves a diversion by the boys and how quick-like you and these other people can get a move on. I ought to say that it's not without risk."

"I'm eager to hear the details," Mel said. "But first, is there any sign yet of the colonel?"

"Alas no, ma'am. Now let me tell you what's going to happen and what you have to do."

CHAPTER 43

FROM HIS HIDING PLACE in the greenery, Johnny saw Sergeant Clegg and two other troopers come charging hell-bent out of the blinding sun—whooping and screaming, sabers twirling. As they descended onto their unsuspecting enemies, there were screams and grunts and exclamations of terror.

The knot of Steppe Warriors at the front steps of the old headquarters building was caught completely off-guard. Not a one managed to draw a sword or nock an arrow before three ghostly heads flew off of three sets of etheric shoulders. It was a horrible thing to see. But what else could they do, Johnny thought. Mel and Dame Honoria's lives were at stake.

The sergeant and the two privates lingered long enough to inflict several more wounds. The only cost to the attackers was an arrow sticking out of Private Moody's shoulder.

Then up into the sky the Zenith troopers soared, galloping west at full tilt.

In short order, better than twenty more Steppe Warriors erupted out of the old plantation offices like angry fire ants—just as Finn had predicted. They leapt onto their stout little horses, then flew off in pursuit of Clegg and his men, soaring into the bright blue sky.

WHILE BAO and one of the troopers slipped beneath Sir Roderick's old headquarters to join the captives, Johnny, Nina, and the other horse soldiers tiptoed up the front steps and into the building. It wouldn't do to go blasting in, Finn had advised. Better to keep the element of surprise. Johnny couldn't have agreed more.

To get to the old office where Bao told them they'd find Mel and Dame Honoria, they had to go down the main corridor, then make a left turn. Johnny, gripping his machete, followed Finn. The other troopers came behind, with Nina trailing to the rear. But before they made the left turn, Johnny stuck his head around the corner. What he saw stopped him in his tracks.

There were two Steppe Warriors down at the end of that hallway—one of whom he recognized.

It was a Steppe Warrior from Jadetown, a friend of that fellow Johnny had pulverized back on General Tang Boulevard. Johnny doubted that the ghost soldier with the moon face would be very gentle, should he happen to get his hands on Mr. John Joshua Graphic.

Johnny backed up a few steps and told Finn what he'd seen, whispering in the ghost's ear.

WHEN THE MOMENT CAME, neither of the Steppe Warriors noticed Lieutenant Finn's ginger-bearded face peering out of the wall behind them. But Johnny saw it all, peeking around the corner.

"Now, boys!" Finn yelled, surging toward the two Steppe Warriors.

The Steppe Warrior from Jadetown barely had time to unsheathe his blade before Finn's cavalry saber came swinging down.

The ferocious momentum of Finn's attack drove the wraith back up the hallway toward Johnny. He was amazed that the Steppe Warrior managed to keep his head from being sliced off.

Back at the other end of the hallway, the second Steppe Warrior had managed to slow the troopers' onslaught. The blades clanging against each other made a terrible racket.

Just at this juncture, a door down the hallway cracked open and out popped Mel's head. She looked away from Johnny at first, then right at him. "Johnny!" she screamed. "Behind you!"

He spun around and found himself facing a Steppe Warrior who was sneaking up on him—only about ten feet away. For a second or two they gaped at each other. Then, not even thinking, Johnny charged at the ghost with his machete upraised.

The Steppe Warrior backpedaled in the direction he had come from. He stopped and waited for Johnny's first blow, then started raining down strikes on him.

Johnny's blade was heavy and clumsy, but he miraculously managed to parry the Steppe Warrior's strikes. *This guy*, Johnny thought in a rush, *must not be very good, if I can make a fight out of it.*

Just then the "guy" came at Johnny with a malevolent look on his face. Johnny grimaced and prepared for the assault, ready to repulse yet more sword strikes. But the Steppe Warrior's eyes focused behind Johnny, and he quick-footed it backward before launching himself up through the ceiling.

For a second or two, Johnny thought that he and his machete had bested the Steppe Warrior. But, in fact, his precipitous retreat was caused by the arrival of Lieutenant Finn and his troopers.

Finn regarded Johnny with a grim smile and a nod. "Not bad, for a beginner. " He resheathed his saber. "But best you not try to do that again, if you divine my meaning. Now, let's get our folks out of here."

Almost breathless, Johnny nodded. "Okey-dokey, Lieutenant. No more sword fights. Swell idea."

That's when Nina came rushing down the building's main corridor. "Can somebody please tell me what's going on?" she asked, sounding a bit over-anxious.

They marched back down the side corridor just as Mel and Dame Honoria emerged from their "prison cell." The old lady was too quick for Johnny and had him in a sweaty, snuffling embrace before he could back out of range. His sister gently slugged him on the shoulder. Mel looked from Johnny to Finn and back again.

"Pretty good job, you two," she said with a cockeyed grin. "I have a feeling it wouldn't have ended well if you hadn't rescued us."

Johnny shook his head. "Well, you're not entirely rescued yet. We've got about four miles to cover before dark, to get back to the flying boat. With about thirty or forty Steppe Warriors still on the loose. Hate to say it, but we're definitely outnumbered." He then scowled as the three white-coated scientists came out into the hallway—a middle-aged man and woman, and a young guy who looked as if he could still be in high school. "Have these people told you anything?"

Mel shook her head. "They're totally mum. Won't even tell us their names. I think they're more scared of whoever sent them here than they are of us."

Johnny cleared his throat and everyone looked at him. Time to go to work again.

"Let me just get a quick shot of you," he said to his sister, "and Dame Honoria and the scientists. We'll need it for your story."

Dame Honoria and Mel moaned in quick succession about how absolutely dreadful they looked, but reluctantly agreed to Johnny's request—if only to get it over with.

BY MIDAFTERNOON, they all were making their way southward, on the rocky trail that snaked through the coral hills. Sergeant Clegg and his raiding party had rejoined the main group. All the living people had clambered up into the saddles with Zenith troopers, to speed their passage along this very difficult path. Johnny had to stifle a grin, seeing the alarmed expressions on the faces of the scientists and Nina. As far as their own senses were concerned, they were bobbing along up in thin air.

Johnny felt incredibly relieved that no one had gotten hurt. So far. But he could tell that something had happened to Dame Honoria on Old Number One. She ought to have been expounding and pontificating, even in these dire circumstances. She was definitely not her normal, bossy self. But why?

When they emerged from the rocky path, everyone but Dame Honoria and the woman scientist dismounted and started hiking under their own power. An hour or so later they came upon Marchiano and Ozzie Eccleston, still locked in their pugnacious embrace. Both specters looked as if they'd been on a steady diet of vinegar. Sour, resentful expressions were etched on their faces.

Dame Honoria's former servant wailed for his release. Johnny, Mel, and Finn talked it over and decided that they couldn't risk having Ozzie find his Steppe Warrior friends and give them away. Mel ordered Marchiano and another Zenith trooper to bring Ozzie along to the beach, then release him as soon as their aeroboat took off. Each trooper gripped one of his arms.

Not that it mattered.

For when they were within a hundred yards of the beach, Private Schultz—a wiry ghost with a heavy Barovian accent, who had been sent forward to scout with another trooper—came rushing up to them.

"Dare are Shtep Varriors out dare," he whispered urgently. "Vaiting for us. Upon de vatter. Tventy or dirty."

"Have they taken the flying machine?" asked Mel. "Do you know if Uncle Louie and Danny are safe?"

"I do not know, Commander Grapheek. I left Private Boo out zere to keep an eye upon zem."

"Can't go forward," Johnny stated grimly. "And there may be Steppe Warriors back the way we came. So we're in another jam, huh?"

CHAPTER 44

SLIPPING OFF THE GHOST HORSE, Dame Honoria hobbled forward to join her godson and his sister. The little girl ghost tagged along behind her.

"Don't you worry, Johnny," said Dame Honoria, her deep, resonant voice a bit tremulous. "We shall get out safely." There were tears in the corners of her pale blue eyes. "You are such a fine young man. So talented, so determined, so energetic, so upright. I wish I had a son like you."

Johnny blinked at his godmother. What was *that* all about? He had never seen Dame Honoria speak so emotionally in all his life. *Something* was up with her.

He was about to ask what their plan ought to be, when another ghost trooper burst out of the undergrowth. Johnny saw the look of fear on Private Boo's baby face and his heart dropped. He knew the situation had just gone from bad to worse.

"They're headin' right fer us, Commander," exclaimed Boo. He snapped off a quick salute, as he skidded to a halt before Mel. "Comin' off the water and into the jungle. We'd best turn around and run."

"Are you absolutely sure?" Finn snapped.

"Afeared so, sir."

"In my opinion, ma'am," said the lieutenant, "Private Boo has given us the only choice we have."

"You think we should go back toward the coral hills?"

"I do, Commander Graphic."

Mel gave a fatalistic nod. "We're heading back inland," she shouted. "The Steppe Warriors are coming."

Everyone turned around and the two white-coated scientists on foot at the rear of the group suddenly became the leaders. The first of them—the slender youth with thick blond hair and wire-rimmed spectacles—began gasping for air, as panic took hold of him.

"I've gotta get out of here!" he screamed.

He started running down the narrow track, back in the direction they'd come from.

Johnny had a clear view of what happened next.

The young man in the white coat couldn't run very fast on the jungle track and had only made it fifty or so feet, when an arrow shot out of nowhere and went *thwuuump* into his chest.

As if he'd hit a stone wall, the young man came up short, turned and faced the others, and toppled over backward, like a rag doll. His dying face was a mask of bewilderment. The arrow that pierced his heart remained solid for a few seconds, then evaporated.

By the time Johnny had dashed up, a wraith that was an exact twin of the young man—right down to the white lab coat and spectacles—was standing over the body, semi-transparent, his feet floating a few inches over the ground.

"C-c-c-can anyone," the brand-new ghost stammered, "t-t-t-tell me what j-j-j-just happened?"

Johnny was about to explain, when a dozen mounted Steppe

Warriors appeared above them, bows drawn and arrows nocked. Almost simultaneously, each of the blue-coated troopers reached for his revolver. But Mel shouted, "NO! One murder is enough! Troopers, stand down."

A Steppe Warrior descended to the ground, dismounted, and swaggered toward the bedraggled captives, sword in hand. *Uh-oh*, thought Johnny, *it's the wraith from Jadetown.*

The ghost surveyed Mel and Nina and Dame Honoria. Then he stepped up to Johnny, looking him up and down.

"My name is Temur," the Steppe Warrior said. "Now drop your blade."

Johnny didn't see how he could do otherwise—as much as he wanted to fight—and threw his machete aside.

"I wouldn't have thought a midget like you could have defeated my friend back in Jadetown," Temur said. The wraith glared pointedly at him, then brought the tip of his sword right under Johnny's nose and delicately clipped it.

"YOW!" Johnny yelled, jumping backward. He rubbed his nose and his hand came away smeared with blood. He had no idea the end of the nose was so sensitive.

Mel snarled and darted up between Johnny and the specter. "Leave him alone!"

Temur laughed at her. "It will go much worse for him in just a little while."

Mel straightened her shoulders and visibly tried to buck herself up. "You had a chance to kill me back in the headquarters building, along with the others. Why didn't you?"

Temur brought his face within inches of Mel's.

Johnny was sick of Steppe Warriors mistreating his sister. He took a step toward the dreadful ghost. But Dame Honoria gripped his arm firmly and muttered, under her breath, "No, Johnny. Not just yet."

"The khan ordered us to keep you alive," the Steppe Warrior continued. "I do not know why. But he's gone now and said we can slaughter you all. Except for the old woman. So, I have something special in store for you, *Mel-a-nie*." He said her name as if it were some dreadful profanity.

As Mel shuddered and backed away, Johnny stepped to her side. He had to stall this Steppe Warrior. The more time they could kill—a rotten turn of phrase, but painfully accurate—the better their chances of coming out of this alive. It was a long shot, but it might be the only shot they had.

He hurled his taunting questions at Temur. One after the other.

"Do you *really* believe the bomb will free ghosts from the ether? *Really?*

"How come supposedly great warriors like you guys go around murdering innocent, defenseless people?

"Why have two ordinary kids from Zenith been able to twist the great khan into knots?"

Johnny could see his stinging questions had an impact. He didn't want to go too far and provoke a violent outburst. But he had one more thing to say.

"These people helped you with the bomb." Johnny nodded at the engineers in their white coats. "Why have you treated them so badly?"

"It was never in the khan's plan that they would survive," Temur answered, visibly tamping down his temper. "Now that we know how to make the weapon, we don't need them."

"Did you say you're killing all of us *except* Dame Honoria?" asked Johnny, not quite sure he'd heard the Steppe Warrior correctly.

"Did I not speak clearly?" Temur answered, smirking.

Now it was Dame Honoria's turn. The old lady drew herself up a little taller. "There's a reason why I've received this special consideration, Johnny. And I'm not proud of it."

CHAPTER 45

BEFORE SHE EXPLAINED HERSELF, Dame Honoria sniffled a bit. She wiped her hands on her filthy silk robe, then mopped her nose with the back of a sleeve.

"My dears," she said, looking right at her godson and his sister, "it's my Percy. My sweetums. *He* is the khan. One and the same. I found out several days ago. I talked to him."

Johnny was stunned. Dame Honoria's change of character now made perfect sense. How do you tell your godson and his sister that your own son, your own flesh and blood, is trying to murder them? You don't, at least at first. He couldn't blame her for clamming up.

"I know how distressing this news must be," Dame Honoria said with a sigh of resignation. "I still can hardly believe it. The darling baby whose nappies I changed every day has become a megalomaniac who wants to blow up the world."

"But if it's really Percy," Johnny said, "he's gotta know what happened to Mom and Pop." Hope surged inside him. "He was with them that night on Okkatek when they disappeared. He could tell us what he knows."

Johnny looked at Mel's wide-eyed expression and he realized

that she must be thinking the exact same thing. Maybe *this* would be how they'd find their parents—through Percy Rathbone. But Dame Honoria threw cold water on his hopes. "I've asked him about that. I've asked him why he never contacted anyone. But he refuses to answer."

Clearly Temur's patience was wearing thin. "Will you all *shut your mouths*. The khan has commanded us to release the old woman. But the rest remain. The black-haired girl stays and fights me unto her death. After I have taken her head, the rest of you die."

Johnny's heart fell into his stomach. This was worse than anything that had happened to them so far. To die at twelve and a half, without knowing what happened to Mom and Pop—it was too cruel.

Temur turned his head and finally noticed the wide-eyed Ozzie Eccleston, still in the firm grip of Marchiano and another Zenith trooper. He peered at Mel. "Tell your soldiers to release that man. The khan requests his presence."

Her face the very picture of defeat, Mel gave a curt nod and told Marchiano, "Do what the man says, Corporal. Let Ozzie go."

With grimaces of disgust, the two troopers did just that, and Ozzie—with an air of sneering contempt—flew up into the sky and away.

It practically broke Johnny's heart to see the devastated look on Mel's face. She glanced from Dame Honoria to Nina to himself. As if she were saying goodbye to them forever.

This can't be happening, Johnny thought. He had to do *something!*

WHEN JOHNNY AND THE OTHERS emerged out of the jungle shadows onto the broad sandy beach, their Steppe Warrior captors herded them to the left, while Mel and Temur went right.

The black-haired girl and the warrior wraith faced each other, sabers drawn.

Without any warning, the specter charged at Mel, raining down a cascade of strikes—sending her skittering backward and off balance.

Johnny winced and blinked at every clang and clank, desperately wanting to put a stop to this madness, but not knowing how. The Steppe Warrior clearly had no intention of letting this become a long, drawn-out struggle.

With one final, brutal stroke, he smashed the old army saber out of Mel's hand, sending it flying. Mel sprawled backward onto the sand.

Mel was defenseless! She was going to die!

The wraith hefted his blade for a two-handed, sidearm chop through that thin, white, living neck, when—

BOOM! BOOM! BOOM!

Thunderous gunshots!

Johnny couldn't believe who he saw landing on the sand, right between Mel and her would-be executioner.

Colonel MacFarlane and Buck!

The colonel aimed his revolver at Temur.

Up above hovered almost every other missing Zenith trooper. Repeating carbines and six-shooters drawn all around. Many of them aimed at the head of the Steppe Warrior who was about to take Melanie Graphic's head.

"Move the slightest little bit, sir," the silver-bearded officer growled, "and we'll blow your ugly noggin to smithereens!"

To Johnny, the next few silent seconds felt like an eternity. The Steppe Warriors had their arrows aimed at him and Nina, at Dame Honoria and the scientists. The troopers floating above had the Steppe Warriors in their sights. Johnny had never seen the colonel so furious—as if he were ready to take on hell itself. One itchy finger, and the six living people on this beach could all die.

Finally, the colonel spoke. "Now, what I would suggest is that we all lower our weapons and have a little parley among ourselves."

Wiping blood from the cut on his nose, Johnny looked all around. Against the odds, all those military ghosts sensed the wisdom of the colonel's advice and stood still as statues.

"I have terrible news for you, sir," the colonel said, staring straight into Temur's black eyes. "I have seen and heard what the etheric bomb did to the spirits who hoped to truly die."

Several of the Steppe Warriors muttered excitedly to each other, and squinted all the harder at Horace MacFarlane.

"Your khan," the colonel said, "has not told you the truth."

CHAPTER 46

JOHNNY WISHED he could get a picture of the colonel, the very image of unstinting heroism. Alive or dead, what a man!

"I repeat," the colonel said. "Let us put our weapons down."

Temur scowled at the colonel, but nodded and sheathed his curved sword. Simultaneously, the colonel holstered his pistol. All the other soldiers there slowly lowered their weapons.

The colonel nudged Buck forward, until they were a little bit in front of the Steppe Warrior.

"Tell us what you found, bluecoat," said Temur.

The colonel didn't need to clear his throat, but did, for dramatic effect. "We all saw the bomb explode. A green fireball miles wide. A colossal mushroom cloud. But…" He gravely shook his head.

"But what?" asked the Steppe Warrior.

"You had hoped the detonation would blow you all the way to your final resting place. Any sensible ghost would wish for that. Am I right?"

"The Eternal Blue Sky," said a teenaged Steppe Warrior. The boy's expression alternated between joy and dread. "At last we'll go to the Eternal Blue Sky."

"What did you find, old man?" Temur said, his voice laden with suspicion. *"Out with it!"*

The colonel described how he, Schecter, and Underwood had flown into the mushroom cloud. How the debris had battered them and scattered them heaven knows where. Schecter and Underwood had vanished utterly—still missing in action.

Johnny stifled a gasp. Those two, they had been his friends. Schecter had taught Johnny how to play poker and Underwood had rescued him once, when he'd gotten stuck out on a boulder in the middle of a rushing stream. He might have drowned, but for Private Underwood.

"Next thing I knew, I was huddling on the ocean floor, with Buck here." The colonel ran his fingers through the ghost horse's mane. "Pitch dark and dead quiet down there. Then it began. And I still shudder to think of it."

Johnny couldn't help jumping in. "What? What began, Colonel?"

"I started hearing voices, Master Johnny, a galaxy of voices. All talking at once. Mostly different, but some the same. As if there were ten or a hundred of the same person. They got inside my head. A chorus of the damned. They came raining down on me." The colonel gazed at Temur. "Do you understand, sir?"

The warrior, his face suddenly very gloomy, shook his head. But Johnny thought he *must* understand. He just didn't want to admit it.

Mel pulled herself up and took a few reluctant steps toward her nemesis. "I think the colonel is saying, Temur, that the ghosts in the bomb were blown to bits, but not to the Eternal Blue Sky."

Johnny's stomach did a flip-flop. Nothing more hideous could happen to a ghost. Shredded to little pieces, but still cognizant, still capable of feeling pain—and utterly helpless.

"Every atom of their being," the colonel continued grimly, "was screaming with regret. All those ghosts. All those thousands. Torn. Ripped apart. Destroyed but not freed."

At first, Temur looked dismayed, but then came rage. "*These are lies! Dirty, miserable lies!* The khan promised an end to our curse."

"He told us we'd live forever in the Eternal Blue Sky," whined the young Steppe Warrior.

"Either your khan didn't know what would happen or he told you an untruth," the colonel said.

"Your word alone is not good enough," grunted Temur. "Give us proof."

The colonel nodded. "Thought you might want something like that." He leaned over and opened his saddle bag. He reached inside it, grabbing something. Bringing his closed fist around, he snapped it open, scattering a handful of fine gravel over Temur's head.

"What sort of foolery is this?" Temur snarled.

With no warning, a look of absolute pain came over his face. "ARRRGGHHH!" he cried, then stared up at the colonel. "No! NO! It cannot be!"

The Steppe Warrior swayed on his feet and groaned. "I hear hundreds of voices, every one screaming in agony." He crumpled to the ground and huddled in a fetal position, quivering and quaking.

Then Johnny slapped *his* hands up to *his* ears, trying to shut out the thin, horrible keening of the ruined spooks. Somehow, it seeped into his brain and bones and muscles. Dame Honoria and Mel wore expressions of horror on their faces, as well.

Some of the Steppe Warriors looked as if they were going to sob and shriek. Some tried to remain stoic, their faces rigid and brittle. Still others shook their heads miserably and rode slowly away toward the coral hills.

Now the ancient horse soldiers looked like ordinary ghosts, robbed of hope—vague, diaphanous, without the capacity to touch and affect the real world. Percy Rathbone's hold on them had ended. Their agreement with "the khan" had been violated by this deception.

As the Steppe Warriors faded away, Johnny noticed Bao whispering into Dame Honoria's ear. The old lady's face first showed a look of surprise, then grim determination.

"I believe we have one more job to do before we leave this wretched island," she boomed. "Melanie, Johnny, Colonel Mac-Farlane, I need to speak with you."

CHAPTER 47

GRITTING HIS TEETH—as he always did when he went flying with the colonel and Buck—Johnny was the first to spot the little rowboat. The tiny vessel was heading out to a two-engined floatplane in the big lagoon at the north end of Old Number One.

Despite feeling utterly worn out and starving, Johnny had been determined to go with the colonel on this one last vital mission—to capture the khan. The news photographer in him could hardly wait to snap a shot of Percy Rathbone getting his comeuppance.

When Johnny had told Mel and Dame Honoria that he planned to go with the colonel, neither of them argued. After all, Percy's deal with the Steppe Warriors on the island had ended once they had witnessed the horrific effect of the etheric bomb. The ancient ghost soldiers presented no further danger. The colonel even figured that it would take only three troopers—himself plus Finn and Marchiano—to apprehend Percy and his blonde accomplice. The rest would stay and guard Mel, Dame Honoria, and Nina.

The ghost horses and their riders circled down toward the solitary rower. Johnny could tell from Dame Honoria's description that it was Percy. The now-dethroned khan flailed with the oars in a desperate attempt to reach the floatplane. From the door of the aircraft, a woman in an aviator helmet, with copious blonde hair sticking out every which way, urged the rower on.

"Harder, Percy!" she screamed. "Row harder!"

"So it's really him!" Johnny exclaimed, from his perch behind the colonel.

"So it would seem," the colonel returned. "Now we have the scoundrel."

Suddenly, someone in the floatplane pulled the blonde woman back and began firing at Johnny and the troopers.

More quickly than Johnny thought possible, Finn and March-iano returned fire, shooting holes in the aluminum skin of the airplane. In the midst of the gunfire Johnny managed to see the shooter just before he ducked back inside the floatplane. Ozzie, that rat!

With a brisk hand signal, the colonel directed Corporal March-iano down to the water—right between the rowboat and the floatplane. The corporal skidded to a halt atop the gentle waves and aimed his carbine at the open door of the plane.

Even though he was trapped, Percy kept rowing.

"Stop, Mr. Rathbone, or we shoot!" the colonel bellowed from above.

But the grim-looking culprit paid him no heed.

The colonel barked an order to Finn. "Shoot holes in the boat, Lieutenant."

In rapid succession, Finn fired a dozen shots through the thin wood planking of the boat's bottom. Almost immediately, water began to gush into it.

Percy threw down his oars and stood. He cupped his hands to his mouth and hollered to his blonde friend, who had reappeared in the airplane door. "Get away, Pamela! And keep a good eye on

Mummy!"

"No, Percy, no!" the woman wailed.

But Percy didn't respond. He just stood there, frozen in place in the sinking rowboat. He made no effort to swim away. It appeared that the mighty khan intended to go down with his ship.

Johnny knew he had work to do. It was now or never, one shot only. "Colonel, can you hover for a minute?" he shouted in the old officer's ear. "Steady as possible?"

"Consider it done, Master Johnny," the specter replied, lightly tugging on Buck's reins.

Pulling his left hand from the belt around the colonel's waist, Johnny took his camera in both hands and aimed it at the rowboat below. The little vessel was rapidly filling with water.

Just as it started to slip beneath the surface, Finn swooped down and grabbed Percy by the collar of his safari jacket, tugging him up toward the saddle.

At that precise instant Johnny pressed the shutter.

Finn hauled the dripping khan up over the saddle and barked a few intemperate words at him. Percy had the good sense to not struggle.

Thrilled beyond belief, Johnny yelled, "Gotcha, you bum!" right in the colonel's ear.

With mechanical roars, the floatplane's two propellers both started to turn. Johnny could see the blonde woman through the front windshield, in the pilot's seat, a dismal look on her face. She turned the aircraft out to sea and began taxiing away.

"We've gotta stop that floatplane," Johnny shouted. "They're gonna get away."

"There aren't enough of us, Master Johnny," the colonel said. "We have Mr. Rathbone. That'll have to do for now."

Though he felt bitterly disappointed that Ozzie and the woman were getting away, Johnny understood. They would still be flying back to Mel and Dame Honoria with the biggest catch of all.

THE VERY INSTANT that Buck touched down on the beach back at the opposite end of the island, Johnny leapt from the saddle and rushed over to Percy—whom Finn had unceremoniously dumped in a heap on the sand. Percy's face was sullen beneath his pith helmet.

"What happened to my parents on Okkatek Island?" Johnny demanded. "You were there. You know. *I know you know.*"

Percy peered peevishly at Johnny as he picked himself up, dusting sand from his clothing.

Mel rushed up next to Johnny, with the same imploring expression on her face, followed by Dame Honoria.

"Percival, do you not even possess the common decency to answer these youngsters?" scolded the old lady.

Percy beamed a treacly, sarcastic smile at his mother. "Apparently not, Mummy." Then he regarded the Graphics. "Sorry, darling children, can't help you. Too, too bad about Will and Lydia."

Johnny couldn't even sputter a retort. It seemed pretty clear that "the khan" wasn't about to give them any satisfaction. Johnny supposed he shouldn't be surprised. After all, this man had caused a whole lot of misery. And it didn't seem as if he intended to stop anytime soon.

CHAPTER 48

SATURDAY, NOVEMBER 2, 1935

AIRBORNE APPROACHING GORTON ISLAND

TO DAME HONORIA the flying boat seemed like a little bit of heaven, as it winged its way back to Gorton Island early the next morning. For as soon as the big engines started up, deliciously cool air began seeping out of the ventilation ducts into her private compartment in the back of the aircraft. She sighed with pleasure, feeling the moisture on her skin begin to evaporate.

Never in her life had she endured such hardships as in the last several days. The physical demands of her harsh captivity had been very nearly more than she could stand—as a woman pushing on toward the age of sixty and not in the fittest condition.

But more daunting was the emotional strain, which had sent her to the very brink of insanity. And the cause of it all was sitting right opposite her in this little cabin. He was bound hand and foot, but ungagged—in the hope that he might decide to say something useful.

The khan, Percival Roderick Gorton Rathbone, smelling all musty and earthy, glowered nonstop at "the old mater," as he used to call her. Though his voice had not changed one iota, his ever-glum face was even glummer than Dame Honoria could have imagined.

Truth be told, he had always had a grim sort of demeanor about him, even as a youngster. His late father once observed, only half in jest, that Percy seemed to have been born fifty years old, as a hanging judge. What Dame Honoria couldn't explain, however, was Percy's fine new head of hair and his new physique—much like that of a weight lifter. He had to have been engaged in some kind of intense keep-fit program. Perhaps he had taken up rugby.

At least she knew who Percy's female companion was. When Johnny reported that Percy had called her "Pamela," a bell went off in Dame Honoria's head. Pamela Worthington-Smythe had once worked as an assistant for Dame Honoria's secretary. The pretty blonde had been fired six years ago, when it became apparent that she had set her sights on Percival and his potential inheritance.

"Now Percival," said Dame Honoria, "why should you have told Miss Worthington-Smythe to keep an eye on me?"

"Because we're both so very, *very* fond of you," her son answered, his voice dripping with sarcasm.

Sighing, Dame Honoria recalled a time when Percy had seemed a good young man struggling for a good cause—as a tireless campaigner for the rights of ghosts. He'd even published a book on the subject, though it sold only a few dozen copies, which left him quite embittered.

Now, Dame Honoria could hardly believe that this creature—her only child—had hatched one of the most dastardly plots in human history. No one had ever devised such a powerful explosive as the etheric bomb. Was Percy's only goal the dispatching of ghosts to their final rewards?

Or might he have had some darker purpose in mind?

Nothing forced home the terrible reality of Percy's misdeeds more powerfully than the funeral of that poor young scientist. His name had been Franklin Fforbes and they had buried his corpse just off the beach, in a spot garlanded with tropical blooms. Dame Honoria had recited her favorite prayer. Fforbes' ghost, though a bit tongue-tied at first, had given his own eulogy—a few touching, bittersweet words about having left the world far too soon.

And how uncouth of Percy, to not answer Melanie and Johnny's repeated questions about their parents. He had been there on Okkatek Island that dreadful night five years earlier. He had vanished with Will and Lydia. How could he not know *something?* How could he be so cruel, to not share the facts?

As the aeroboat cruised along, Dame Honoria tried to engage her son by telling him items of interest that had happened back in Gilbeyshire since his disappearance. Retainers who had died or retired. Marriages, births, deaths. Local scandals and gossip. A childhood friend of his who had stood for parliament. The ongoing and rather costly restoration of Wickenham's decrepit west wing. And so on.

Percy's responses were mostly on the order of "Eh" and "Um" and "Oh." He was clearly not interested in reminiscences from home. It was *not* the affectionate reunion his mum had hoped for.

There had been only one real moment of connection. For some unaccountable reason, Dame Honoria started to recite a tiny piece of verse that she hadn't thought of in years. Something that Percy had composed for her as a small child. Memory being a funny old thing, it popped right back into her head. She spoke the first lines.

"Mummy loves her little man,

And always likes to feed him..."

She stared at him hopefully, beseechingly, and for a change he obliged her, finishing the final couplet:

"Cakes and tarts and apple flan

Because he is her sweetum."

Dame Honoria was staring at him silently after that when someone rapped sharply on the cabin door. She tottered to her feet and cracked it open. It was young Miss Bain.

"Nina, my dear," she said. "Please come in. What can I do for you?"

Nina tiptoed in and warily eyed the scowling Percy, only a few feet away. It gave Dame Honoria a chill to see the look of revulsion that came across the girl's face. Whether it was due to Percy's alarming appearance or because of his campaign to murder those who were essentially Nina's family, she could not say. The fact remained that at the moment, no one felt very fond of Percival Rathbone. Not even his mum.

"This is yours," said the girl, looking at Dame Honoria. She handed over a small leather case. "Found it in your cave. You wouldn't want to leave it behind, I bet."

Dame Honoria opened the case and smiled for the first time since she laid eyes on her son. "Oh my goodness gracious, my diamond. The Star of Gilbeyshire. Thank you, Nina. I had quite forgotten about it."

She gave the girl a quick hug and tucked the case into the pocket of Danny Kailolu's rain jacket—which he had loaned her to wear over her filthy and odoriferous silk robe.

The famous suffragist watched the bright-eyed young lady—so very smart and earnest—step out of the cabin. Then she once again scrutinized the unfathomable brown eyes of her son.

Something in one of the cobwebby closets at the back of her mind stirred and stretched and threw open a door of memory. And she shuddered, finally understanding what it was.

Her Percival had always had blue eyes.

CHAPTER 49

SATURDAY, NOVEMBER 2, 1935

GORTON ISLAND

HIS MUTTON-CHOP WHISKERS all aquiver, Sir Chauncey Holyfield greeted Johnny and the others at the dock on Gorton Island. Johnny thought the novelist was a funny-looking old fellow—much like one of his eccentric characters that provided comic relief. Nina, a big fan, was particularly excited to shake the ghost author's invisible hand.

"My dear old girl," Sir Chauncey said sheepishly, as he helped pluck Dame Honoria up out of the black rubber dinghy, "profuse apologies for abandoning you. I am deeply mortified. Heroism not my cup of tea." He gave her a quick hug and peck on the cheek.

"You left me out to hang, Chauncey," she grumbled, scowling at him. "And if you want to make up for it, I'll expect you to work harder than you ever have before."

"Of course, Honoria, of course," said the ghost. Then he took a closer look at the peculiar figure frowning up at him from the dinghy. On either side of this creature sat two blue-coated ghost troopers. "Good grief, who—or should I say *what*—is that?"

"Sir Chauncey, I would like you to meet my son, the khan. Percival Roderick Gorton Rathbone."

"Hello, Percival, so good to finally meet you. Your mother has had so many wonderful things to—" Sir Chauncey came to a dead stop and pivoted to look at Dame Honoria. "Did you say *khan?*"

She nodded tiredly.

The best-selling author blinked in amazement at the dour person being helped up out of the dinghy by the ghost troopers. "You mean," he peeped, "that your sweetums is the homicidal psychopath behind the Gesellschaft murders?"

Dame Honoria shut her eyes and nodded again.

THE MISTRESS OF GORTON ISLAND had asked Johnny and Mel to come out onto the white sand beach after dinner. The sun was setting over the Rotonesian mainland, a glorious seascape with multi-hued clouds dotting the sky. A lovely, mild breeze came off the water.

Johnny, his pant legs rolled up to his knees, loved the sensation of the sand between his toes. It felt to him, after they arrived on Gorton Island, as though they were on vacation. But he was positively drooping in his tracks. He needed a long night of shut-eye. His sister, in the boldly-colored silk summer dress that she had bought in the Orchid Isles, didn't look much livelier.

"I don't know what you needed to talk about, Dame Honoria," said Mel. "But can you tell us, has Percy said anything about Mom and Dad? *Anything?* Even the least little bit?"

"Yeah," Johnny put in, "Percy might be our best chance of finding them, if they're still alive. And he's being a real creep about it!"

"I know," Dame Honoria answered with resignation. "We can only hope that he has a change of heart very soon."

"So," Mel said, "what did you want to talk about?"

"Melanie, you've seen Percy in the past, years ago in Gilbey-shire," the old lady replied. "But you never knew him as I did. Until this morning I'd not put two and two together. I had encountered Percy only once on Old Number One, before the colonel took him into custody. I recognized his voice immediately, of course. But physically he's changed. Bigger, stronger, not at all like his old self."

"Anyone can go on an exercise program and build up muscles," said Johnny, kicking at the white sand.

"That's what I thought, as well. But I noticed other things, too. He used to have a weaker jaw and a slightly receding chin. Exercise cannot account for that. Nor the dank forest smell Percy exudes whenever he comes into a room. Most peculiar."

"Where are you going with this, Dame Honoria?" asked Johnny, now waking up. This was beginning to sound a little weird.

"I don't like that look on your face," Mel told her.

"Bad news and my features don't go well together, do they?" The noblewoman gave a desolate chuckle. "This morning I took a close, hard look at my son and finally something very obvious leapt out at me. I don't know how I could have missed it earlier."

Mel regarded her old friend. "Yes, what was it?"

"The color of Percy's eyes has changed. From blue to brown."

Johnny shook his head. This made no sense. "It's impossible to change the color of your eyes, once you're old enough. Some babies' eyes can change color, but not adults'. Right?"

"Correct. And do you know what I think it means, my dears?"

"Maybe he's someone pretending to be Percy," Mel suggested with a hesitant tone. "Someone living who knows a lot about your son. Someone who can imitate his voice. Enough to fool a very hopeful mother."

"I wish it was so, my dear. But this person knew things that only Percival could have known. He was able to recite part of a poem my son composed as a little chap. How could an imposter have known it?"

Johnny pondered that. Dame Honoria was right. Even if this person—supposing he wasn't Percy—had somehow held Percy in captivity for five years, he couldn't fool Dame Honoria. Because it would have been quite impossible for the culprit to have learned every little obscure detail from Percy's childhood.

So if this wasn't someone else pretending to be Percy, if it really was Percy, but he didn't look remotely like his old self, unless—

"Percy's got a new body," Johnny blurted out.

"My thoughts exactly," Dame Honoria agreed gravely.

"If he's gotten a new body it means his old one died. On Okka-tek Island or somewhere else."

The old lady nodded again, shutting her eyes firmly against the tears that tried to seep out. It appeared that she hated to even think about her Percy dying. Despite all the vile things he had done, he still was her sweetums and thinking of his death must have pained her greatly. Any mother would feel the same, Johnny imagined.

"Which means he didn't pass beyond the ether," Johnny continued. "He became a ghost."

"I believe so," Dame Honoria concurred.

"And as a ghost, Percy somehow took over someone else's body. Hard to imagine taking over a living person's body. So probably he possessed a body that had just died."

"I confess that I am thinking along the same lines, Johnny," the old lady said.

"But that's supposed to be impossible. Right? First Impossible Thing. No ghost can come back to life."

"It's *supposed* to be that way," said Mel. "No ghost should be able to reanimate and inhabit their own dead body. But we never considered the possibility of a ghost possessing somebody else's dead body."

"Highly improbable," said Dame Honoria. "But sitting upstairs in my house, held prisoner, is evidence that such a thing may have taken place."

"It seems Percy has found a way," observed Mel. "He's a very, very smart man. His mother's son…"

Dame Honoria sniffed and acknowledged Mel's sideways compliment with a quick smile. "And in the world of fantasy and legend what do we call a dead body that has come back to life? Or unlife, if you prefer?"

"The technical name for it," said Mel, "would be 'revenant.'"

A strange feeling that combined dread with exhilaration surged through Johnny. He was witnessing a historical moment, an occasion when the whole world changed. Something new and frightening had come into being. A horror that used to exist only in comic books and radio serials now, it seemed, had become real. What it meant, he couldn't say. He was only a kid with a camera. But this would be an event that he would remember forever.

"There's another word you can use," he said. "Percy is a *zombie*."

CHAPTER 50

SUNDAY, NOVEMBER 3, 1935

GORTON ISLAND

"MY NAME IS SPELLED F-R-A-N-K-L-I-N F-F-O-R-B-E-S. Two f's in the surname. Eccentric spelling, I guess. The second f is silent. I am twenty-one…erm…*was* twenty-one years old. Got my degree from Albertville Polytechnic, in metallic engineering. Graduated just six months ago. Not a very long career, eh?"

The slender wraith with thick blond hair grinned nervously at Mel and Johnny, then jabbered some more.

Johnny, Mel, and the ghost were sitting around a bamboo table on Dame Honoria's front verandah. Danny was behind Mel, leaning against one of the beams that supported the roof. Every once in a while he hovered in over her shoulder, to read her notes about what the ghost had said. Johnny was glad that Mel could have some time with Danny. It seemed she liked the guy, and so did Johnny. Mel hadn't had much luck with boyfriends, but maybe this time would be different.

This, however, was no romantic date. Johnny wondered how

they were ever going to extract the important facts out of this poor ghost, if he wouldn't stop babbling on and on without getting to the point. Mel was too polite. If you're a real newshound, you've got to be a little pushy. Otherwise you'd never get the story.

Johnny took a deep breath and rapped his knuckles sharply on the table. Franklin Fforbes and Mel both stared at him quizzically.

"I think we have enough background information, Mr. Fforbes," Johnny said evenly. "Can we please move on to the actual events that brought you to this unfortunate situation?"

The wraith gave a nervous laugh. "I apologize. I do tend to blather. And please call me Frank."

"Sure thing, Frank. But we've gotta get your story down before you go floating off."

"I assure you that I have no intention of floating off. Miss Graphic said she'd help with my family. My present circumstance will be a terrible disappointment to them."

"Understood, Frank. Now let's begin with how you were recruited into this secret project. When was your first contact with government agents?"

The specter ran his fingers through his dense blond hair, then scratched vigorously behind his right ear. "Here I am, all— all— all *dead*. And I'm still itching. I just don't understand how—"

Johnny groaned with exasperation. "*Frank!*"

Franklin Fforbes grimaced. "Sorry. Okay, the question was, how did I get sucked into this disaster? Well, late last winter one of my professors called me into his office to meet a man who needed a metallic engineer. He called himself Mr. Smith, and he said he represented an important government research project. It paid very well. If I got the job, I had to swear—under penalty of imprisonment—to never tell anyone what I did. It sounded exciting."

"What did Mr. Smith look like, Frank?"

"I can tell you, he gave me a little chill. He was a tall man, kind of tubby. His head was perfectly, shiny smooth, not a hair on it. He had a white pencil mustache. He had what I would call piggy eyes. And one of his hands twitched constantly. He didn't seem like a man you would want to mess with."

Johnny and Mel's eyes locked and simultaneously they pronounced, "Santangelo."

IT TOOK EVEN LONGER to get answers out of the two scientists who were still among the living.

The woman was named Doctor Doris Dinglemann. Stout, red-faced, and loud, she sounded like a badly played trombone. The man was tall and willowy, with tightly drawn features and washed-out blue eyes. His voice was soft and reedy. Emil LaGrange let the woman do most of the talking—as if he were used to it. It turned out they were far more afraid of the people they worked for than the people who had rescued them. So mostly they refused to answer Johnny and Mel's questions.

But they became especially agitated when Johnny started reading them what Franklin Fforbes had said about the etheric bomb.

"He can't do that, can't say that," Doctor Dinglemann bleated. "He signed an oath of absolute secrecy."

"He's dead," Mel spat. "Thanks to the people who sent you here. And there's nothing anyone can do to him anymore. He's released from any legal obligations."

Suddenly Johnny remembered something that Miss Beale, the *Clarion*'s managing editor, had told him about—a technique that reporters can sometimes use to get reluctant interview subjects to help with stories.

"Okay, Doctor Dinglemann," he said, hoping this would work.

"If you're afraid of the big bald guy with the white mustache—"

Both the man and woman went utterly pale.

"—you don't have to say anything. But if you agree with what Frank told us, all you gotta do is nod. Disagree—shake your head. Don't know—shrug your shoulders. We just want confirmation. You don't have to say a word. Simple as that. Then if someone asks you what you told us, you can say, 'Nothing. Didn't say a word.' And you'll be telling 'em the straight truth."

Doctor Dinglemann and Emil LaGrange whispered in each other's ears, then stared at the brother and sister. They didn't look the least bit happy, but both of them nodded.

PERCY RATHBONE spent the two days before their departure locked in the upstairs guest room, guarded by Zenith troopers. He preferred a diet exclusively of meat—mostly canned mackerel and tuna, as that was all that Dame Honoria had in her larder.

Johnny, Dame Honoria, and Mel tried twice to loosen his tongue. The first time produced nothing but a few useless, monosyllabic responses. But the second time he provided tiny slivers of information and one expression of semi-regret.

"Your etheric bomb did a terrible atrocity to thousands of the ghosts, for whom you claim to be an advocate," said Dame Honoria. "How do you feel about that?"

Percy sighed, and with those new, unreadable brown eyes, he contemplated his mother. "Unfortunate, of course, Mummy, that they didn't pass beyond the ether. I wish that they had. But they suffer for a greater good. No different than soldiers suffering in war."

"And what good is that?" snapped Johnny.

He knew all too well that Percy had always despised Will and

Lydia Graphic, and their kids. Mel had told Johnny her theory was that Percy believed they had wormed their way into his mother's affections—somehow displacing him.

As if to confirm it, Percy almost snarled at Johnny. "We mean to free the ghosts from their subjugation, and give them a place to live upon this earth—dead *and* undead alike."

It was almost too incredible. If Percy was a zombie or a revenant, and therefore undead, he had just declared openly that there would be more like him coming. The looks on Mel and Dame Honoria's faces showed the same shock of realization.

"By 'we' do you mean yourself and Miss Worthington-Smythe?" asked Dame Honoria.

Percy thought a moment before answering, then nodded. "Yes, of course, Mummy, that's exactly what I mean."

"And perhaps you can explain what that woman is doing in this rather incriminating sketch which Melanie and Johnny have shared with me," Dame Honoria continued. From a pocket she withdrew the rolled-up drawing that Mongke Eng had left behind, then showed it to Percy. "You will recognize Will and Lydia Graphic. By the look of it, on Okkatek."

A black expression flitted across Percy's face. "That blasted contessa," he growled. Then he composed himself. "Who's to say it's even real? She may have faked it. Made it up out of her imagination."

Johnny suddenly lost his temper. "You're lying, you rotten creep! You know what happened to our parents and you're keeping it a secret. If they're dead, tell us. If they're alive, tell us where they are!"

The zombie only smiled, which made Johnny even angrier. Not wanting to give Percy the satisfaction of seeing how riled he was, Johnny simply shut his mouth and looked away.

But Dame Honoria had one last comment. "What baffles me, Percy, is how you persuaded the Steppe Warriors and other ghost assassins into following you, as their khan, their leader. Why in the world did they believe you?"

Percy shook his head, as if he couldn't quite believe how dense Mummy could sometimes be. "They haven't had a khan, a ruler, in centuries. No one else had tried to help them to escape the ether, to go to their Eternal Blue Sky. So when I came along... Well, when people are desperate and hopeless, they'll turn to any leader who offers them a better future."

The three interrogators were just leaving the room when Johnny heard a barely audible comment come out of Percy's mouth.

"Oh, poor Mummy," the prisoner hissed in a whisper. "You have no idea what sweetums has in store for you."

Out in the hallway, Johnny immediately told Dame Honoria and Mel what he'd just heard.

The old lady winced. "Oh my dear, he is a handful, isn't he?"

CHAPTER 51

JOHNNY PEERED out into the night, staring at the black-top rushing beneath the headlights of the big newspaper truck. He was squeezed in between Mr. Cargill and the bearded truck driver. They had left Zenith at three o'clock in the afternoon and it was now about midnight. They were out in the middle of nowhere and wouldn't arrive in Capital City for another seven hours.

A lot had happened back home while Johnny was away. Mr. Cargill had been thrown in jail for printing their stories on the etheric bomb. He'd told Johnny it wasn't too bad, being stuck in the hoosegow. He'd been able to play poker with the other inmates and didn't have to eat any vegetables—Mrs. Cargill being awfully big on vegetables. He served five days, but he said it had been worth every minute of it to get those stories into print.

Johnny felt a little apprehensive about their current mission. He figured that once the government realized what was in the *Clarion* Extra edition, Mr. Cargill might get hauled off to the clink *again.*

It all had to go like clockwork, like a military operation.

Mr. Cargill decided to personally hawk the Extra edition in front of the Parliament building in Capital City. The newsies—boys and girls who sold newspapers in the street—had the assignment of spreading out across downtown. Over thirty of them were following along in a bus behind the truck. Johnny would go with a newsie he knew and take pictures of the operation.

The chief also arranged for the World Press Association to send the stories out on the wires at 8 a.m. Plains Central Time. That's when copies of the Extra edition would start selling in Zenith, as well.

Radio stations owned by Mrs. Throckmorton—owner of the *Clarion* and Mr. Cargill's boss—would lead their news with Johnny and Mel's big scoop every hour on the hour.

After mobbing a breakfast diner on the outskirts of town, Mr. Cargill's troop of newsies deployed around Capital City's business, government, and retail districts. The chief took a bag of papers and headed for the Parliament building. Johnny hiked east with his newsie pal Tom Krajnc, making for the front entrance of the Ministry of War.

If enough members of Parliament read the story and were upset by the current government's secret involvement in the etheric bomb scandal, they might vote to bring the government down. It was called a vote of no confidence. That would finish Scofield as etheristics minister and Patterson as war minister.

JOHNNY HAD ON HIS SUNGLASSES and his urchin disguise that he'd used for the goldbricking sewer workers story. He didn't want anyone to recognize him, especially any ghost assassins. Lieutenant Finn and Sergeant Clegg had come along, too, just in case—following along a few paces behind.

Johnny hiked with Tom to a spot outside one of the main entrances to the massive Ministry of War building. A heavy stream of government workers, military officers, and bureaucrats flowed around them.

Johnny and Tom were both too nervous to talk. But Johnny kept an eye on his pocket watch. Mr. Cargill had been adamant about that.

No one was to start selling the newspaper until 8 a.m. sharp. Together, the two boys counted down. When the second hand swept past the 12, Johnny nodded. Tom hauled the first copy out of his canvas bag and started shouting. Like most newsies, he had a piercing, powerful voice.

"EXTRA! EXTRA! GUMMINT HELPS MAKE SUPER BOMB. IMPIL-CATED IN ETHERIST MURDERS. THE LATEST NEWS AND PITCHERS FROM MELANIE AND JOHNNY GRAPHIC. ONLY A NICKEL. ONLY IN THE *ZENITH CLARION!*"

Eyes wide with surprise, a woman in a severe black overcoat dropped five pennies in Tom's grimy hand and grabbed that first copy.

Johnny snatched an Extra out of Tom's bag and his breath caught as he scanned the front page.

WORLDWIDE ETHERIC BOMB CONSPIRACY REVEALED! GOVERNMENT IMPLICATED!

In smaller type below came the subheadlines:

SCOFIELD ORDERED MURDER OF PHYSICAL ETHERISTS TO PREVENT SPREAD OF BOMB TECHNOLOGY

ROGUE ETHERIST RATHBONE CAPTURED, HANDED OVER TO AUTHORITIES

PRIME MINISTER'S INVOLVEMENT IN QUESTION

WHEREABOUTS OF OTHER BOMBS UNKNOWN

FIRST ZOMBIE IN HISTORY

Beneath it were Mel and Johnny's bylines and three of his shots: Mel and Dame Honoria right after their liberation on Old Number One, looking bedraggled and shell-shocked. The picture of Percy Rathbone being hauled out of the sinking rowboat by an invisible Lieutenant Finn. And a view of Doris Dinglemann and Emil LaGrange in the back of the flying boat, seeming very surprised and unhappy to be caught on film. There were also smaller photos of Minister Scofield, Minister Patterson, and Peter Santangelo.

Two other stories shared the front page. The first was headlined:

HORROR OF THE ETHERIC BOMB REVEALED

**Exclusive Account
by Col. Horace MacFarlane,
First Zenith Cavalry Brigade, Deceased**

And the second proclaimed:

"MY SON IS A ZOMBIE!"
A MOTHER'S ANGUISH
**Exclusive Personal Account
by Dame Honoria Gorton Rathbone,
M.E., D.E., R.S.C.E.**

Suddenly aware again of where he was, Johnny looked up and saw that Tom had been practically mobbed, as people pushed in around him to snap up copies of the provocative Extra edition.

CHAPTER 52

TUESDAY, DECEMBER 3, 1935
CAPITAL CITY

JOHNNY FOUND HIMSELF sitting cross-legged on the floor in the parliamentary committee chamber in Capital City. He had his Zoom 4x5 in his lap. Four other photographers sat on his left and three more on his right.

Johnny felt as if he had been dropped into the middle of a bee-hive that morning. Hundreds of people crowded into the chamber to watch members of parliament grill the accused scoundrels.

Appearing first before the committee was the former minister of etheristics, Hubert Scofield. He refused to answer any questions, on the grounds of his right against "self-incrimination." Mr. Cargill later told Johnny this meant Scofield didn't want to admit he had done anything illegal. The chatter around Capital City was that Scofield would have a very hard time keeping his sorry keister out of Bonewood Scrubs Prison.

Later in the morning, it was Peter Santangelo's turn. As his left hand twitched incessantly, the tall, flabby man repeated the same thing over and over. He had only been following the orders of his boss, Hubert Scofield. And how could he have known that those orders may have broken the law?

Santangelo managed to keep his voice expressionless and his pale face bland—even when he made eye contact with Johnny. But beads of sweat kept appearing on his bald head, no matter how often he tried to wipe them away with a handkerchief.

This hardly seemed like the same guy who had threatened to throw Mel and Johnny in jail. Who had been incredibly rude and snotty. Who had gotten himself walloped with a broom by Mrs. Lundgren. Who had seemed really scary the times Johnny had met him. Today the bum almost came across as a decent, ordinary guy. But Johnny knew otherwise.

From his position on the floor, Johnny could see Mel, Uncle Louie, Nina, Dame Honoria, and Mr. Cargill off to the side, in the spectators' gallery. They all wanted to be a part of this historic event. In fact, Mr. Cargill was scribbling notes, having assigned the story to himself.

It had taken less than a week after the *Clarion* Extra edition had come out for the old government to collapse. Investigators for the new coalition government quickly discovered what Scofield and Mabel Patterson had been up to. It was bad enough that they had conspired with Percival Rathbone, pouring millions of hidden dollars into a secret campaign to build a doomsday bomb. But worse yet, they had approved the murders of members of the Hausenhofer Gesselschaft, who might have helped rival nations make their own etheric weapons.

When it was her turn to testify later that day, the former minister of war took her place before the committee. Even though Mabel Patterson faced long imprisonment in the Frozen Falls Women's Correctional Institute, the haughty politician with the bulldog face sat there stolidly. She offered no information, answering most of the questions by saying, "That topic is classified because of national security."

During a brief break in her testimony, the other photographers grabbed the chance to stand up and stretch their legs. Only Johnny remained seated cross-legged on the floor, his Zoom 4x5 in hand, ready to shoot.

Patterson didn't budge from her chair, waiting for the questioning to resume. She surveyed the standing photographers with an expression about as friendly as a rattlesnake's. Her hooded eyes suddenly moved down and locked on Johnny. A look of volcanic hatred erupted across her face as she recognized him. Her blubbery lips formed a distorted scowl. Her eyes widened. Her nostrils flared. Her brow furrowed.

But only for a few seconds.

Long enough.

In a single, smooth motion, Johnny lifted his camera, framed the shot, and pressed the shutter. The flashbulb dazzled the whole room.

Instantly Mabel Patterson's face shriveled up, like a deflated balloon.

For the next few days Johnny's picture of the furious ex-minister of war appeared on front pages around the world. No one else had gotten the shot.

THAT EVENING, at a bustling restaurant called Everton's Chophouse in downtown Capital City, Mr. Cargill explained what was probably going on behind the scenes in the new government. Johnny and the rest listened intently, nibbling at their dinners.

"The officials don't want to do any more than throw Scofield, Patterson, and Santangelo in jail. The new government figures the public is nervous enough, what with etheric bombs and zombies on the front pages. They want this whole incident to fade out of the news entirely. Did you notice that the questions weren't very probing today? And darned few new facts came out. That's their plan.

"But at the same time, it wouldn't surprise me if behind the scenes the folks at the Ministry of War are scrambling to figure out how many bombs Percy made. And how they can make 'em, too. Apparently, most of the scientists that Patterson and Scofield sent to help Percy died when the first bomb exploded."

Dame Honoria shuddered and Johnny felt sorry for her. Yet more victims of her little sweetums—now safely ensconced in a high-security prison cell in Zenith. Of course, she was a victim, too.

"So I bet you that Dinglemann and LaGrange are being pushed hard for everything they know," Mr. Cargill continued. "I mean, if there happened to be another war with the Old Dominion, the bomb would be useful to have."

"They'd even *think* about a third Border War?" exclaimed Uncle Louie. "That's just nuts!"

"Have any of those people actually seen what war is like?" asked Dame Honoria, shaking her head.

Their shocked reactions didn't surprise Johnny. After all, Uncle Louie had witnessed terrible things in the trenches in the Great War. And Dame Honoria had volunteered as a nursing assistant in a military hospital in Royalton during the worldwide conflict.

"At least the new PM," Mr. Cargill said, buttering his hot popover, "seems to have his head on straight. I've heard Mr. Sunderland has no desire to start another conflict with the Old Dominion." The chief took a bite and turned to Dame Honoria. "So, do you have any more ideas about your son's zombie thing? Do you think there might be more of 'em out there?"

She didn't even bother to look up from the lobster she was

picking at. "I wouldn't call what Percy's done a solution to the First Impossible Thing—bringing ghosts back to life. He's not really alive, nor is the body he's occupying. But it's more than ghosts could have hoped for. So, I think we're going to see more zombies very soon. *Lots* of them."

CHAPTER 53

FRIDAY, DECEMBER 6, 1935

ZENITH

JOHNNY WALKED into the crowded bar room, making his way through a haze of cigar smoke. Several people congratulated him on his great front-page shot of Mabel Patterson's fearsome scowl. "It was nothing," he mumbled modestly, "just doing my job." He hopped up on a bar stool and ordered a hamburger with cheese and mayonnaise, deep-fried string potatoes, and a mug of Henderson's Root Beer.

The Morning Edition Bar and Grille was the most popular place in town for newspaper people to gather. There you could see everybody from big-name columnists down to cub reporters. Kids weren't usually allowed in. But Carlton Cargill made sure his star photographer could come there for a sandwich and a root beer. Besides, other newsmen and newswomen about town were getting used to him. What seemed odd a few months ago—a twelve-and-a-half-year-old news lensman—didn't seem so odd anymore. Johnny liked that.

The bartender—a burly former printing press operator named

Buddy—plonked down a huge hamburger on the counter and drew a mug of Henderson's root beer with a big, foamy head. Johnny thanked him and slapped a dollar bill and some change onto the bar. He wolfed down a big bite, munched on a string fry, then took a gulp of root beer. He licked off the foam mustache that formed on his upper lip.

"Pardon me," said a vaguely familiar voice, "but aren't you Johnny Graphic?"

Johnny twisted around and saw a smirking face regarding him, someone from the Great East, though the accent sounded more like Royal Kingdom—haughty and snooty. He examined the short, thin man for a few seconds. The fellow wore a gray winter coat over a cream-colored summer suit.

Then it hit Johnny. The guy was Rotonesian. But something was wrong about him. Dark, cold, penetrating eyes. Rotonesians were warm, friendly people. At least the people Johnny met there had been. Not this guy. And he had on way too much cologne. And the voice—why did it sound so familiar?

"Who wants to know?" said Johnny, narrowing his eyes.

The Rotonesian doffed his plaid slouch cap. "Lately I go by the name of Prakoso."

"You have another name?"

The diminutive man nodded and squeezed himself between Johnny and the next stool. He leaned confidentially toward the boy. "I do."

The photographer began to feel suspicious about the game his unwelcome companion was playing. "Uhhh, what is it?"

Prakoso took a shelled peanut from the bowl on the bar, cracked it open, popped the two nuts into his mouth, chewed, and swallowed. "Johnny, you have no idea," he sighed, "how good they taste after all these years."

Johnny felt something cold and unsettling deep down inside him. "What's…your…other…name?"

The man chuckled ominously. "Ozzie."

Involuntarily, Johnny sucked in a quick breath of air. This was not good. Ozzie had been a ghost. Now he wasn't.

"Of course," the little man said, "we met only briefly on Gorton Island and Old Number One. Not much fun for either of us, what."

Johnny was dumbfounded. "You're a *zombie?*"

"We prefer to call ourselves the reliving. Not so many nasty connotations. None of this nonsense." He crossed his eyes, opened his mouth wide, and stuck his arms out straight ahead, miming a lumbering walk. "Apart from our earthy smell and the rotten skin tone, we're not all that different from the never-been-deads."

"Wha-wha-whadaya want?"

"I have a letter to deliver."

"Who to?"

"The powers that be, old chap. Prime minister, king, queen, president, grand poobah. Whatever it is you have here. It's very important that—"

"This palooka buggin' ya, sport?" Buddy the bartender had stopped directly in front of Ozzie and scowled down at him.

Johnny couldn't think of anything he wanted more than for Ozzie Eccleston to go away. But he had to find out what the zombie wanted. "It's okay, Buddy."

The bartender looked unconvinced, but walked away. Ozzie snorted. "As I was saying, this message is of existential importance to—"

"'Existential'?" Johnny squeaked.

"Means a question pertaining to one's very existence. Life or death. The wrong answer could, in fact, lead to the doom of hundreds of thousands of good citizens of the Plains Republic."

Yup, Johnny thought, *this is bad*. "What do you want me to do?"

And Ozzie told him.

"How about I meet you back here tomorrow," Johnny said. "Same time. I'll try to get an answer."

"Excellent, young sir. Now what would you think about buying your old friend Ozzie a hamburger sandwich?" He hopped nimbly up onto the stool next to the boy.

Johnny nodded, still dazed. "Um, okay. How do you like your burger? Medium? Well done? Rare?"

"Actually, raw. *Perfectly raw*."

IT WAS A CLEAR, COLD Sunday afternoon, two days later. A few minutes before the appointed hour, Johnny, five other living people, and a ghost gathered around the long meeting table in the board room of the *Zenith Clarion*.

At the head of the table sat Carlton Cargill, grumbling certain words that children weren't meant to hear or allowed to speak. The new Regional Director of Etheristics, Wilton Crider, sat next to him. Dame Honoria paced along the side of the table by the door. She wore a drab brown lady's suit and a peculiar woolen beret that looked like a stack of overcooked pancakes. Also at the table were Uncle Louie and Mel. Colonel MacFarlane leaned against the wall, arms crossed, looking very much on edge.

Johnny sat on the side of the table by the broad picture window that overlooked Zenith Bay, brooding. When would this nightmare ever end!

At exactly two o'clock, one of the newspaper's security guards ushered in the little Rotonesian, who reeked of cheap cologne. Ozzie almost walked right into Dame Honoria. Both juddered to a halt, a look of shocked recognition on their faces.

Dame Honoria spoke first—in a tone that could have frozen all the water in Zenith Bay. "Johnny tells us that you're in there somewhere, Ozzie."

A dark, frightening grin spread across the round Rotonesian face.

"Well," she continued, "you're going to have to prove it."

Ozzie bowed slightly from the waist. "Of course, ma'am. I'd expect nothing less."

"The voice sounds right, anyway," said Dame Honoria. She indicated a chair for Ozzie/Prakoso. She walked around the table and sat facing him.

"I shall ask you things that only my father's majordomo might know," she said. "Things too obscure for even the most meticulous briefing."

Ozzie crossed his arms and said, "Ask away, Mrs. Rathbone. Ask away."

"My father's favorite drink?"

"He was a claret man, your old dad. He had to have his Chateau Greysolon close at hand. The '97, of course."

Dame Honoria's eyes widened a bit, then squinted. "The name of the budgie I kept on Gorton Island?"

"MacTavish. A blue budgie. Miserable little blighter never missed a chance to bite me."

The zombie successfully answered several more of Dame Honoria's questions and she finally nodded to Crider and Mr. Cargill.

"Thank you, Mrs. Rathbone," Crider said. "Naturally, Mr. Eccleston, we have many things we'd like to ask you. But the first is simple: *What is it you want?*"

The zombie reached inside his jacket and pulled out a buff-colored envelope. He slid it across the empty table toward Crider. "A little message for your government."

Crider grabbed the envelope, ripped it open, extracted a sheet of paper, and began to read.

Johnny's heart dropped like a stone when he saw Crider's ruddy complexion turn a sickly white.

When Crider finished reading, he stared at Ozzie with a stunned expression. "Good heavens, man. You can't be serious."

The Rotonesian zombie grinned a shy little smile. "Oh, but we are, Mr. Crider. We are. *Deadly serious.*"

CHAPTER 54

TUESDAY, DECEMBER 10, 1935

ZENITH

JOHNNY WASN'T SUPPOSED TO tell anyone about the secret meeting in the boardroom of the *Zenith Clarion*. But he didn't think it was right that his best friend couldn't know about the terrible news. After all, Nina had risked her life, too, on their journey across the Greater Ocean. So he arranged to meet her after school at their favorite soda fountain. "A top-secret meeting," he had whispered in her ear.

He was on the Oakley Avenue streetcar in East Zenith when he noticed that the girl ghost Bao was tailing him. He spotted her a couple of times, flying along in the rain, a good hundred feet behind the streetcar. Lately, the ghost had been following him around the house a lot, looking weirdly moony when they made eye contact.

Dripping from the rain, Johnny stepped into Shep's Super Soda Shop—all glass and mirrors and stainless steel and colorful vinyl upholstery. For a moment no one bothered to look at the new arrival. But when some girls in the nearest booth noticed him, they almost shouted in unison, "It's Johnny Graphic!"

That unleashed a torrent of greetings: "Hey Johnny!" and "Hi Johnny!" and "Look who's here!" and "Where've you been?" But there were also a few catcalls and boos and one loud, rude raspberry. Not everyone was impressed with Johnny Graphic the Newspaper Big Shot.

A moment later, in came Nina Bain in her yellow rain slicker and yellow fisherman's hat.

Her entrance provoked fevered speculation. Johnny could hear joshing words about "boyfriend" and "girlfriend" and even the dreaded "First comes love, then comes marriage…"

Both blushing fiercely, they settled into the last booth in the back. The very skinny Shep magically appeared with a tray. He unloaded their regulars—a vanilla shake and La Concha hamburger for Johnny, and a Cozy Island hot dog and strawberry malt for Nina. "Both of 'em on the house, Johnny," said Shep. "Don't be a stranger now."

After they cleaned their plates and drained their glasses, Johnny leaned toward the center of the table. Nina leaned in, too, eager to learn the forbidden knowledge.

"We have to talk softly, Sparks," he said. "It'd be really bad if anyone overheard. And whatever I tell you has gotta be super, duper, *duper* secret. I mean, *you can tell no one*."

"Absolutely, not a peep." Nina's eyes were glittering with anticipation.

Johnny recounted everything that had happened at the top of the Clarion Tower. He had both elbows on the table, chin resting on his knuckles. He spoke intensely but very quietly. They were almost nose-to-nose. Johnny could hear other kids chattering about them. He hoped they didn't think he and Nina were whispering sweet nothings to each other.

"So Ozzie hands the letter to Crider. He reads it. Crider almost looks like he's going to…well…like…*barf.*"

"What was in the letter?" she asked with an impatient look.

"Do you know what an 'ultimatum' is?"

"*Of course I know.* A demand for something, backed up by a threat of some kind."

"Well, this ultimatum's a doozy."

"How so?"

Johnny leaned even closer toward her. "They want whole cities reserved for ghosts and for zombies. All the living get kicked out. First out of Zenith. Then Silver City, Molderdam, Tor Chan, Ville de Rivière, Royalton."

Nina gasped. "That's totally crazy!"

"No argument there, Sparks. Nutty as a holiday fruitcake."

"And what if the government doesn't agree?"

"If Zenith isn't emptied of every living human by the end of this year, they'll blow us all up with another etheric bomb."

When Nina gasped, kids in the nearby booths instantly looked their way. Johnny knew there were a lot of nosey parkers around, trying to overhear their conversation. He put an index finger to his lips, signaling to Nina that she should lower her voice.

"The end of the year is just a few weeks away," she whispered.

"Right again, Sparks."

"And even if the government agreed, where would everyone go?"

"I know it sounds impossible. There are over a million people in Zenith. That's a lot of folks to turn into refugees."

Nina knit her brows. "But I thought ghosts would have known by now that the bomb won't kill them absolutely dead. Why would they agree to go into it?"

"Because the ghosts in the second bomb were already in it when the first bomb exploded. They don't know what happened to all those other poor palookas when it was detonated."

"But I love Zenith," Nina groaned. "Everything about it. The lake, the parks, the libraries, the museums, the movie houses, the stores downtown. To have it blown up by maniacs and zombies—well, it's the most horrible thing imaginable."

Johnny almost felt guilty, telling her the terrible news. It wasn't easy being one of the very few people on earth who had actually seen the etheric bomb in action. And now they both had to carry around the awful secret of a second bomb.

"What do you think the government's going to do?" she asked with a note of desperation.

"Mr. Crider said he didn't know. But he made Mr. Cargill promise not to print anything until a decision was made, until he could give an official okay. If any of us blabs, we get tossed in the clink."

"Seriously?"

"You betcha, Sparks. *Seriously*. Even if you're just a kid."

"Then why are you telling me?"

"'Cause there's no one in the world I trust more than you. You won't go around blabbing it. And besides, like I said, you deserve to know."

She rewarded him with a wobbly grin.

"Anyway," he continued, "it just absolutely killed Mr. Cargill, not being able to break the biggest story in years. But he agreed. If news of this got out, there might be panic. Anarchy. A lot of people could get hurt."

"So what happens next?"

"If the prime minister decides to give in, I suppose they'll force an evacuation of Zenith."

"That's hard to imagine. Based on just a single letter? What if it's a trick?"

"We thought of that. That's why Mr. Cargill believes the new prime minister will probably decide to do nothing. Call Ozzie's bluff. If it is a bluff."

"He has a bad choice or a worse choice," observed Nina. "Maybe they could try to stop the bomb from getting here."

"Remember, Sparks, no one even knows what the thing looks like. Franklin Fforbes and the other two scientists never saw the actual bomb. Neither did Bao. Bigger or smaller than a bread box? It's anyone's guess. It might even be here already."

Nina's dark eyes widened. "Johnny, maybe we ought to get out of town!"

Johnny stared at his friend, surprised. "But what if we're the only ones with a chance to stop it, Sparks?"

Frowning miserably, Nina whispered, "I don't want to lose my family again."

"Me neither," Johnny sighed. The possibility that his parents might still be alive had been on his mind a lot lately. And this blasted bomb business was preventing any efforts to go searching for them. Johnny could never forgive Percy Rathbone for the huge mess he had made.

Johnny figured they looked awfully gloomy as they headed out of the soda shop. That didn't stop a giggling, scrawny girl—slouching in a booth by herself—from hollering, "Be sure to invite us to the wedding! *Ha-ha-ha!*"

Johnny was approaching the door when he heard the loud slap of a hand on skin. He pivoted around to see the scrawny girl looking this way and that, her cheek rapidly turning red. She angrily sputtered, "Who did that? Who did that?"

Out of the corner of his eye Johnny spotted Bao flying up through the ceiling—shaking her hand as if something had just hurt it.

He groaned. What was that all about? He needed to have a serious talk with that little girl ghost.

CHAPTER 55

IN THE DAYS FOLLOWING his conversation with Nina, Johnny felt almost as if the encounter with Ozzie the zombie had never actually happened. The idea that all of Zenith could get blown up into a giant mushroom cloud seemed bizarre. Ridiculous. Absurd.

Because wherever Johnny went, the city looked perfectly normal—no different than he had seen it in any other holiday season of his young life. People bustled about in their winter hats and gloves and overcoats, lugging shopping bags full of holiday gifts. On the street corners bell-ringers collected nickels and dimes for the poor. Jolly holiday music filled the air. Colorful decorations and lights hung on every downtown street lamp. Kids all over town looked almost giddy, longing for the presents that awaited them in a few short days. Even the adults were smiling.

But, of course, Ozzie *wasn't* just a figment of Johnny's imagination. He was as real as real could be. And if the odd-smelling little creature had told them the truth, a second etheric bomb could be here in Zenith *right now.*

For the first time since he'd finished school, Johnny wondered if maybe some secrets were too big for a twelve-and-a-half-year-old. He knew he wasn't the only one feeling the weight of this dreadful knowledge.

Nina, usually bright and upbeat, had become uncharacteristically glum. Everyone had figured out that she knew about the ultimatum. But like Johnny, they all trusted her to keep the secret.

Uncle Louie's big, square, happy face had gone gray and sad. He hadn't cracked a joke in ages.

Dame Honoria tried to look and sound cheerful, but couldn't quite pull it off. No matter what she did, her guilt about Percy was there for everyone to see. But still, she seemed relieved that her son was safely locked up in the bowels of the National Building.

Mel kept to her room, except when she joined them to eat. Danny had been in town between flights, but she wouldn't even go down to the Babbitt Aeroboat Port to see him. She just talked to him on the phone for a minute in a dull, flat voice, then dashed back upstairs to work on her equations. She was desperate to figure out what the bomb might look like and how it might be disarmed.

Johnny and Mel were also making plans for a winter trip to the Old Continent to hunt down the Contessa di Altamonta. She was the ghost painter who had made that mysterious drawing of their parents in captivity. Since Percy had clammed up utterly, the contessa's knowledge was vital to shedding some light on what happened during that fateful expedition on Okkatek Island.

For her part, Bao had confessed to Johnny that she had been eavesdropping on him and Nina at the malt shop. She had hovered right behind him during the entire top-secret conversation. And she had slapped the girl who wanted to come to Johnny's "wedding."

The only good laugh Johnny had had lately was when Bao had asked him a very solemn question. "Johnny, you aren't really getting married, are you?"

The girl in the malt shop was just making a bad joke, he explained. Heckfire, he was only twelve and a half. Besides, who would want to marry him? Then the thought occurred that maybe centuries ago, in Bao's tribe, twelve-and-a-half-year-olds actually did get married. Now that was *really* scary.

Johnny made the little ghost promise to never spy on him again, adding that "Being dead is no excuse for being rude." Bao nodded earnestly and swore that she was a good girl, she really was. Then she started to cry—a quiet, tearless sob—which made Johnny feel like a mean old bully.

Later, he asked Mel about Bao's strange behavior. His sister rolled her eyes. "You big dope," she laughed. "She has a huge crush on you."

JOHNNY TRAMPED UP Birchwood's long driveway in the chilly drizzle, after an assignment at city hall. In his head he went over what he needed to say to everyone. Normally, he wouldn't feel comfortable ordering around Uncle Louie or Dame Honoria or even Mel. But these sure weren't normal times. He had to do something—even if it proved to be in vain. Let no one ever say that John Joshua Graphic would allow his favorite place in the world to get blown up without a good fight.

He went up the front stairs and stepped inside the big brick house—vigorously wiping his soaked shoes, setting down his camera pack, and throwing off his wet raincoat and hat.

"Hello, Master Johnny," said Mrs. Lundgren, from the front hallway.

Too preoccupied to even say hello, Johnny asked, "Is everyone home?"

"Yes, indeed," the ghost housekeeper said. "Even Dame Honoria and Sir Chauncey."

Within five minutes Johnny had gathered family and friends around the kitchen table. Mel looked irritated at being dragged away from her research.

"What's up, sport?" Uncle Louie asked.

"Yeah, Johnny, where's the fire?" Nina added.

Dame Honoria was sphinx-like, revealing none of her thoughts. Colonel MacFarlane stood by the refrigerator, at ease.

"After I dropped off my film of the mayor's press conference, I had a word with Mr. Cargill," explained Johnny.

"About the bomb threat?" Mel said.

He nodded.

"Any good news?" asked Nina, sounding hopeful.

He shook his head. "Mr. Cargill can't even get Mr. Crider to return his calls. Miss Beale says none of her sources in Capital City shows any sign of even knowing about the ultimatum. It's clear everyone's being kept in the dark, or otherwise we'd be hearing rumblings about something big coming down the pike.

"Mr. Cargill thinks that if the government was gonna do anything, they'd have done it by now. He thinks they plan to call Ozzie's bluff. They won't evacuate Zenith. It's like they're daring Percy's gang to set off the bomb!"

The minute he said "Percy's gang," Johnny regretted it. Not that it wasn't true, the way he referred to Percy Rathbone. He was the boss of a gang of criminals, terrorists. But he knew how it hurt Dame Honoria. She gave a little shudder when he spoke that phrase.

Everyone around the table looked helpless.

"As you know," Dame Honoria said, her gaze downcast, "I have visited with Percy several times, down in the prison cells of the National Building. He remains stubbornly uncommunicative."

"Did you mention Ozzie's ultimatum?" Johnny asked.

"Yes. I told him about the demand for a ghost-only city. At that, Percy smiled and nodded, as if he thought it a capital idea. Then I added that unless the city was evacuated by the end of the year, an etheric bomb would be detonated and Zenith wiped off the face of the earth."

Dame Honoria paused for a moment and looked Johnny right in the eye.

"A curious thing, though. While he seemed pleased about the ultimatum, he was genuinely surprised when I mentioned that Zenith is the target. It's almost as if he had previous knowledge of the plan, but not that it would be carried out here."

"Maybe the plan changed, once he was captured," said Johnny.

"That was my thought, too," said Dame Honoria. "I wonder if, by bringing Percy here, we unwittingly provoked his followers to bring the bomb to Zenith, as well."

Johnny was thinking the same exact thing and now he had to push hard for some action.

"Then we have to find the bomb and destroy it," he said grimly. "Before it destroys us."

Mel shook her head. "I wish we could, Johnny. But it would make looking for a needle in a haystack seem like child's play. The city's way too big; they could hide the bomb anywhere. We don't even know what it looks like."

Johnny slammed his hand on the table, rattling cups and saucers. "*But we have to try!* If Mom and Pop are alive, I don't want them coming back here to find us dead and Zenith a smoking wasteland."

"What do we do then?" asked Nina.

"It's a long shot, maybe, but I have an idea," Johnny responded.

"Okay, John," said Uncle Louie. "Shoot."

"We have the colonel and the Zenith Brigade on our side," he said. "What we've gotta do is send them out to recruit as many other ghosts as possible and then hunt through every house, every office, every factory, every building in Zenith. They can go anywhere. Nothing can stop them. We get a big map of the city and coordinate the search from here. We don't tell the other ghosts about the bomb itself. Word could get out and start a panic among the living. But we direct them to hunt for Steppe Warriors or other suspicious ghosts. Seek out weird devices that have been hidden away."

Everyone else at the table suddenly looked deep in thought.

Then Uncle Louie said, "I like it. It's worth a shot."

"We have to do something," said Nina.

"I agree with Nina," Dame Honoria pronounced. "We have to make an effort."

Mel didn't seem convinced, but she twisted around and looked at Colonel MacFarlane. She simply said, "Colonel?"

Johnny stared eagerly at the Border War cavalryman, knowing full well that he was the key to the whole enterprise. If he didn't think it would work, it would never happen.

The ghost officer drew himself up a little taller as a slight grin showed itself among his whiskers. To Johnny he looked almost alive again.

"When would you like us to start, Commander?"

CHAPTER 56

WEDNESDAY, DECEMBER 18, 1935

ZENITH

WHILE COMMANDER GRAPHIC, Dame Honoria, and Johnny mapped out the bomb hunt, the colonel, Finn, and Clegg recruited ghostly searchers. The number of wraiths who volunteered surprised the colonel. More than ninety came just from the ghost ghetto out at Mount Pleasant Cemetery. Given the chance to do something useful—though not told exactly why—hundreds of ghosts eagerly pitched in.

One such willing recruit, called Sakima, was a native of the region, having lived and died there centuries before the white men came. The colonel figured that Sakima would have an eagle eye for spotting dodgy types such as Steppe Warriors. Unfortunately, when it came to looking for the bomb, the dead native seemed quite bewildered. Asked to alert the colonel if he found any suspicious metallic objects, Sakima led the horse soldier first to a typewriter, then to a sewing machine, and finally to a waffle iron.

The colonel found an eager troop of recruits up on the dusty, unused top floor of a bicycle factory. A dead teacher named Mrs.

Hokkanen held class there every day of the week for a clutch of ghost children. Mrs. Hokkanen enthusiastically took up the colonel's assignment as an opportunity to instruct the dead youngsters about technology and science—by leading daily field trips in search of "peculiar devices and machinery."

Perhaps the most enthusiastic and well-qualified searcher was none other than Franklin Fforbes. No one had thought to tell the young ghost about the planned citywide hunt until the colonel ran into him in the garage behind Birchwood.

In the end, all manner of ghosts answered the colonel's call— from longshoremen and lumberjacks to nuns and nurses.

ONCE ALL THE PLANS were laid out, the colonel spent twenty-four hours a day riding slowly through every part of the Bowery, his assigned territory. Through basements and boiler rooms. Garages and warehouses. Filthy old tunnels full of pipes for steam, electric power cables, and water, with mobs of rats scurrying about. He asked every wraith he came across the same questions: "Seen any strange new ghosts about? Any peculiar machinery? Anything at all odd?"

Not one of the scores of ghosts whom the colonel talked to knew anything about suspicious new spooks. Nor bizarre technology that might signify a plot. Some lacked any interest whatsoever, muttering answers such as, "Nah, don't know nothin'" or "What's it matter, we're all dead anyway." But more than a few wraiths were curious.

A drowning victim from the end of the last century—still dripping ghostly lake water and draped with aquatic weeds— seemed particularly interested. To her bosom she clasped the specter of a baby, who cried softly but incessantly.

"Why do you want to know, sir?" she asked eagerly. "Is there some danger to the living?"

The colonel knew he couldn't say too much. "Very possibly, ma'am. Any clues or inklings could end up saving lives."

"What is the danger, exactly?"

"I cannot say, ma'am. But it'd be a very bad thing, were it to occur. I think you'll agree that we ought to look after the living as best we can. Something you've seen or heard could make a difference."

"Well, sir, I certainly'll try—" She blinked at him expectantly.

"Oh, sorry, ma'am. Rude of me." He doffed his campaign cap. "They call me Colonel MacFarlane. If you notice anything, you'll find me down at the great equestrian statue by the aerial bridge. Every day at noon and midnight. Tell your friends, as well. Umm, your name?"

"Mrs. Ruth Johnson. Went down with the wreck of the *Peacemaker*. November, 1893."

"The little one. It's yours?"

She shook her head. "It's a he and his name is Oscar. Died of scarlet fever, poor dear. I found him in the house where he passed, just up the hill here in Zenith. Crying like he is now. On and off, day and night. The new lady of the house could hear him, and he made her life there a misery. She asked me if I'd take the little fellow. That was thirty years ago."

"Why does he keep crying?"

"It's a terrible thing, being the specter of a six-month-old."

"What do you mean, Mrs. Johnson?"

"He doesn't understand what's happened to him. And he wants something I can't give him, something no one can give him."

"What's that?"

"He wants his mama."

CHAPTER 57

MONDAY, DECEMBER 23, 1935

ZENITH

EVERY MORNING throughout the holidays Johnny pulled himself out of bed at six, threw on his clothes, and trotted down to the mailbox at the end of the driveway. He'd yank out the morning's *Clarion* and scan the front pages for news related to the ultimatum and the etheric bomb. But there was never even a hint that anything was going on.

Just ordinary bad news. An earthquake here. A hurricane there. Workers' strikes at the railroads. Little wars in little countries he'd never even heard of. Nothing *really* important.

Today, however, he spotted a small story about a special training event the Army was conducting at the military base north of Zenith. That's an odd deal, he thought. The Army wouldn't normally call up reserve soldiers right in the middle of the holidays. He wondered if it had anything to do with the bomb ultimatum. Of course, he had no way of finding out.

Whatever the Army was up to, Johnny doubted that it could help. What could a few hundred soldiers do, if the etheric explosive went off?

For that matter, what were the odds that the colonel's ghost searchers would ever find the bomb, given that there were millions of places to look?

Johnny was beginning to give up hope. It seemed dreadfully possible now that this would all end very badly.

Kaboom!

No more Zenith.

No more Uncle Louie.

No more Mel.

No more Nina.

No more Johnny Graphic.

All gone.

"IT'S MAKING ME *CRAZY*," Johnny grumbled. "The waiting. The not-knowing."

It was right after breakfast. Bundled up against the cold, he and Nina rocked to and fro on the porch swing in back. It was almost freezing and their breaths made little geysers of white mist.

"Me too," she said.

They swung silently for a few moments, staring out at the broad back lawn with its border of birches and pines. The trees looked ragged and sodden and hopeless. Much like Johnny felt.

"So you actually saw Ozzie again, huh?"

Johnny sighed and nodded. "He was at the Morning Edition on Friday. Walked right up and sat down next to me at the bar, yakking like we were old pals. Told me how much he enjoyed the moving picture shows and nightclubs around town. Then he hit me up for another hamburger."

Nina looked amazed. "Did you buy him one?"

"Well, sure," said Johnny. "I didn't want to make him mad."

"I guess that makes sense."

"In a weird way, I was kind of happy to see him. I figure he wouldn't be hanging around if he knew the bomb was about to go off. Because now that Ozzie's in a real body—even if it's a dead one—he'd get blown to bits just like the rest of us."

"Does he still smell funny?"

"Yeah, he does. Not real bad. Kind of mildewy. The only time it got smelly was when he burped."

Nina stifled a quick giggle.

They rocked a bit more until she broke the silence.

"Any more news about your trip to the Old Continent?"

"Yeah," he said. "We're leaving in mid-January. That is, if we're still alive. Mel's got the aeroboat tickets and she's set up an itinerary. We go from here to Neuport to Royalton to the Confederazione di Ducati. Hopefully we'll track down the Contessa and find out about that drawing of our folks."

After a momentary silence, Nina asked, "So, are you nervous about getting your award from Mr. Cargill on New Year's Eve?"

Johnny had almost forgotten about that. It had been announced in the *Clarion* last week that he and Mel would receive Newshawk Awards at the paper's New Year's Ball. Because of the importance of their stories, they were being named the *Clarion*'s reporter and photographer of the year.

Dame Honoria had hauled him, Nina, and Mel downtown to Mahl's Department Store to get outfits for the big evening—a tuxedo for Johnny and gowns for the girls. Dame Honoria even had her necklace with the big black diamond, the Star of Gilbeyshire, cleaned. She wanted it to sparkle perfectly for the New Year's celebration. Danny Kailolu was flying in just to take Mel to the ball—something that had finally improved her mood.

The idea of a New Year's ball and a newspaper award seemed

kind of frivolous, considering what was going on behind the scenes. Still, Johnny knew there was nothing he could do that wasn't already being handled by the colonel and his ghost searchers. He might as well go to the ball and pretend that everything was okay, everything was normal.

"Yeah," he finally answered darkly. "I guess I do feel nervous. But not about getting the award."

CHRISTMAS MORNING came and went. Gifts were given and received—including the jewelry that Dame Honoria had secretly bought the day they'd gone to Mahl's Department Store. Silver cufflinks for Johnny to wear with his tuxedo. A pearl necklace for Mel. Nina received a heart-shaped gold locket, containing an old photo of her mother and father that Uncle Louie had found.

Nina also got a handmade bamboo fly-fishing rod. Mel received three scientific biographies that she'd wanted. And Johnny found a new Ritterflex camera under the tree. The amazing twin-lens reflex would allow him to take twelve shots without reloading.

But the smiles were forced, the *thank you*'s somehow muted, the hugs especially clingy and intense. Instead of festiveness, this holiday season was draped with sadness and a longing for more carefree days.

Over the following week, life in the big brick house proceeded typically enough, but under a dark cloud of gloom.

Uncle Louie went back to work at the aeroboat port. His stature as a mechanic had risen considerably, now that his co-workers had read all about all those hair-raising adventures he had flying across the Greater Ocean.

Nina, having caught up on her schoolwork, spent hours at the Central Public Library, doing research for the historical novel she planned to write. Sir Chauncey himself—through Dame Honoria—had promised to help her plot it.

Johnny urged Mel to get in touch with Megatherian Studios in La Concha, to see about reviving the etheric film project. Even though they had earned a good amount for their photos and stories, they needed more money to pay for Birchwood's mortgage and upkeep. Mel's movie research was the best chance they had of making big bucks. In the meantime, she had started to go out again to help people with their ghost problems.

Dame Honoria wore several red pencils down to nubbins, editing the manuscript of *Beatrice Periwinkle*, with Sir Chauncey and the ever-present Bao at her side.

For his part, Johnny roamed around Zenith with various *Clarion* reporters, shooting press conferences and traffic accidents and holiday events. After his brief fame earlier in the autumn, it seemed now that no one much noticed him. Which was fine. He was in no mood for the jolly bantering that went on this time of year.

At home, no one said another word about fleeing Zenith before the New Year's deadline. It was as if they all felt accountable for the city being the target of the reprehensible plot. And they had to see it out, for better or worse.

Of course, Johnny and the others stopped regularly in the spare bedroom, where a four-by-six-foot city map covered a folding banquet table. Neighborhood by neighborhood, Dame Honoria and Mel crossed off one block after another, as the colonel, Finn, and Clegg came back with their reports.

But apart from Johnny's sighting of Ozzie, there was no sign of any more zombies or unusual ghosts. No sign of a weird contraption that could be an etheric bomb. And the deadline for the ultimatum that Ozzie had delivered was ticking ever closer, minute by minute.

But the work done by the colonel and his ghost volunteers did result in one positive outcome—actually, several positive outcomes.

The Zenith Police Department had received a flurry of mysterious, anonymous tips about the locations of hideouts belonging to criminal gangs, drug dealers, and moonshiners. A kidnapped businessman was found and rescued. A counterfeiting ring was busted up. The loot from a big bank robbery turned up in the attic of an ex-convict. No one ever took credit or claimed the rewards for these tips. Every newspaper in town speculated about them. *Who were the secret crime fighters?*

Johnny, of course, knew.

But he would never tell.

CHAPTER 58

THE BALLROOM'S DOUBLE DOORS swung open promptly at seven and the New Year's Eve revelers poured in. The men were all attired in black tuxedoes or tailcoats. The women created a veritable rainbow with their elegant gowns of many colors.

Dame Honoria and Bao led the Graphic party in, followed by Uncle Louie and his "gal pal," Flo Zuckerberg. Trailing behind came Nina and Johnny, with his camera backpack over his shoulder. Johnny believed that he always ought to have his camera at the ready, even if he was about to get blown up.

The circular ballroom of the Hotel Splendid was one of the grandest public spaces in all of Zenith. From the vaulted ceiling far above, a quartet of enormous bronze chandeliers threw golden light into every corner. Hanging among them were nets containing thousands of balloons, awaiting release at the midnight hour.

Normally Johnny would have enjoyed being in the midst of such opulence. But tonight he was just going through the motions.

He tried his darnedest to be polite as people congratulated him on his award, but his smile felt frozen and insincere.

The Graphic party sat at a table near the bandstand and were soon joined by Carlton Cargill and Mrs. Cargill—a little brown-haired woman in a dark blue dress. Johnny could hardly believe that this diminutive, quiet lady could make the chief eat all those vegetables.

Mrs. Throckmorton arrived a few moments later. The publisher of the Zenith *Clarion* was tall and thin, with a narrow, severe face and perfectly white, waved hair. Sitting down, she pronounced in a surprisingly deep voice, "So, Carlton, this is the famous Johnny Graphic."

Johnny was astonished. He'd never heard *anyone* call the boss anything but "Mr. Cargill" or "Chief."

"Indeed it is, Mrs. Throckmorton." Mr. Cargill beamed at Johnny. "The youngster who, with his sister Mel, doubled our circulation through October and November."

"And brought down a government, to boot," added the publisher with a smirk of satisfaction. "Finally we meet." She reached across the table and shook hands with Johnny. Mr. Cargill then introduced her to Uncle Louie, Nina, and Flo.

Turning to Dame Honoria, the newspaper publisher made her own introduction. "Dame Honoria, we met after your talk at the Zenith Women's Club last fall. Count me a great fan."

"Kind of you to say so," said the old suffragist.

Normally that type of compliment made Dame Honoria puff up a bit, but Johnny could see that she was putting on a brave front, just like the rest of them.

Mrs. Throckmorton peered at him. "And I suppose you have some of your spooks with you tonight."

Johnny nodded, pointing up at the nearest chandelier. "Colonel

MacFarlane's sitting up there with Sergeant Clegg."

"And the ghost that Dame Honoria found on the island? The little girl? Is she with us?"

"She sure is, Mrs. Throckmorton. Over there." Johnny pointed at the bandstand.

Standing right between two saxophone players, Bao looked both baffled and enchanted.

"And we have no further word on the difficult problem we all face?" asked Mrs. Throckmorton.

Dame Honoria shook her head. Johnny gloomily shook his, as well.

"Hey folks, we made it."

Everyone at the table looked up.

There stood Mel, wearing a grin as broad as Johnny had ever seen on her. Danny Kailolu had an arm around her shoulder and his smile was just as big as hers. She looked swell in her emerald green gown and fancy hairdo. And he looked terrifically sharp in his dress uniform. If anyone deserved a good time tonight, it was Mel. And she appeared determined to have one.

AT EIGHT O'CLOCK a gourmet meal was served by a regiment of waiters and waitresses in short white jackets. First came the appetizers—lobster cocktail, smoked salmon on tiny squares of toast, and caviar on rye crackers. Johnny knew that caviar—fish eggs—was an elegant, expensive treat. But boy, one taste was all he needed. He finished every drop of his cream of celery soup, though. Then came lamb chops with mint jelly, and boiled new potatoes with parsley. There was a butterhead-lettuce salad with his favorite dressing, Thousand Island. From the dessert trollley he picked a big piece of red devil cake with whipped cream and a cherry. By the time he pushed that final plate back, he felt absolutely stuffed.

Then the moment arrived for the presentation of the News-hawk Awards. And Johnny felt almost as nervous as if he were being pursued by a regiment of Steppe Warriors.

"Every New Year's Eve," Carlton Cargill boomed into the microphone up on the bandstand, "we honor the *Clarion* contributors who've done the most to advance journalism. This year's winners amazed the whole world and helped bring down a corrupt government. So, without further ado, I present the Zenith Clarion Newshawk Award for Reporting to Melanie Graphic."

Even though she'd known about the award for weeks, Mel had a bad case of the jitters. Neither she nor Johnny enjoyed public speaking. Nonetheless, she climbed up to Mr. Cargill's side and took the award, a miniature gold-plated typewriter.

The vast ballroom erupted in applause. Then a chant began: "Speech! Speech!" Mr. Cargill tugged the young etherist over to the microphone.

Mel straightened up her shoulders, set her jaw firmly, and narrowed her eyes with a look of steely determination.

"Evil things were afoot this past autumn, and the world had to know the truth. But what I did was only a small part of the effort. We were able to tell this story thanks to the courage of Mr. Cargill and Mrs. Throckmorton. We were able to fly halfway around the globe because of Zephyr Lines and our wonderful pilots, Danny Kailolu—"

When he saw Mel shoot a special smile right at Danny, Johnny grinned, too.

"—and my uncle, Louie Hofstedter. And I want to give special recognition to our radio operator, Miss Nina Bain."

Johnny reached over and slapped Danny on the shoulder. The pilot blushed and shrugged an "Aw shucks" sort of shrug. Uncle

Louie gave two thumbs up as Flo kissed him on the cheek. Then Johnny winked at Nina and offered her a crisp salute.

"But without Colonel Horace MacFarlane and the ghost troopers of the First Zenith Cavalry Brigade," Mel continued, "I would not be standing here and no one would know the true story. So, don't thank me, thank them."

As the applause faded, someone shouted, "You looked so good in your mustache, Miss Graphic. Where is it?"

Mel leaned toward the mic again. "In the trash can."

The crowd roared with laughter.

Mr. Cargill took back the microphone. "Now it's time to present the Newshawk Award for Photography to the young man who accompanied his sister on that dangerous expedition across the Greater Ocean. Johnny Graphic!"

Feeling his cheeks starting to burn, Johnny climbed up on the bandstand and accepted the little gold-plated press camera. Stepping up to the mic, he said the first thing that came into his head. "Holy maroley, everyone. Thanks!"

He started to turn away, when he thought of something else. He grabbed the microphone again.

"More than anything, I want to thank the chief, Mr. Cargill, for trusting a twelve-and-a-half-year-old to get the job done."

"*YE-OUCH!*" NINA YELPED.

"Sorry I stepped on you, Sparks," mumbled Johnny as he clumsily fox-trotted her backward across the oak parquet dance floor. "Told ya so. I got two left feet."

She managed a grin through her grimace. "That's okay. Who cares about a broken toe, anyway?"

Not wanting to be a total party pooper, Johnny danced with Nina one more time and then with Dame Honoria once. He thought it a shame that only a few partiers could see Mel waltz around the circular dance floor with Colonel MacFarlane. The rest gazed in wonderment at the slender, black-haired girl in an emerald-green gown dancing the waltz exquisitely—all alone.

Over the course of the evening the ballroom had gotten quite warm. Johnny and Uncle Louie took off their tux jackets. Dame Honoria slipped off the ivory-colored jacket that she wore over her burgundy gown, revealing the Star of Gilbeyshire, which glittered dazzlingly on her ample bosom. Again and again, people stopped by the table to admire the giant gem.

Johnny found he couldn't stop checking his pocket watch. The first minutes of the new year were close at hand—the deadline set out by Ozzie's ultimatum. Johnny surveyed the big ballroom, looking for signs of imminent doom. He had no idea what those signs might be, but he hoped he would recognize them when he saw them.

Finally, midnight was only seconds away. The music stopped. Two waiters brought a huge clock up onto the stage. Everyone rose to their feet. A moment later the bandleader and his pert blonde singer counted down the final seconds of 1935 in unison, as revelers twirled noisemakers and tooted plastic horns.

"Ten. Nine. Eight. Seven. Six. Five. Four. Three. Two. One."

The instant the second hand hit twelve, hundreds of voices screamed as one. "HAPPY NEW YEAR!"

The netting far above opened up and thousands of balloons began drifting down.

And nothing happened.

A slight, tiny, wonderful bit of relief crept through Johnny's entire body. They had made it to midnight and no humongous explosion.

Zenith was safe.

Ozzie's threat was just a big bunch of hot air. Nothing more. Johnny felt almost light-headed.

"Hey," he said turning to Uncle Louie and Nina, "we're still alive! How about that?"

CHAPTER 59

NEVER IN A THOUSAND YEARS did Bao think she would see such a magnificent sight as this vast, beautiful chamber, full of people in splendid, colorful gowns and tunics. She'd never heard any kind of music like this. Horns blared, pipes piped, drums pounded, and a woman sang words in a twittering birdsong.

Until just yesterday, Grandmother had said that Bao couldn't come. But the little girl ghost begged and begged and begged. She promised to be good and not misbehave the way she had at the malt shop. Grandmother had been very cross about that and required Bao to stay in the house until told otherwise.

Mel observed with a chuckle that Bao had been "grounded." Whatever that meant, Bao didn't think it was very funny. Still, she had behaved perfectly every minute of every day since Grandmother's scolding.

Now looking out into the great chamber, from the middle of the band, Bao thought that the dancing looked like glorious fun—even though she had no idea how to do it. She hoped that Johnny might ask her to dance and show her the steps. But she lost sight of him and the others.

She got her wish, though, when the ghost of a young man came up to her. Grinning and laughing, he stood two heads taller than her and wore a white suit of some kind.

"Miss," he said, "you look like you're not from around here. How'd you end up in Zenith?"

When Bao finished telling him her story, he shook his head in astonishment. "You are one well-travelled little spook, aren't you? Well, on behalf of the ghost community of Zenith, I want to welcome you with a dance around the floor. Will you honor me?"

Bao was delighted *and* mortified. "But I don't know how."

"Easy enough to learn. Let me take your hands."

He clasped her right hand in his left, and her left in his right.

Bao's eyes widened and she smiled shyly. And she could feel his hands, which meant that somehow the two of them had a connection.

"Now I'm the fellow, so I lead. You just watch my feet. I'll move them in a pattern to the beat of one-two-three, one-two-three. And you just do the same thing, but backward."

A few minutes later Bao and the young man—who said his name was Melvin—were waltzing around the circular dance floor. Bao stumbled a few times and got distracted when they danced right through the bodies of living people. But for a little mountain girl who'd never danced in her life or her death, she did reasonably well.

The mystery of their physical connection was solved as they danced. Melvin told how he had recently helped Colonel Mac-Farlane on the city-wide search for ghostly interlopers and strange technology. He and Bao were on the same side, both fighting for a good cause.

After saying goodbye to her new friend, Bao flew up to the great lamps hanging above the ballroom for a visit with the colonel. He noted that she might hurt her face, grinning so hard. Her only reply was a burbling giggle. She had never felt gladder that she had decided not to go into the bomb.

Finally, Bao ended up back among the horn and pipe players, just about the time the music stopped. The man who had been leading the musicians waited while a big, round timepiece was brought up on the platform. He said something and everyone in the giant chamber went silent.

Then he and the woman singer started to speak, both at the same time.

"Ten. Nine. Eight. Seven. Six. Five. Four. Three. Two. One."

Suddenly, hundreds of voices were screaming, "Happy New Year!"

From her perch on the bandstand, Bao could just barely see Grandmother sitting at a nearby table. The little ghost was eager to tell her about Melvin and how she had learned to dance the waltz.

Then Bao looked down from Grandmother's face and saw the gigantic black jewel that dangled from her neck.

Bao had seen it once before, on that terrible island.

In the hands of the khan.

She hadn't put two and two together until this very instant.

As gaily colored balloons began wafting down, Bao managed to scream, "The bomb! *It's the bomb!*"

Almost at the same instant something horrible rose up through the platform directly in front of her.

A Steppe Warrior! With bleeding, empty eye sockets!

CHAPTER 60

WEDNESDAY, JANUARY 1, 1936

ZENITH

"WHAT WAS THAT?" Johnny asked, peering at the bandstand—though it was hard to see anything in between all the falling balloons. He and the others were back at the table.

"Wha'd you say, Johnny?" asked Mel, smiling and swaying dreamily, with Danny's arm around her shoulder.

"Someone screamed, Sis. Sounded like Bao." Johnny yanked his Zoom 4x5 from the backpack and got a firm grip on the leather strap. Just in case. But then he thought better of it. He'd already wrecked one camera. Instead, he stood and grabbed one of the party chairs and folded it flat. It would make a clumsy weapon, but a decent shield.

That's when he saw _what_ Bao was screaming about.

"_Oh hell!_" Johnny swore.

Then it was Mel's turn to see the empty-eyed wraith treading toward them, right through the falling balloons. She gasped as if she were having a heart attack and wiggled away from Danny.

Out of nowhere, Bao came flying like a rocket at the Steppe

Warrior. But with a powerful slap of his hand he batted away the little girl ghost. Howling in pain, she skidded off beneath the bandstand.

Johnny gripped the folding chair tighter and walked around the table, heading for Burilgi. "Dame Honoria, Uncle Louie," he shouted over his shoulder. "Steppe Warrior!"

Uncle Louie's face suddenly registered furious comprehension. He picked up a chair, folded it, and got a good grip. "Now tell me where to swing this thing," he growled, and tramped after his nephew.

"What's going on?" sputtered Flo Zuckerberg.

"Just stay behind us, kiddo," Uncle Louie commanded, "and maybe we'll get through this alive."

All the people near Johnny's table were looking at him and Uncle Louie with notable anxiety—apprehension showing on their faces. Johnny knew it was futile to tell them to move to a safe distance. Because if things went badly in the next few moments, a safe distance was about fifty miles from Zenith.

Carlton Cargill took command in a way that only a big-time newspaper editor could do. "Ghost attack!" he bellowed. "Evacuate the ballroom!"

The festive first moments of 1936 quickly turned to unruly panic. Everyone was yelling and screaming.

People crushed toward the doors. Some were trampled and hurt and had to limp away. The blonde band singer kicked off her high heels, hoisted her gown, jumped down from the bandstand, and darted away like a football halfback.

Mel, Johnny, Dame Honoria, and Uncle Louie faced the Steppe Warrior—who had stopped about fifteen feet in front of them, knee-deep in balloons. Two other Steppe Warriors appeared at his side, arrows nocked in their bows.

Out of the corner of his eye Johnny saw Bao pop up beside Dame Honoria and nudge her on the shoulder. The old woman started to scold the little wraith. "Not now," she snapped as Bao floated up and jabbered desperately in her ear. Then Dame Honoria turned as white as a sheet.

"My heavens no!" she exclaimed, covering her giant jewel with her hand. She turned to Johnny, just to her right. "My diamond!" she whispered into his ear, her eyes wide with horror. *It is the bomb!"*

The realization hit Johnny like a truckload of bricks. They had been searching for weeks for the blasted thing and it had been right under their noses all the time. In fact, in the bedroom right across the hallway from his!

"What would you have us do, Burilgi?" growled the warrior on the right.

"Kill the boy and girl!" hissed the eyeless Steppe Warrior.

The bowmen pulled back their bowstrings and aimed their arrows. But before they could shoot, the colonel and Sergeant Clegg came down on them like falcons, striking the bows right out of their hands and slamming into them. Johnny thought he could actually hear bones breaking.

The colonel and sergeant backed away, sabers drawn, ready to charge again. But the two ghost assassins launched themselves first, howling, twirling their swords. Blades clanging, the four ghost soldiers battled off around the curve of the ballroom.

Johnny started to say something, but Mel cut him off. "They're never going to stop, Johnny," she said, her voice trembling. "They're never going to quit until they've blown themselves and us all to bits."

Turning to Burilgi, she cried, *"Don't you understand?* The bomb doesn't end your misery. It only smashes you into little pieces. You stay in the ether, with all the horrible pain and no control—worse than before."

"Lies," the specter bellowed. "LIES!"

"It's a waste of time to argue with him, Mel," shouted Johnny. "Percy has brainwashed this stupid spook and he won't be satisfied until he's destroyed all of us!"

CHAPTER 61

MEL IGNORED JOHNNY'S ENTREATY. "Please believe me," she begged the Steppe Warrior. "You've been deceived about the bomb. I'm telling you the truth."

The Steppe Warrior grinned his skeletal grin and shook his head. "I should trust you instead of the khan?"

He paused for a second, then snapped his left hand open. Something flew out of it, fluttering next to him.

Johnny squinted hard. It was a miniature, one-armed Steppe Warrior. Only a few inches long. He remembered her from the fight in the upstairs hallway.

Checheg.

He knew that ghosts could control their size, but he wasn't sure what good a dinky little ghost like her could do in a fight. Why would she be so small?

Then a dreadful thought occurred.

What if she was the trigger! What if she had shrunk down small enough to squeeze into the great diamond and set off the explosion!

As if to confirm that horrible intuition, Checheg made a bee-line straight at Dame Honoria and the Star of Gilbeyshire.

Bursting balloons under foot, Johnny bounded toward the tiny, flitting etheric figure.

The shrunken ghost of Checheg tried to dodge him. But too late.

Johnny swung his folding chair as hard as he could, as high as he could.

With a sickening *thunk*, he walloped the tiny wraith straight through the giant mural behind the bandstand.

Johnny's momentary triumph was interrupted by a screeching voice that sounded like his sister. "Johnny, look out!"

He twirled to see the eyeless Steppe Warrior charging at him, curved blade upraised.

Johnny hefted the folded chair out in front of himself just in time to receive Burilgi's first overhand strike.

The blow rattled Johnny right down to his toenails. Flakes of paint and chips of wood flew everywhere, and even his unetheristic friends shuddered to see the chair vibrating violently in thin air.

Johnny returned the favor by jamming the chair into the Steppe Warrior's face—again and again in rapid succession. The assault bashed Burilgi's nose flat and blocked his sword arm.

The empty-eyed specter backed away, intending another charge. What he didn't count on was an attack from his left.

It came suddenly, shockingly.

Bao flew at him wielding a weapon that she had found nearby—an abandoned tenor saxophone. Swinging it with the un-expected form of a home run hitter, she smashed it into his left knee with every drop of energy that her little body possessed.

Burilgi rounded on Bao as she flitted away, only to be hit a glancing blow on the top of his head by Johnny and his folding chair. The impact made the Steppe Warrior's leather helmet fly off his head.

Burilgi leapt high into the air and came down on the scurrying girl ghost. He kicked hard, connected with Bao's head, and sent her scudding away—struck senseless. Then the Steppe Warrior climbed like a monkey up toward the ceiling, and dived at Johnny, his blade extended.

Johnny saw Burilgi coming. He tried to lift the battered chair up over his head, but it slipped out of his grasp, breaking several balloons with loud pops as it hit the floor.

He heard Mel shriek, *"Above Johnny's head. Now!"*

Out of the corner of his eye Johnny saw Uncle Louie—a hammer thrower back in high school—grunt and heave one of the folding chairs. Johnny's only thought came in a flash: *Hope it doesn't break my skull.*

The piece of party furniture made for an ungainly missile. But Uncle Louie was so strong that it covered the distance in just two seconds, in a flat, neat trajectory.

It winged the Steppe Warrior's sword arm. Deflected him just enough to keep the blade from piercing Johnny's neck.

But not enough to prevent a nasty slice across Johnny's chest, cutting open his tuxedo, shirt, and undershirt, lightly skittering over his ribs.

Suddenly bloodied, he hollered in pain, frustration, and rage.

Kicking off her fancy shoes, Mel rushed forward to help him. Uncle Louie and Danny followed close behind. The two men tugged Johnny back toward the table. Meanwhile, Mel stopped to help a woman who was lying amid the balloons, holding her leg and sobbing dreadfully.

Sitting in the chair, dazed from the pain of his wound, Johnny watched as Dame Honoria—with a kind of steely calm—slipped her silk brocade jacket back on, then buttoned it up. She took Nina's hand with both her hands and whispered something in the girl's ear.

Nina looked up at Dame Honoria, then at Johnny—who was blinking back at her, his hands stained with blood from his chest wound. He was afraid Nina might start to cry, as she reached into her purse. Poor kid. She never deserved to get caught up in this mess.

Nina fussed around with her purse's contents, then withdrew a handkerchief, which she handed to him. As he muttered a shaky thank you and wiped his hands, he looked back in the direction of the bandstand and groaned.

Burilgi had somehow grabbed Mel and held her from behind—in a deadly embrace.

His dagger was pressed to her throat, where it drew a bead of blood.

CHAPTER 62

SEEING THE BLOOD on his sister's neck, Johnny thought about rushing to her rescue. But that adult voice in his head told him, *not so fast*. If he tried anything heroic, Mel could get badly hurt. Or worse.

"Dame Honoria, come over here!" Mel wailed, her features a picture of dread. "Please!"

"Of course, my dear," Dame Honoria answered. She turned her head sideways. "Come with me," Johnny heard her whisper to Nina, "but draw no attention to yourself."

The two walked slowly toward Mel and her captor, wending their way amid the debris.

Johnny, Danny, and Uncle Louie shuffled along behind them, utterly disheartened and exhausted. Flo Zuckerberg, for her part, looked as though she wanted to kill someone but didn't know whom or with what.

By this time the colonel and the sergeant had managed to dispense with their adversaries. They stood a dozen feet from Mel, helplessly eyeing the wicked blade held directly over her jugular vein.

As Dame Honoria and Nina came up within a few feet, Burilgi

hissed, "Give me the diamond, old woman. Now!"

Dame Honoria eyed the ghost and Mel.

"It was around my neck just a few minutes ago," she whimpered, sounding weak and beaten. "Now it's gone. Came off somehow. Clasp broken. Somewhere around here." She turned and swept a hand across a landscape of overturned tables, mangled chairs, and many, many balloons.

By now almost every other party-goer had escaped. At the far end of the ballroom, by the entrance doors, Carlton Cargill was trying to keep several police officers from barging in.

The Steppe Warrior betrayed no emotion. He seemed to be pondering Dame Honoria's revelation.

"Perhaps you've hidden it in your jacket, old woman," the ghost said in a tone as cold as ice. "Let us see what's inside your pockets."

Dame Honoria obligingly turned her pockets inside out, revealing no necklace. "And I suppose," she said with a sigh, "you'd like to see what I have in my handbag."

Looking every inch the defeated old crone, she unsnapped the top of her black sequined purse and held it open for viewing.

Burilgi seemed almost to be squinting, as he looked inside the bag. "Empty it."

Dame Honoria nodded and pulled item after item out of the handbag and threw them aside.

A small mirror. Several tissues. A compact. Reading glasses. Lipstick. A tiny bottle of Gorton's aspirin. Then she tipped the bag upside down, to prove there was nothing else inside it.

"The diamond must be somewhere around here," she said, scanning the floor nearby.

Suddenly Burilgi's head shifted slightly to the left and down. If he'd had eyes, they would have drilled holes right through Nina Bain. "You, girl," he pronounced with frightening intensity, "open your bag."

Dame Honoria flinched and Johnny suddenly realized what she must have done. She had to have given the diamond to Nina. And now the ghost had the girl in his crosshairs.

With a look of terrible sadness, Dame Honoria conveyed to Nina what the ghost wanted.

Nina's eyes opened wide and she gulped. "M-m-m-me?"

"Open it now," the ghost ordered, "or my dagger slices a little deeper."

Mel quaked uncontrollably, her face a deathly white—a terrible contrast to the very red blood trickling down her neck.

Dame Honoria repeated what Burilgi had said.

"*Please, Nina,*" sobbed Mel.

"There's nothing…in here…but my things," Nina said breathlessly.

"Tell the girl to show me," Burilgi growled. "*Empty the bag.*"

Johnny transmitted that order.

"Okay," squeaked Nina, unsnapping her purse.

Johnny shut his eyes for a few seconds. He couldn't stand to see what was about to happen. Then he thought the better of it. He had to watch the nightmare unfold.

Nina pulled open the top of her purse and removed its contents.

Out came a tiny vial of perfume. A tin of breath mints. A compact. A coin purse. Then a pair of gloves that matched the color of her dress.

"That's all I have," she said, looking defiant. "See?" Gulping, she walked up closer to Mel and the specter that she couldn't see. She spread the top of the purse wide open with both hands. The spook peered intently at the inside. Then she tipped and shook the thing again, to make her point. All that wafted out were a few flecks of lint.

Johnny was astonished. He was torn between relief that the diamond might be safe and dread that his sister might die.

But what had Nina done with the Star of Gilbeyshire?

Did she even have it in the first place?

And *where was it now?*

CHAPTER 63

WHEREVER THE BLACK DIAMOND might have gotten to, Johnny's most pressing concern now was how to save his sister's life. And, as his brain churned, he had to admit that he had only one idea. And not a very good idea, at that.

Johnny managed to make eye contact with Colonel MacFarlane—who looked as if he were about to explode with frustration. Because he couldn't think of anything else, Johnny made a fist with his right hand and punched it an inch or two forward. Which he hoped the colonel would interpret to mean "Attack!" The ghost soldier understood, but subtly shook his head. Just then a voice like a dull ax scraped over slate startled Johnny to attention.

"You have five minutes to find the jewel, or the girl dies," Burilgi announced, squeezing Mel even more tightly.

Dame Honoria nodded, wiped her profusely sweating brow, and repeated Burilgi's demand.

Johnny and Nina and the others began to sift through the debris that littered the ballroom floor near their table, when another voice cut through the gloom.

"No!" Mel yelled. "Stop! All of you!"

Startled, Johnny and the others pivoted around to stare at the captive young woman. What could she possibly be up to?

"What happens to me isn't important," Mel said. "You can't let this monster have the diamond!"

In response to her outburst, Burilgi growled and lightly flicked the edge of his dagger against another spot on her neck.

Mel winced in pain but didn't scream. She kept talking, though so quietly and delicately that Johnny had to strain to hear her. As if she were speaking only for the ears of the empty-eyed wraith.

"We etherists have tried for years and years to convince the living that ghosts shouldn't be feared, that ghosts were just like them—only dead. We've tried to give ghosts purpose and fulfillment. Something to make the emptiness tolerable.

"But in a few short weeks you and Percival Rathbone and your other ghostly thugs have frightened millions. Killed innocent people who loved and cared for ghosts. Condemned thousands of specters to a doom worse than anything they could have imagined. Now even more people hate ghosts, fear ghosts. The damage you've done will take years to mend."

The dagger seemed to move, and the thought flared in Johnny's brain: *Is this the fatal cut?*

But nothing more happened. His racing heartbeat slowed slightly.

"And your so-called khan?" Mel continued. "A fraud, a charlatan, a confidence trickster. Nothing he's told you is the truth. He's just a wretched, despicable human being. Well, former human being.

"And you threaten my city with utter destruction. *My city!* Well, go ahead and kill me and be damned, you miserable excuse for a ghost. But when you do, don't expect any mercy from my troopers here."

Colonel MacFarlane and Sergeant Clegg both nodded: *Order*

received and understood.

In the midst of all this, Johnny heard the bullhorn voice of Carlton Cargill from across the ballroom. He was arguing with the police chief. "Listen, O'Reilly, you all charge in there and you'll get that girl killed!"

The Steppe Warrior pulled himself taut. "A very pretty little speech. But unless I get that jewel, *you die in one minute.*"

At just that instant Mel's face changed utterly.

Her mouth opened in a gasp of surprise.

Her eyes widened.

A shudder resonated through her whole body—as if she were about to have a seizure.

Burilgi seemed taken aback and he loosened his grip on her.

Then the most remarkable and wonderful thing Johnny had ever seen in his entire life happened.

Two small, ghostly hands popped straight up out of Mel's chest.

They grabbed the Steppe Warrior's etheric dagger.

They yanked it out of his hand.

Then, bearing the blade, Bao shot up toward the ceiling like a rocket.

With a furious grunt, Mel twisted violently and slipped from the grasp of a startled Burilgi. She part-danced, part-staggered away, screaming, "*Get him, get him!*"

Both the colonel and Clegg came at Burilgi with flurries of powerful roundhouse punches. The Steppe Warrior hadn't even the time to draw his sword.

Clegg pummeled Burilgi about the head and shoulders, and buried a nasty left hook into the Steppe Warrior's mid-section again and again. The colonel attacked his kidneys from the back.

Johnny had seen boxing matches and fights at school, but nothing nearly this brutal. The two dead cavalrymen were burning with rage.

All that the eyeless assassin could do was to fend off the blows and, finally, try to plunge through the ballroom floor. He nearly made his escape.

But the colonel—whose lightning quick reflexes hadn't been dulled by all those decades in the ether—managed to grab a fistful of Burilgi's pigtail. He held on with fierce tenacity, preventing the Steppe Warrior from slipping deeper into the floorboards. Then he yanked powerfully on the pigtail, ripping out a handful of hair by the roots.

Burilgi vanished.

"Clegg, after him!" bellowed the colonel.

Clegg dived down through the oak, as the colonel rushed to Mel's side, still gripping his grisly trophy.

Though his chest hurt like heckfire, Johnny wanted to jump up in the air, hug the colonel, and shout *hurray*. For the moment, they had defeated Percy's minions.

CHAPTER 64

"BUT WHERE'S THE DIAMOND?" cried Mel, after receiving hugs from Dame Honoria and Uncle Louie. "This is all pointless if we don't find the Star of Gilbeyshire! Zenith could still get blown up!"

Johnny was thinking the exact same thing. He looked anxiously from Mel to Dame Honoria to Nina. Where was the gem?

Dame Honoria turned to Nina, a look of profound worry on her face. "My dear," she asked breathlessly, "what did you do with it?"

Nina looked around warily. "Are the Steppe Warriors gone?"

"For the time being, I should think so," Dame Honoria answered. "Now Nina, where did you put the diamond?"

"It's in here." Nina held up her purse and snapped it open for Dame Honoria to examine.

The old lady shook her head. "But there's nothing there. Nothing at all, except—"

"Except a zipper," said Nina with a self-satisfied smile. "I showed him the inside of my purse, but I was guessing that the Steppe Warrior had never seen a zipper before."

With that, she unzipped the small side pocket inside the purse.

She withdrew the Star of Gilbeyshire, resplendent and glittering in its titanium setting.

"Oh, Nina!" exclaimed Dame Honoria, picking the girl up in a tremendous hug. "*You are a genius!*" Then her face went somber. "But..."

Johnny's smile faded quickly at Dame Honoria's use of that certain conjunction. "Yes, but *what?*"

"But we now have in our possession what is surely the deadliest weapon in existence," Dame Honoria said. "And we have to decide what to do with it."

"Even though the new government is a big improvement, I'm not sure I'd trust them with an etheric bomb," said Mel, dabbing at the cut on her throat with a napkin.

"Precisely," Dame Honoria agreed. "That's why we have to destroy it. Immediately. Irrevocably."

"But how?" Johnny asked. "It's a diamond. Hardest substance on earth."

"Hard but brittle, John," observed Uncle Louie. "Not indestructible."

"But what happens to all the ghosts inside it?" asked Nina. She held up the necklace and tried to see inside the big black stone. "Can we free them?"

"I think I have an answer to all that," said Mel, "now that we know the dimensions, the approximate weight, and the atomic structure of the bomb. Dame Honoria, what I'm thinking is—"

Mel huddled with the old lady. They started talking in terms so technical and abstruse that Johnny had no idea what they were saying. There were various noddings and shakings of heads. Several equations and formulae were scrawled on paper napkins picked up off the floor.

In the middle of all that technical chitchat, Johnny grabbed a couple of quick shots of the devastated ballroom. Injuries or not, he still had a job to do. Mr. Cargill would expect some pictures.

Mel and Dame Honoria soon reached a consensus. And they would have to move quickly. They'd need to rely on Mr. Cargill and Mrs. Throckmorton to spring them from the anticipated attentions of the police. They'd require a quick visit to the hospital, to take care of Johnny's new wound and check out Mel's neck.

Then a thought popped into Johnny's head: where had Bao gotten to? He looked around the disordered ballroom and there she stood, up on the bandstand, peering pensively from behind the overturned bass fiddle.

Johnny shuffled over through the balloons, right up to the edge of the bandstand platform. "Bao, what's the matter?"

The little girl ghost frowned and tiptoed slowly over to him. Her chin trembled and she had that about-to-cry look—never mind that she couldn't. She held up her right palm and whimpered, "I cut my hand."

There was a nasty gash at the base of her index and middle fingers, where the dagger had cut her. Even though the wound didn't bleed, a ghost being a ghost, it had to hurt something awful. Johnny wondered if there was any way to give her stitches. Mel or Dame Honoria might know.

Johnny surprised Bao and himself by reaching up, grabbing her by her tiny waist, and lifting her down from the bandstand. He'd never tried to hold up a ghost before and she was surprisingly light—though solid enough to feel real. He set her down on the dance floor and gave her a quick embrace. So what if she had a crush on him.

"You were fantastic, you know," he said. "Amazing. How did you think up that move?"

Now she was smiling again, beaming, staring intently up at

him. "I couldn't let him hurt Mel. I was the only one small enough to go up through her body without being seen. Except for cutting my hand, it was easy."

Johnny beamed back. "Bao, you're the bravest little girl I've ever met. Now I think there are some folks over there who'd like to thank you."

CHAPTER 65

THE LONG, BLACK Kaiser Coronation limousine sat for several minutes just inside the entrance to the vast Acme Iron Works in West Zenith. It was the middle of the night, but angry red light erupted occasionally from the black, hulking structures spread across the landscape. The sounds of mechanical rumblings and metallic percussions were all around. Johnny could almost feel the vibrations in his bones.

Everyone had jammed into the passenger compartment. Johnny was squeezed in with Mel, Nina, and Flo in the backward-facing seat. Dame Honoria sat with Mr. Cargill, Uncle Louie, and Mrs. Throckmorton in the forward-facing seat, also mashed tightly together. Danny sat up front with the chauffeur.

Johnny could see Colonel MacFarlane up on Buck, just between the limousine and the steel mill's guard shack—with Bao in the saddle in front of him. She was jabbering away, just as any kid might have done after such an exciting evening.

There came a rap of knuckles on glass and everyone turned to see a young, stoutly built man, clad in a red-and-black wool jacket over denim work overalls. A hard tin hat rested atop his head.

Uncle Louie rolled down the window.

"We have an okay from the president of the company," announced the young man, still looking baffled by his late-night encounter with a limousine full of bedraggled New Year's Eve revelers. "He said anything Mrs. Throckmorton should need, we ought to help with."

It didn't surprise Johnny that Mrs. Throckmorton was on Acme's board of directors. As the owner of the *Clarion* newspaper, she had to know all the big wheels in Zenith's business circles. And it sure came in handy tonight. No other factory in town had a super industrial steel press. It helped, too, that it only took a call from Mrs. Throckmorton to the mayor to get them out of the police station.

"Our night superintendent'll be joining us at Shed Number 3," the young man said. "Now if you'll just have your driver follow my truck."

SHED NUMBER 3 was as big as two football fields and lay dormant during the night shift. Circles of light came down from fixtures far above. The massive pieces of machinery looked like slumbering iron giants. Being there gave Johnny the idea of suggesting a photographic essay on those magnificent machines, for the *Clarion*'s Sunday rotogravure picture magazine. He could have a lot of fun shooting in there.

The stout young worker introduced himself as Gus Gunderson, but said everyone called him Gizmo. He was the night mechanic and explained what some of the machinery did. Johnny had never seen anyone with so many tools hanging from his tool belt.

After a few minutes, the night superintendent arrived. He was a trim, middle-aged man with a pencil mustache and wire-rim spectacles. He had on a heavy brown canvas jacket and a silver-colored hard hat. He told Mrs. Throckmorton that he was always glad to help a member of Acme's board of directors.

"It's my understanding," Mrs. Throckmorton said, "that you have a large mechanical press in here that can squash iron flat."

"We do," he said. "We call it the Super Stamper. But first, would you folks mind putting on these tin caps? Safety first, you know." The superintendent pointed to a rack of hard hats just inside the door.

Johnny almost laughed. If the superintendent knew how spectacularly dangerous his late-night visitors' cargo was—and how trifling the notion of a tin hat was in the face of the etheric bomb—he'd probably have a stroke.

"Now if you would tell me what you need, Mrs. Throckmorton," said the superintendent, after everybody donned their metal hats.

The white-haired millionaire didn't answer, but Dame Honoria did. "We need to demolish a certain small object beyond any hope of repair. To dust, if possible. Nina, show the gentleman our problem."

Nina snapped open her purse and withdrew the Star of Gilbeyshire, holding it up at arm's length for the superintendent to see.

He stared at the big black stone, dazzled *and* flummoxed. "Ma'am," he said slowly, "my Super Stamper'll certainly pulverize even a diamond. But why would you want to? That gem has gotta be worth tens of thousands of dollars."

"Half a million pounds, actually," sighed Dame Honoria.

The superintendent whistled. "But why destroy it?"

"We can't tell you that," Mel said.

"In fact," said Mrs. Throckmorton in the iciest tone possible, "*we were never here.* If you or Mr. Gunderson or your security guard at the front gate should speak so much as one word about our visit, you will all be out of a job. Do you understand?"

The superintendent did indeed seem to understand and nodded vigorously, as did Gizmo Gunderson.

That was the moment when Johnny saw something tiny and fluttery and semi-transparent fly out of the left pocket of Uncle Louie's overcoat.

Before anyone could react, the diminutive specter darted toward the black diamond in Nina's hand, shrinking as it went.

Johnny screamed, "Nina, hold it tight!"

He closed the space between himself and his friend in two leaping strides, just as the little ghost's single arm began to merge into the black diamond.

It was Checheg! Again!

Nina did just what Johnny told her to, grasping the necklace's titanium chain forcefully with both hands.

Johnny caught the little wraith by the legs, with his right thumb and forefinger, and pulled backward with both hands, with all his might, beginning a terrible tug of war with Nina.

The power that was sucking the ghost into the diamond shocked Johnny. The gem was starting to glow and turn a livid shade of green.

Johnny didn't know if he could stop it from exploding!

CHAPTER 66

THE TINY GHOST'S HEAD and shoulders had disappeared almost entirely into the green-tinged black diamond, when Dame Honoria rushed up behind Johnny. She took him in a bear hug, tugging him backward. A random thought flew through Johnny's head: *She's surprisingly strong for an old lady.*

For her part, Mel grabbed Nina by the waist to help her pull against Johnny and Dame Honoria.

Among all the dreadful things that had happened in the last few months, nothing came close to frightening Johnny more than this.

If Nina or he were to collapse or lose their grips, the tiny wraith would be sucked right into the etheric bomb.

And would somehow trigger it.

And then everything would be finished.

Nina and Johnny, Mel and Dame Honoria, everyone here and the whole city.

Gone in a flash of hellish green fire.

Realizing what was probably happening, Mr. Cargill suddenly barked out that more help was needed. He ordered Uncle Louie and Flo to pull behind Nina and Mel. He directed Danny to pull behind Johnny and Dame Honoria, then joined in himself. It had become a struggle with a whole city and a million lives at stake.

"*Gotta rip her outta there,*" grunted Johnny through gritted teeth. "*Gotta! Just GOTTA!*"

"*It's like,*" Mel gasped from behind Nina's left shoulder, "*the bomb...is giving...the ghost...super...strength.*"

Johnny caught a brief glimpse of the colonel and Bao off to the right, both glowing green—more brightly than he'd ever seen ghosts glow—trying to stagger away from the diamond. It almost seemed as if some super-powerful force of gravity was grabbing at them. The bomb wanted to consume them, as well!

"Don't know how much longer I can hold on," Johnny cried. "My hands are burning!"

"Mine too!" screamed Nina.

"We have to keep trying!" bellowed Dame Honoria.

Now the Steppe Warrior's chest was almost entirely inside the black diamond. It seemed that nothing could stop the inevitable from happening.

With shocking abruptness, Gizmo Gunderson, the night mechanic, materialized out of the darkness on the far side of the pool of light that illuminated the fateful tug of war. He was gripping an ice pick in his right hand as he strode up to Johnny and Nina.

The young mechanic brought the tip of the ice pick down within an inch of the tiny ghost and stabbed a hole right through her.

Checheg flew out of the black diamond like a shot, wailing in anguish, instantly regaining her normal stature. She had a gaping fissure right through her stomach, and her face was a mask of pure agony. She zoomed away, through half a dozen pieces of heavy machinery.

Gone, disappeared, vanished.

At the instant the tiny ghost gave up the struggle, everyone on both sides sprawled backward into heaps on the filthy concrete floor. The Star of Gilbeyshire flew out of Nina's grasp and skittered off into the shadows, its livid green glow extinguished.

Sitting in a big blotch of grease, his fancy overcoat ruined forever, Johnny was amazed that the tug of war had ended as unexpectedly as it had begun. They'd caught another huge break, thanks to Gizmo Gunderson.

Johnny hopped up and tried unsuccessfully to levitate Dame Honoria, who was way too much of a handful. Uncle Louie came over and gently hauled the celebrated suffragist to her feet. Mel and Nina clambered up as well, dazed as they gazed at each other. The two began to blubber and embrace. Flo and Danny stood there shaking their heads in wonderment, while the superintendent merely looked appalled.

His heart still pounding, his face beet red, Johnny approached Gizmo, who also looked flushed and a little shaky. "Hey, thank you. You saved a lotta lives tonight."

The young mechanic seemed startled. "Did I? Really?"

Johnny nodded.

"You know, I could see ghosts all my life," Gizmo said. "Only it brought me nothing but grief. Kids would beat me up, make fun of me. I mean, no one here even knows. This may be the only time it's been good for anything."

Johnny clapped him on the shoulder and shuffled back to Mel, who still was very upset.

"When will it *stop?*" she sobbed. "I am so very, very *tired.*"

"Me too," groaned Nina.

"Young ladies!" Dame Honoria boomed, dusting herself off. "We haven't the luxury of weeping or dawdling. We still have to destroy the jewel, the sooner the better. Will someone please find the blasted object. And you—" She pointed an imperious index finger at the superintendent. "Please see to it that the Super Stamper, as you call it, is fully operational."

They all slogged off into the shadowy maze of giant machinery. "How many times in an evening does a guy have to save Zenith?" Johnny muttered, to no one in particular. "Jeez Louise!"

THE SUPER STAMPER stood a good three stories tall. The dark, hulking machine had well-oiled steel shafts at each of four corners, upon which the tempered steel top plate—about the dimensions of four billiard tables—rode down onto a bottom plate. The device could exert two thousand tons of pressure.

Right at the center of the bottom plate sat the black diamond known around the world as the Star of Gilbeyshire. The pear-shaped gem still seemed far too small and inconsequential to blow up a city of a million people.

The bedraggled party-goers were gathered on one side of the huge press.

The superintendent looked nervous and not very happy to be there. Next to him, Gizmo Gunderson simply appeared dazed. A bashful smile kept breaking out on his face.

Mel and Danny leaned against each other—her arm about his waist, his around her shoulder. Johnny was holding Nina's shoulder as well, primarily because she seemed in danger of collapsing in a heap. Floating up above were the colonel and Bao.

"Mr. Superintendent, if you please," Dame Honoria intoned.

"Yes, ma'am," he said, flipping several switches on the control panel and turning a dial.

The Super Stamper vibrated to life.

Then the superintendent mashed down on a large green button.

The top plate began rumbling downward.

Twelve feet. Eight feet.

Johnny sure hoped that Mel and Dame Honoria knew what they were doing. It would be terrible if instead of destroying the bomb by crushing it, they set it off. But it was too late to worry about that.

The top plate got to four feet. One foot. One inch.

Suddenly there was a muffled, brittle *CRAAACK*, followed by a CRUUUNCHing sound.

And in less than a tiny fraction of a heartbeat, Johnny and the others were enveloped in a howling green hurricane of ghosts.

CHAPTER 67

A TIDAL WAVE OF GHOSTS surged in all directions!

In only a couple of seconds, Johnny saw hundreds of transparent spectral faces flash past him.

Children and old people. Men and women. The recently dead and ancient wraiths. All colors and all races.

They showed emotions ranging from delight and joy to abject fear and loathing, as they swirled around Johnny and the others. Laughing, shouting, sobbing, shrieking. The noise was overwhelming.

Out of pure reflex, Johnny threw himself and Nina onto the hard concrete. She yelped in pain and angrily bopped him on the ear. Mel toppled Danny, too, afraid for their lives. And Dame Honoria—apparently loath to spend any more time on the filthy factory floor—merely covered her head and crouched.

Even those who couldn't see ghosts flowing through them felt a powerful electrical charge. Uncle Louie later told Johnny that he could sense every hair on his body trying to jump to attention. His eyes had burned and his ears had rung; his fingers and toes had tingled. Flo's auburn hair stood up like a fright wig.

For several long minutes, ghosts kept geysering out of the

demolished diamond. Many flew up through the metal roof of Shed Number 3 and vanished. But others lingered amid the giant machines, wailing and jabbering and trying to make sense of things. Dozens of times Johnny heard the same question: "Why aren't we really dead?"

The whole shed seemed to be swimming with ghosts. Johnny couldn't imagine that anything like this had ever happened before.

After a while Dame Honoria gathered him and the others around her, and motioned for the superintendent and Gizmo Gunderson to join them.

"Gunderson, my lad," said Carlton Cargill, clapping an arm around the man's shoulder, "you did something very big here this evening. First-class work. *First-class!* Good job that you could see ghosts."

The young man beamed and shrugged. "It just seemed like the thing to do. Lucky I have an ice pick on my belt."

"Hats off to you, too, Superintendent," said Mrs. Throckmorton.

The superintendent smiled a quizzical smile, as if he wasn't at all sure what he was being thanked for. "I don't suppose you could tell me, um, what we just, uhhh, did here tonight?"

Mrs. Throckmorton gravely shook her head, as did Dame Honoria and Mel and Johnny.

"However," said the newspaper publisher, "I'm going to speak with management and arrange that you and Mr. Gunderson both shall have bonuses for your efforts tonight. But remember, you must never tell anyone what happened here. *Never!*"

WHILE THE OTHERS went to warm up in the superintendent's office, Johnny, Mel, Dame Honoria, the colonel, and Bao wandered amid the gigantic machinery of Shed Number 3.

They had to tell the remaining ghosts about the true, terrible cost of the etheric bomb.

"As long as ghosts believe they can escape the ether," Mel said, "there's a danger that someone will make more etheric bombs. We have to spread word throughout the entire ghost world that being in the bomb only makes your predicament worse. Far worse."

Johnny jumped in. "If these ghosts tell other ghosts who tell other ghosts who—"

"Then we might be able to throw gravel into sweetums'..." Dame Honoria grimaced and shook her head. "I mean into *Percy's* gears. We don't know if his cronies are planning to make any more, even without him. But we must try to put a stop to it."

Johnny hunted through every nook and cranny of Shed Number 3, training a flashlight here and there. His feet were frigid, his fingers freezing, his nose red, and his breath making little fountains of condensed moisture. He wondered if he would ever warm up again. Altogether, he and the others spoke to hundreds of wraiths.

Some of the ghosts Johnny talked to were relieved to be out of the bomb. ("It vas terribly cramped in der," stated a Barovian field marshal. "Like zardines in de can. Poor dizipline, much pushing und shoving. Danke, mein Junge.") Some were angry. ("You have ruined everything!" shrieked an Onango tribeswoman with many brass rings around her neck. "Now I will never escape this hell!") And others looked as if they would kill themselves—*if only they could*. ("Heaven," moaned a rotund medieval monk from Ville de Riviere, "eez all zat I wanted.")

It was almost on to breakfast time when the whole crew felt they had done everything they could. They were about to head out the door when the little mountain girl caught sight of the back of a wraith ambling around behind one of the many bulky machines.

She made a gasping noise and ran over to try to catch a glimpse. Johnny trotted after her.

Up she flew, for a bird's-eye view.

She looked down and squealed with joy.

"Evvie," she cried, "*is that you?*"

Beaming with delight, Bao turned to Johnny. "It's my friend Evvie. We flew across the ocean together."

Johnny saw the ghost of a young man in safari duds stop in his tracks, twirl around, and look up. What had been a scowl on his face turned into a giant grin.

"Bao!" the specter laughed, hands on hips. "My dear old girl! Where *have* you been?"

CHAPTER 68

JOHNNY TRUDGED ALONG the rocky shore of Great Lake early in the afternoon of the second day of the new year. The sky was a bright electric blue, the air crisp and clear and almost down to freezing. A frigid wind whipped in off the water, prompting him to pull his fedora down over chilly ears. A few hundred feet away automobiles and trucks made a steady hum, cruising up and down the busy Lake Highway.

The top headline of that morning's *Clarion* had proclaimed:

NEW YEAR'S BALL
GHOST ATTACK: FURTHER
DETAILS EMERGE

Positioned beneath it was one of Johnny's pictures showing the Hotel Splendid's demolished ballroom.

Just like the initial story that ran on New Year's Day, the follow-up article said nothing about how close Zenith had come to utter annihilation—not once but twice. Neither story even hinted at the etheric bomb nor the incident at the Acme Iron Works.

Johnny crunched to a halt on the rocky shore and stared out across the big lake—so big that you couldn't see the other side. The wind died down and now it didn't feel as nippy.

Just twelve months earlier, as an eleven-year-old, Johnny had been so keen to test out of school that he had studied for hours every night. But being a grown-up—at least when it came to the news photography business—hadn't exactly been a picnic in the park.

So much had just been, well, scary. Or sad.

Scary—Ghosts trying to kill his own sister.

Sad—Spooks getting shredded to bits without escaping the ether.

Scary—Percy and Ozzie hijacking the bodies of the dead, becoming the first zombies.

Sad—Still not knowing if he and Mel would ever see their parents again.

Scary—A million people coming within a hair's breadth of getting blown to smithereens.

Sad—Seeing a great old lady getting betrayed by an ungrateful wretch of a son.

Johnny thought it was loathsome, the way Percy had used Dame Honoria's Star of Gilbeyshire for the second bomb. Dame Honoria had said that she believed Percy intended her to carry the gem back to the Royal Kingdom. What means of transport could be safer and more secure? And back home, almost certainly, Percy would issue his ultimatum and, if necessary, blow up the capital city of Royalton.

What really made Johnny's blood run cold was that Percy knew his own mother would die a horrible death.

It was a wickedly clever plan. Obviously, once Percy had been captured, his confederates—probably Ozzie and Miss Worthington-Smythe—improvised and made Zenith their target.

But maybe one of the worst things about what had happened was that now, even more living people believed that ghosts were *all* bad, *all* dangerous. Just because of Percy and a few rotten spooks.

Johnny had read about anti-ghost bigots who wanted the authorities to chase ghosts out of cities—to research how they could actually be "exterminated," as if they were noxious bugs or something. Most ghosts were decent people who'd just caught a bad break. They deserved sympathy, not hatred. That's what Mom and Pop had always said.

For now, though, Johnny thought it would be nice to really, truly get back to normal. Take ordinary news pictures of ordinary news.

No more dangerous adventures for a long time, thanks very much. Just the trip to the Confederazione with Mel to track down the contessa and hear the story behind that picture she drew—the sketch that showed Lydia and Will Graphic in captivity. Johnny didn't want to let his hopes get too high. But maybe, just maybe, he and Mel would find their parents alive and well. To have them back in their lives again—he couldn't imagine how swell that would feel.

"Master Graphic."

Johnny nearly jumped out of his wingtips.

There behind him was Colonel MacFarlane, up on Buck, wearing a severe expression.

"Whadaya need, Colonel?" Johnny asked, a little sharply. He wanted to be alone, wanted to think. And the stitches in his chest make him kind of grouchy. That sword wound sure hurt.

"You're required back at the house," the colonel pronounced

gravely. "Immediately."

"Immediately?"

"Indeed so."

Johnny groaned. He liked to avoid flying with the colonel and Buck. "What for?"

"Something important, is all that the commander told me. She ordered me to find and fetch you."

CHAPTER 69

JOHNNY CLAMBERED DOWN off Buck right at the front steps, bolted them three at a time, and dashed inside. He had no idea what the emergency might be. *Another ghost attack? Another etheric bomb? More zombies?*

Seated on the big leather sofa in the living room were Carlton Cargill and his managing editor, Maude Beale. Mel, Uncle Louie, and Nina were standing by the fireplace, beneath the portrait of Lydia and Will Graphic. Dame Honoria sat in the rocking chair near the china cabinet, going back and forth. Hovering nearby was Bao, who, in honor of her undaunted bravery, had been promoted by Dame Honoria to the position of personal ghost assistant.

Everyone had smiles on their faces. *So, not bad news, at least.*

"What's going on?" Johnny asked, after saying hello to his boss and Miss Beale.

Mel cleared her throat and looked as if she might break into a little celebratory dance.

"Well?" he said.

His sister took a deep breath. "Mr. Cargill and Miss Beale have a proposition for us."

"Oh?" was all that Johnny could think to say.

"John, my lad, your efforts and the efforts of Miss Graphic this past autumn have not only been heroic acts of first-class journalism, but have been a terrific boost for the *Zenith Clarion*." Mr. Cargill punctuated his words by stabbing the air with his unlit cigar. "Our circulation has risen nearly fifty percent and we've collected hefty fees from the World Press Association for the use of your stories. Mrs. Throckmorton is delighted."

"And if Mrs. Throckmorton is delighted," put in Miss Beale, "the chief is delighted."

Johnny puffed up a little bit and grinned at Mel and Uncle Louie. It felt awfully good to know the chief valued his work that much. But there were two things he had been curious about.

"Mr. Cargill," he asked, "what was the government doing about the threat? And do they know that we destroyed the bomb?"

His boss nodded slowly. "I have confidential word that our military and police agencies went on high alert. The mobilization of soldiers at the Zenith army base was part of that effort. Mr. Crider of the Ministry of Etheristics informed me—and you can share this with no one else—that Prime Minister Sunderland himself sends you his thanks."

Now *that* would have been fun to tell his friends about back at Falkland Junior High. A kid getting thanked by the most important person in the country. But he understood why it had to remain top secret.

"We hardly want any more zombies wandering among us," Mr. Cargill continued, "or more etheric bombs threatening other innocent metropolises. Nor do we want certain photographers and their sisters getting sliced to pieces by malevolent specters. However newsworthy these items might be, we don't need more of that kind of trouble."

Johnny was bubbling with curiosity. Where was the chief

headed with this? "Mel said you had a proposition, Mr. Cargill. What kind of proposition?"

Mr. Cargill regarded him intensely. "In a couple of weeks you and Melanie plan to fly to the Confederazione di Ducati to hunt for the contessa, the ghost artist who drew the mysterious picture of your parents. Correct?"

Johnny nodded. "Yeah, Mel's already got the airline tickets, via Neuport and Royalton. On Zephyr Lines."

"Well, then, my young friend, you'd better get a refund," said Mr. Cargill.

"I don't understand," replied Johnny, scrunching up his face in bafflement.

Mr. Cargill chuckled. "If you agree to our proposal, Johnny, the *Clarion* would like to send you and Melanie to write and photograph a series of reports on the hunt for Will and Lydia Graphic. Our readers have expressed a big interest in the story, and so has the World Press Association. They want to know what happened to your mom and dad nearly as much as you and Melanie do.

"Not only will we pay you for your articles and photos, as usual, but we'll provide you with a flying boat. We'll cover the expenses for the journey. And we'll pay the mortgage on your house all through 1936. Melanie's already agreed. All you have to do is say yes."

Johnny's jaw dropped. He and Mel could do everything they'd planned to do. Find the contessa and go wherever the clues she provided led them. On whatever schedule they chose. And all they had to do was write stories and shoot photographs. What could possibly be better? Then a gloomy thought entered his head.

"What about Uncle Louie and Nina? Do they get to come, too?"

Nina's bubbling giggle gave him his answer. "Yes, we do!" she exclaimed.

"They're gonna let you out of school again?"

"They sure are," she said proudly.

Uncle Louie laughed and nodded. "Nina did such a swell job making up her schoolwork this fall, that the principal gave the okay the minute I got her on the phone. Said it was a fantastic educational opportunity for a young lady, traveling to the Old Continent.

"Anyway, I'll be co-piloting and Danny'll be back in the captain's seat. We get a Gianelli Z-509 this time, one with long-distance tanks. Flies faster, higher, farther, and cheaper than a Como Eagle. A lot more cramped, though. No sleeping cabins. And Nina operates the radio again."

Nina beamed at Johnny and let out a spontaneous yip of delight.

"And I shall be returning home with you," said Dame Honoria in that uniquely sonorous tone of hers. "Bao is eager to see Gilbey-shire, as well. And we're bringing her friend Evvie, Lord Hurley of Evansham, back home to have a reunion with his family. I once met his younger brother, the present Lord Hurley."

"But what about Percy?" Johnny asked. "I thought you were going to stay here and try to help the authorities question him."

"I saw Percy again this morning, Johnny," replied Dame Honoria. "I believe he needs to spend more time in solitary reflection. I shall return to help when he shows some sign of contrition."

Johnny turned back to Mr. Cargill., "And no one's seen Ozzie?"

Before the editor could answer, Dame Honoria sniffed in a haughty and dismissive manner. "The little weasel's probably trying to cadge more free hamburger sandwiches from strangers in disreputable pubs."

Mr. Cargill shook his head. "We and the authorities have

pictures of his present appearance. But no one's spotted Ozzie since your last encounter with him, Johnny."

Still, even with villains like Ozzie on the loose, Johnny figured that things had turned out well—considering the terrific dangers they'd encountered. He looked around the living room, a ridiculously big smile spreading across his freckled face. Here was everybody he cared about. His sister and uncle. His godmother Dame Honoria. His best friend Nina. His bosses.

And now they would be having a new adventure. But this time, the reward at adventure's end wouldn't be the prevention of some titanic disaster, but the mending of a broken family.

The boy photographer turned to face Mr. Cargill.

"Count me in, Chief," he said. "When do we leave?"

EPILOG

SATURDAY, JANUARY 4, 1936

ZENITH

PERCIVAL RODERICK GORTON RATHBONE shifted awkwardly, sitting on the edge of his prison cot, questing for a position that would bring comfort.

He wasn't the first ghost to take over a newly dead body. But he was the first in many centuries. Hijacking a fresh corpse was easy—once you had someone to teach you how.

Not that there weren't challenges.

For a start, becoming a zombie hurt. In the muscles. The bones. The organs inside. A kind of burning, tingling sensation that flowed from one end of his new body to the other. Terrible itching of the hair follicles. Sleep that came only in brief snatches. Fingers and toes that were constantly numb.

But a zombie body was stronger and more durable than a living body—able to sustain punishment an ordinary person could not take. However, no one was indestructible. Given enough damage, even a zombie would release the ghost at its core.

He had just started pacing his cell—for at least the hundredth time—when he heard a ghostly "Pssst-pssst" emanating from a shadowy corner.

He peered in that direction and was gratified to see the fearsome features of the Steppe Warrior Burilgi protruding from the varnished cement wall. Making sure none of the guards had their eyes on him, Percy went over to have a jaw wag with his old henchman.

He heard a remarkable story of miserable ineptitude. The second bomb. Unexploded. Destroyed. All that effort gone to waste. Zenith would have been the perfect target for a grand blow-up. Even better than Royalton.

The Graphics' hometown. Burnt to a cinder. Along with Mummy. How delicious. And it would have gotten him out of this zombie body and the prison that it was in.

"And is everything prepared for my return home?" he asked.

"Yes, Khan, it is," the ghost replied. "Ready to move at your command."

As he told Burilgi what had to be done, Percy noticed something odd.

"What happened to your pigtail?"

The Steppe Warrior grumbled and showed no sign of wanting to answer.

"Very well, then," Percy said, going down on his knees and holding his head erect. "Do it."

Burilgi tensed like a steel spring, then whipped his blade from right to left, in a blur, striking Percy's zombie head clean off his shoulders.

The detached noggin hit the cement floor with a muffled thud and rolled off into a corner, under the cot.

Within seconds the diaphanous form of Percy's ghost appeared next to the Steppe Warrior—as dour and gloomy as ever.

"Now," he said, "take me to Ozzie and Miss Worthington-Smythe."

The End

APPENDIX 1

THE TWO IMPOSSIBLE THINGS

The First Impossible Thing posits that no ghost may return to life in a physical body.

The Second Impossible Thing posits that no ghost may escape the ether and pass over to the great unknown that claims, upon their deaths, the vast majority of all living creatures.

APPENDIX 2

THE LAWS OF ETHERISTICS

1. Ghosts—also known as specters, wraiths, sprites, spirits, phantoms, phantasms, and spooks—are the sentient remains of deceased humans and animals.

2. Ghosts exist non-corporeally in the forms and with the perquisites in which and with which they died, in a non-material universe parallel but contingent to our own, called "The Ether."

3. Ghosts are creatures of free will.

4. Ghosts may exercise their free will by serving living humans and—thus endowed by living "effectuators"—assume a degree of corporeality required to perform the tasks requested of them in our material universe.

5. Ghosts' corporeality—including use of implements they may have utilized when alive—finds expression as it is needed and

vanishes when it is not, often in the blink of an eye. The duration and efficacy of this phenomenon can vary, however, for reasons not yet understood.

6. Ghosts who are engaged corporeally in any activity that may harm living humans or animals are subject to the same injuries as the living—though they cannot be killed a second time.

7. Ghosts are free at any time to withdraw from their arrangements in service to practicing etherists, and others with the capacity to see and hear them, but thereby lose the benefits of corporeality.

8. Practicing etherists and others with the capacity to see and hear etherians are free to end arrangements with them, thereby terminating the ghosts' benefits of corporeality.

—Adopted this Sixth Day of May, 1896, by the Third World Congress of Consulting Etherists, gathered in Molderdam, Kingdom of the Low Countries. Anna De Waart, General Secretary, presiding.

ACKNOWLEDGEMENTS

During the writing of *Johnny Graphic and the Etheric Bomb*, several individuals were instrumental. Marlo Garnsworthy brought her expertise in kids' literature to the table and made a huge difference by spotting the "elephant in the living room." Kate Collins, an avid fantasy reader, came up with several important tweaks. Jeri Smith was my excellent copyeditor/proofreader. Steve Thomas created both the original book cover and map, and the covers for the new edition of the Johnny Graphic Adventures. Above all, my wife, Sue Wichmann, kept the book on track over these many months.

ABOUT THE AUTHOR

In addition to being the creator of the Johnny Graphic Adventures trilogy, D. R. Martin is the author of four Mary MacDougall historical mysteries and three King Harald canine cozy mysteries—written under his pen name, Richard Audry. He's also the author of the hardboiled PI mystery *Smoking Ruin*. You can follow D. R. at johnnygraphicadventures.com, drmartinbooks.com, and facebook.com/johnnygraphicadventures.

The Johnny Graphic Trilogy

If you enjoyed *Johnny Graphic and the Etheric Bomb*, don't miss the other action-packed tales in the trilogy...

In *Johnny Graphic and the Attack of the Zombies* (Book 2), Johnny and his friends journey to the Royal Kingdom to help defeat an army of zombies—bog corpses reanimated by Percy Rathbone's ghostly minions. Stranded and on their own in hostile territory, Johnny and his companions not only have to save themselves, but scores of abducted kids, as well. Book 2 in the Johnny Graphic Adventures is on sale now at leading e-book sellers and in paperback.

In *Johnny Graphic and the Ghost of Doom* (Book 3), Johnny and his companions fly to Okkatek Island to hunt for his lost parents. But on their arrival, a threatening volcano forces the group to make other plans. Johnny, however, is having none of it and schemes to head off on his own adventure, searching for Will and Lydia Graphic. *Johnny Graphic and the Ghost of Doom* will be on sale as an e-book and paperback in the summer of 2020.

www.ingramcontent.com/pod-product-compliance
Lightning Source LLC
Chambersburg PA
CBHW020919110726
47900CB00001B/220